HURRICANE SEASON

Born in Veracruz, Mexico, in 1982, Fernanda Melchor is widely recognized as one of the most exciting new voices of Mexican literature. In 2018, she won the PEN Mexico Award for Literary and Journalistic Excellence and in 2019 the German Anna-Seghers-Preis and the International Literature Award for *Hurricane Season*.

Sophie Hughes has translated novels by several contemporary Latin American and Spanish authors, including Laia Jufresa and Rodrigo Hasbún. Her translation of Alia Trabucco Zerán's *The Remainder* was shortlisted for the 2019 Man Booker International Prize.

'Repellent yet compulsive, *Hurricane Season* is a hell of a force to be reckoned with.'
— Claire-Louise Bennett, author of *Pond*

'Not only does Fernanda Melchor write with the violent force that the themes of her investigation demand, but on every page she displays an ear and perspicacity rarely seen in our literature.'
— Yuri Herrera, author of *The Transmigration of Bodies*

'Written with pain and enormous skill, in a rhythm at once tearing and hypnotic, *Hurricane Season* is an account of the wreckage of a forsaken Mexico governed by nightmarish jungle law. An important, brave novel by a writer of extraordinary talent, magnificently translated by Sophie Hughes.'
— Alia Trabucco Zerán, author of *The Remainder*

'Melchor experiments with the Latin American Neo-Baroque and with European formalism – in the novel, each chapter is sustained in a long paragraph in which sentences only finish when they really and truly can't carry another clause, articulating a relentless reality in a language openly faithful to that spoken by Mexicans today. Fernanda Melchor isn't interested in revealing what happened, but rather in providing a way to record what is so hard to articulate.'
— Álvaro Enrigue, author of *Sudden Death*

'Melchor wields a sentence like a saber. She never flinches in the bold, precise strokes of *Hurricane Season*. In prose as precise and breathtaking as it is unsettling, Melchor has crafted an unprecedented novel about femicide in Mexico and how poverty and extreme power imbalances lead to violence everywhere.'
— Idra Novey, author of *Those Who Knew*

Fitzcarraldo Editions

HURRICANE SEASON

FERNANDA MELCHOR

Translated by
SOPHIE HUGHES

For Eric

'He, too, has resigned his part
In the casual comedy;
He, too, has been changed in his turn,
Transformed utterly:
A terrible beauty is born.'
— W. B. Yeats, *Easter, 1916*

'Some of the events described here are
real. All of the characters are invented.'
— Jorge Ibargüengoitia, *The Dead Girls*

I.

They reached the canal along the track leading up from
the river, their slingshots drawn for battle and their eyes
squinting, almost stitched together, in the midday glare.
There were five of them, their ringleader the only one
in swimming trunks: red shorts that blazed behind the
parched crops of the cane fields, still low in early May.
The rest of the troop trailed behind him in their underpants, all four caked in mud up to their shins, all four
taking turns to carry the pail of small rocks they'd taken
from the river that morning; all four scowling and fierce
and so ready to give themselves up for the cause that
not even the youngest, bringing up the rear, would have
dared admit he was scared, the elastic of his slingshot
pulled taut in his hands, the rock snug in the leather pad,
primed to strike anything that got in his way at the very
first sign of an ambush, be that the caw of the bienteveo,
perched unseen like a guard in the trees behind them, the
rustle of leaves being thrashed aside, or the whoosh of a
rock cleaving the air just beyond their noses, the breeze
warm and the almost white sky thick with ethereal birds
of prey and a terrible smell that hit them harder than a
fistful of sand in the face, a stench that made them want
to hawk it up before it reached their guts, that made them
want to stop and turn round. But the ringleader pointed to the edge of the cattle track, and all five of them,
crawling along the dry grass, all five of them packed
together in a single body, all five of them surrounded
by blow flies, finally recognized what was peeping out
from the yellow foam on the water's surface: the rotten
face of a corpse floating among the rushes and the plastic bags swept in from the road on the breeze, the dark
mask seething under a myriad of black snakes, smiling.

They called her the Witch, the same as her mother; the
Young Witch when she first started trading in curses
and cures, and then, when she wound up alone, the year
of the landslide, simply the Witch. If she'd had another
name, scrawled on some time-worn, worm-eaten piece
of paper maybe, buried at the back of one of those wardrobes that the old crone crammed full of plastic bags and
filthy rags, locks of hair, bones, rotten leftovers, if at
some point she'd been given a first name and last name
like everyone else in town, well, no one had ever known
it, not even the women who visited the house each Friday
had ever heard her called anything else. She'd always
been you, retard, or you, asshole, or you, devil child, if
ever the Witch wanted her to come, or to be quiet, or
even just to sit still under the table so that she could listen to the women's maudlin pleas, their snivelling tales
of woe, their strife, the aches and pains, their dreams of
dead relatives and the spats between those still alive, and
money, it was almost always the money, but also their
husbands and those whores from the highway, and why
do they always walk out on me just when I've got my
hopes up, they'd blub, what was the point of it all, they'd
moan, they might as well be dead, just call it a day,
wished they'd never been born, and with the corner of
their shawls they'd dry the tears from their faces, which
they covered in any case the moment they left the
Witch's kitchen, because they weren't about to give those
bigmouths in town the satisfaction of going around saying how they'd been to see the Witch to plot their revenge
against so-and-so, how they'd put a curse on the slut
leading their husband astray, because there was always
one, always some miserable bitch in town spinning

yarns about the girls who, quite innocently, minding their own business, went to the Witch's for a remedy for indigestion for that dipshit at home clogged up to his nuts on the kilo of crisps he ate in one sitting, or a tea to keep tiredness at bay, or an ointment for tummy troubles, or, let's be honest, just to sit there awhile and lighten the load, let it all out, the pain and sadness that fluttered hopelessly in their throats. Because the Witch listened, and nothing seemed to shock her, and frankly, what would you expect from a woman they say killed her own husband, Manolo Conde no less, and for money, the old cunt's money, his house and the land, a hundred hectares of cultivated fields and pastures left to him by his father, or what was left of it after his father had sold it off piece by piece to the leader of the Mill Workers Union so that, from then on, he wouldn't have to lift a finger, so he could live off his rents and apparently off his so-called businesses, which were always failing, but so vast was the estate that when Don Manolo died there was still a sizeable tract of land left over, with a tidy rental value; so tidy, in fact, that the old man's sons, two fully grown lads, both out of school, sons by his legitimate wife over in Montiel Sosa, rolled into town the moment they heard the news: heart attack, the doctor from Villa told the boys when they showed up at that house in the middle of the sugar cane fields where the vigil was being held, and right there, in front of everyone, they told the Witch that she had until the next day to pack her bags and leave town, that she was mad if she thought they'd let a slag like her get her hands on their father's assets: the land, the house, that house which, even after all those years, was still unfinished, as lavish and warped as Don Manolo's dreams, with its elaborate staircase and banisters decked out in plaster cherubs, its high ceilings

where the bats made their roosts, and, hidden somewhere, or so the story went, the money, a shedload of
gold coins that Don Manolo had inherited from his father and never banked, not forgetting the diamond, the
diamond ring that no one had ever seen, not even the
sons, but that was said to hold a stone so big it looked
fake, a bona fide heirloom that had belonged to Don
Manolo's grandmother, a certain Señora Chucita Villagarbosa de los Monteros de Conde, and that by both
legal and divine right belonged to the boys' mother, Don
Manolo's real wife, his legitimate wife in the eyes of God
and man alike, not to that trollop, that conniving, homi-
cidal upstart, the Witch, who swanned around town like
Lady Muck when she was nothing but a tart Don Manolo
had dragged out of some jungle hellhole for the sole purpose of living out his basest instincts in the privacy of
the plains. An evil woman, it turned out, because, who
knows how, some say with the devil in her ear, she had
learned of a herb that grew wild up in the mountains, almost at the summit, among the old ruins that, according
to those suits from the government, were the ancient
tombs of men who'd once lived up there, the first dwell-
ers, there even before those filthy Spaniards who, from
their boats, took one look at all that land spread out before them and said finders keepers, this land belongs to
us and to the Kingdom of Castile; and the ancients, the
few who were left, had to run for the hills and they lost
everything, right down to the stones of their temples,
which ended up buried in the mountainside in the hurricane of '78, what with the landslide, the avalanche of
mud that swamped more than a hundred locals from La
Matosa and the ruins where those herbs were said to
grow, the herbs that the Witch boiled up into an odour-
less, colourless poison so imperceptible that even the

doctor from Villa concluded Manolo had died of a heart attack, but those pig-headed sons of his swore blind that he'd been poisoned, and later everyone blamed the Witch for the sons' deaths too, because on the very same day they buried their father, the devil came and took them on the highway, on their way to the cemetery in Villa, heading up the funeral procession; the pair of them died crushed under a stack of metal joists that slid off the truck in front; blood-smeared steel all over the next day's papers, the whole thing more than a little creepy because no one could explain how such a thing could have happened, how those joists had come loose from the fastening cable and smashed through the wind-screen, skewering them both, and there was no shortage of people who put two and two together and blamed the Witch, who said the Witch had put a curse on them, that the evil wench had sold her soul to the devil in exchange for special powers, all to hold on to the house and sur-rounding land, and it was around then that the Witch locked herself away in the house never to leave again, not by day or night, perhaps for fear the Condes were waiting to take their revenge, or maybe because she was hiding something, a secret she couldn't let out of her sight, something in the house that she refused to leave unguarded, and she grew thin and pale and just looking her in the eyes sent a chill through you because it was clear she'd gone mad, and it was the women of La Matosa who brought her food in exchange for her help prepar-ing their lotions and potions, concoctions brewed either with the herbs that the Witch grew in her vegetable gar-den or with the wild plants she sent the women to forage on the mountainside, back when there was still a moun-tainside to speak of. It was also around that time the locals began seeing the flying creature at night, the one

18

that trailed the men returning home along the dirt tracks between the villages, its talons poised to attack, or perhaps to grab hold of them and fly them off to the gates of hell, its terrible eyes blazing; and it was around then, too, that the rumour about the statue began, a statue that the Witch kept hidden somewhere in that house, probably upstairs, where not a soul was allowed to enter, not even the women who visited her, and where it's said she fornicated with it behind closed doors, with this statue that was in fact a giant model of the devil, with a long cock as thick as an arm clenching a machete, a hulking cock which, every night without fail, the Witch had her wicked way with, and that's why she always said she didn't need a husband, and as it went, after Don Manolo's death, the old hag never did meet another man, and was it any surprise when all she did was slag them off, call them drunks and layabouts, a pack of dogs, shameless pigs, over her dead body was one of those wasters entering her house; and the others, the townswomen, were fools for putting up with them, and her eyes would light up as she said all this, and for a second she'd become beautiful again, her hair tousled and her cheeks flushed with excitement, and the women would make the sign of the cross as, out of nowhere, the image of the Witch naked flashed through their minds; the Witch straddling the devil and sinking down onto his grotesque cock, all the way down the shaft, his semen running down her thighs, red like lava, or green and oozing like the strange brews that bubbled away in a cauldron on her stovetop and that the old sorceress would give them to sip from a spoon, to cure them of their ills; or sometimes black like tar, black like the enormous pupils and matted hair of the creature they discovered one day beneath the kitchen table, hanging off the Witch's skirt, a girl so silent and sickly that many of the women prayed to themselves that she would die before too long, be put out of her misery; the same little creature who, some time later, was glimpsed sitting cross-legged at the foot of the stairs, an open book on her lap and her lips silently mouthing every word her black eyes read, and the news spread like wildfire, because by evening people all the way in Villa had heard that the Witch's daughter was still alive, an unexpected turn of events by all accounts, because even deformed runts, the two-headed chickens and the goats with five hooves that might occasionally come out alive, even they croaked in a matter of days, and here was the Witch's daughter, the Girl, as they began to call her, that creature engendered in secret and shame, growing bigger and more robust with each passing day, until she was so strong she could carry out whatever task the mother dictated: chopping the wood, collecting the water from the well, walking to the market in Villa, eight miles there and eight back, lugging shopping bags and crates, never stopping to rest for a second, and certainly not taking any detour or hanging out with the other girls in town, who, more to the point, weren't brave enough to speak to her anyway, they didn't even make fun of her frizzy, matted hair, her tattered dresses or her massive bare feet, they didn't tease her, so tall, so ungainly, as spry as any boy and smarter than most, because people eventually twigged that it was the Girl who handled the household expenses and negotiated the rent with the men from the Mill, men just waiting for the day the Witches slipped up so they could be legally evicted, and who took advantage of the fact that there was no paperwork and not a man alive who would come to their defence, but in fact they didn't need anyone because the Girl, God knows how, had taught herself to manage their finances, and so tight was her hold on the purse strings that she even showed up one day in the kitchen to put a price on the townswomen's consultations, because the old Witch – who at the time couldn't have been older than forty, but looked sixty if she was a day, with all those wrinkles, grey hairs and saggy skin – the old Witch had lost her marbles and was forgetting to charge for sessions, or she'd simply accept whatever the women offered her: a bar of raw sugar, a pound of chickpeas, a paper cone of rotting lemons or a worm-ridden chicken – useless crap, all of it – but the Girl put a stop to that nonsense, she turned up one day in the kitchen and announced in a throaty voice, unaccustomed as she was to talking, that the gifts the women had got used to bringing no longer covered the cost of their consultations and that things couldn't go on like this. She told them that, starting now, prices would reflect the complexity of the request, the ways and means that the mother would have to employ and the kind of magic required to pull off the job, because it was hardly the same thing to cure their piles as to make a man fall at their knees, or, say, to make contact with their dead mother to find out if the old bitch had forgiven them neglecting her when she was alive, right? No, things were going to change around there, and the women were far from happy about it, plenty of them stopped paying their Friday visits, and if they fell ill they went to that mister from Palogacho who seemed to be more effective than the Witch anyway, because people trekked all the way from the capital to see him, famous people from the TV, footballers, politicians on the campaign trail, but then he didn't come cheap either, and since most of the women couldn't even get together the bus fare to Palogacho they were better off telling the Girl, Ah, what the hell, so how's this work, what happens next, because they only had such-and-such amount, and the Young Witch would bare those huge teeth of hers and tell them not to worry, if they didn't have enough they could leave her something by way of a guarantee, those earrings you had on the other morning, for example, or your daughter's gold holy cross, or, if they must, a dish of lamb tamales, the coffee maker, the radio, a bicycle, she accepted all kinds of household goods, and if they were late there was interest to pay because from one day to the next she also started moneylending, at a rate of thirty-five per cent, sometimes more, and everyone in town said all that conniving was the devil's work, because who'd ever known a girl that canny, where else could she get it from, and down the bar they called it daylight robbery, it was about time they turned that bitch in to the relevant authorities, to the police, time they locked her up for loan-sharking, for preying on the poor, who the hell did she think she was, exploiting the people of La Matosa and the neighbouring villages, but when the time came nobody did a thing: who else was going to lend them hard cash in exchange for their sorry belongings, and besides, no one was prepared to make enemies of the Witches because the truth was they were scared shitless. Even the men avoided walking past the house at night. Everyone knew about the sounds that came from inside there, the moaning and wailing that carried all the way to the dirt track, which, in their minds, was the sound of two witches fornicating with the devil, although others thought it was just the Witch cracking up, because by that point she could barely recognize people she knew and from one minute to the next her eyes would glaze over, and everyone said God was punishing her for being such an evil skank, and above all for having birthed that daughter of

22

Satan, because the Witch had always enjoyed keeping the Girl's father a secret whenever anyone asked, and none of them were any the wiser because no one knew for sure when the daughter had been born. Don Manolo had been dead for years, that much was certain, and there'd been no other man to speak of; she didn't ever leave the house or go to dances, and in fact what those women really wanted to know was whether, God forbid, their own husbands had spawned that foul beast of a child, and that's why they'd get goosebumps when, by way of response, the Witch merely stared at them with a hateful sneer before replying that the Girl was the devil's child, and God knows she looked it, especially when you compared her to that painting in the church in Villa, to the kid with his head smashed in and the Archangel Michael pinning him to the floor; above all in the eyes and eyebrows, and the women would cross themselves and sometimes, late at night, they even dreamed that the devil was chasing them with his big cock as stiff as a rod and raring to impregnate them, and they'd wake up with tears in their eyes, bellies aching, and the insides of their thighs all wet, and they'd scurry along to Villa to confess to Father Casto, who'd scold them for swallowing that mumbo-jumbo; because there were those who laughed it all off, saying the Witch was simply mad and that the Girl had been snatched from a nearby village; and then there were those who said that old Sarajuana, who was already getting on in years, used to tell the story of how a group of men turned up at her cantina one night, young kids not from around there, not from La Matosa, and maybe not even from Villa, judging by the way they spoke, and these boys, who were already blind drunk, started bragging about how they'd just come from having fun with some lady in La Matosa, some

bitch they say killed her old man and went around playing the enchantress, and Sarajuana pricked up her ears
to hear them explain how they'd snuck into the house
and beaten the shit out of her, to stop her from moving,
the only way they could take turns banging her, because, witch or no witch, she was a tidy piece of ass, and
you could tell that underneath it all she wanted it, from
the way she squirmed and squealed as they fucked her,
and besides, they're all a bunch of sluts in this dump,
they said. And in the bar there was no shortage of punters who took offence – there never was, as Sarajuana
knew well – who got their backs up at those outsiders
calling La Matosa a dump, and they made a real scene,
jumped the cunts and, right there in the middle of the
cantina, kicked the shit out of those boys, although in
the end no one pulled out a machete, maybe because
they were able to fuck them up with just their bare hands,
or maybe because it was too hot to take the dig to heart,
and there weren't any girls in Sarajuana's to impress that
day, not even those squalid slags who'd come from the
coast to sell themselves for a beer; no one, just them and
old Sara, who by this point was basically one of the lads,
the swarthy-faced kind with their obligatory tashes and
a bottle of beer growing warm in their hand and the hum
of the ceiling fan slicing through the thick heat radiating
from their bodies, and the cassette player, *za-ca-ti-to pal
conejo*, blaring next to the lit taper, *tiernito-verde voy a cor-
tar*, beside the picture of San Martín Caballero, *pa llevarle
al conejito*, and the aloe vera tied with a ribbon soaked in
holy water, *que ya-empiezá desesperar, sí señor, cómo no*, and
aguardiente to rouse the green-eyed monster, the Witch
had explained, to deflect the bad energy back onto the
one who deserved it, the one who'd dished it out. That's
why, in the very centre of the Witch's kitchen table, on a

24

plate of sea salt, there was a red apple struck all the way through with a fillet knife, and next to it a white carnation, which, every Friday morning, the women – those women who woke at the crack of dawn to go and see her – would find withered and shrivelled, almost rotten, tinged yellow by all the bad vibes they brought into that house, a sort of negative energy that, they believed, built up inside of them when times were tough, and that the old girl, with her remedies, could purge them of; a thick yet invisible miasma left floating in the stale air of that musty house, because, well, nobody knew for sure what sparked the Witch's fear of windows, but by the time the Girl was old enough to rattle around in that gloomy living room, next to the kitchen, where no one ever dared go, by that time the Witch had already bricked up all the windows with her own bare hands – using concrete blocks and cement, timbers and wire mesh – and even the front door, made of dark, almost black oak, the door through which they'd carried away old Don Manolo in his coffin and taken him off to be buried in Villa, even this door had been boarded up with planks of wood and bricks, anything to keep a living soul from entering, so in other words access to the house was restricted to a small side door leading into the kitchen from the garden, because the Girl had to get out somehow to collect the water, tend the vegetable patch and run the errands, and since you couldn't lock it, the Witch paid a blacksmith to forge a metal gate with solid bars, thicker even than the ones on the prison cells in Villa, or so he boasted; a gate with a fist-sized lock and a key that never left the old girl's bra, it was permanently pressed to her left breast; a gate that, with increasing frequency, the women would find locked, and since they didn't dare knock they would wait there until they heard shouting, insults and ravings coming from the Witch as she smashed furniture against the walls and floor, or so they assumed from the sounds that reached the yard, while the Girl – as, years later, they would relate to the new ladies working the highway – hid clutching a knife, curled up in a ball under the kitchen table, just like back when she was a little girl, back when the whole town assumed and hoped and even prayed that she'd meet an early grave, be put out of her misery, because sooner or later the devil was coming to claim her and the ground would open up and both the Witches would plunge into the abyss, down into the fiery lakes of hell, the Girl because she was possessed, and the older one because of all the crimes she'd committed with her witchcraft: for having poisoned Don Manolo and putting a curse on his sons so they'd die in that accident; for making the townsmen sterile and weak with her dark dealings, with her black magic; and, above all, for having plucked so many seeds – rightfully planted there – from the bellies of bad women, dissolving them in the poison that she brewed for anyone who asked and the recipe for which she passed down to the Girl in the days leading up to the landslide of '78, when the whole region was on lockdown as the hurricane hit the coast with bitter, thundering force, and day after day rumbling storm clouds pumped the sky with water, inundating the fields and rotting everything, drowning the animals that, blindsided by the gale and the thunder, couldn't escape their pens in time; drowning even some children, the ones no one scooped up quickly enough when the hillside broke away and came crashing down in a tumult of rocks and uprooted oak trees and a black sludge that swamped everything in its path, eventually spilling out onto the coast, but only after having converted two-thirds of the town into a graveyard before the tearful,

26

bloodshot eyes of those who'd survived, thanks to the mango trees that they'd managed to hold on to when the water rushed in, and they'd held on like that for days, clinging to the branches, until the soldiers came and heaved them onto their boats, just as soon as that squall had worn itself out, having already ripped through the sierra, at which point the sun reappeared from behind the grey clouds and the land started to congeal again, and the people, soaked to the bone, their skin covered in lichen like infinitesimal corals, arrived en masse in Villagarbosa, livestock and surviving children in tow, seeking refuge wherever the government would put them: the basement of the town hall, the church vestibule, even the local school suspended classes for weeks to accommodate them; these people and all their crap, their whingeing and their lists of dead and missing persons, among whom the Witch and her accursed daughter were counted, because nobody had seen hide nor hair of them after the storm. It wasn't until weeks later that the Girl appeared one morning on the streets of Villa, dressed head to toe in black, her socks as black as the hairs on her legs, as black as her long-sleeved blouse, as black as her skirt and high-heels and the veil she clipped with hairpins to the bun of dark hair perched on the crown of her head, and the sight of her left everyone speechless, whether out of disgust or amusement it was impossible to say, dumbfounded by the ridiculous figure she cut: in the brain-frying heat, here was that weirdo dressed in black, she must be mad, just ridiculous, a real sight, like those cross-dressers who, every year without fail, showed up at the Villa Carnival, although no one dared laugh in her face because more than a few others had lost loved ones during that time, and on seeing the Girl dressed up like death, on seeing her sunken, solemn gait as she dragged her feet towards the market, they knew the other one had died, the mother, the Old Witch, gone from this world, surely buried in the mire that had swallowed half the town; an ugly death, and yet still better than she deserved, some thought, given the life of sin and simony she'd led; and nobody, not even the women, not even they, the regulars, the Friday callers, had the nerve to ask the bereaved girl what would happen with the business, who would take over the cures, the magic, and it would be years before people started returning to that house among the cane fields, whole years in which La Matosa was slowly dotted once more with shacks and shanties raised on the bones of those who'd been crushed under the hillside; repopulated by outsiders, most of them lured by the promise of work, the construction of the new highway that was to run right through Villa and connect both the port and the capital to the recently discovered oil wells north of town, up in Palogacho, enough work for *fondas* and food stalls to start cropping up, and in time even cantinas, guest houses, knocking shops and strip clubs where the drivers, the travelling tradesmen and the day labourers would stop to take a moment from the monotony of that road flanked on either side by cane fields, cane and pastures and reeds filling every inch of land for miles and miles, in every direction, from the very edge of the tarmac to the low slopes of the sierra to the west, or running eastward to the coast, to its eternally raging waters; brush and brush and more squat brush covered in vines that grew with rapacious speed during the rainy season and threatened to overwhelm homes and crops alike, and which the men kept at bay with their machetes, stooped at the side of the road, or on the banks of the river, or in the furrowed fields, their feet plunged inside the hot earth, some of them too focused or too proud to pay any mind to the rueful glances thrown their way from afar, from the dirt track; to that black-clad spectre who spent her time haunting the remotest parts of town, the plots where crews of new boys – the new recruits, paid peanuts – toiled, smooth-faced and supple as rope, the muscles on their arms, legs and stomachs wrung out from the gruelling labour and the scorching sun and chasing after a rag ball on the local football pitch come evening, and their frenzied races to see who would be the first to reach the water pump, the first to dive into the river, the first to find the coin thrown from the river-bank, who could spit the furthest while straddling the trunk of the fig tree suspended over the warm dusk waters, hollering and hooting, toned legs swinging in unison, shoulders all touching in a row, backs lustrous like buffed leather, shiny and dark like the seeds of a tamarind, or creamy like dulce de leche or the tender pulp of a ripe sapodilla. Skin the colour of cinnamon, of mahogany and rosewood, skin glistening wet and alive, which, from afar – from that tree trunk several yards away where the Witch spied on them – appeared smooth, taut and firm like the tart flesh of unripened fruit, the most irresistible kind, her favourite, the kind she begged for in silence, focusing the full force of her desire in her piercing black gaze, but remaining either hidden in the undergrowth or paralyzed with longing at the edge of the fields, those shopping bags hanging from her arms and her eyes moist from the sheer beauty of all that scin-tillating flesh, her veil raised in order to see them better, smell them better, taste – in her imagination – the brack-ish scent of those young men wafting in the air around the plains, carried along by the breeze that made the leaves on the sugar cane fissle, just like the frayed edges of their straw hats, the tips of their colourful kerchiefs and the flames that lashed through the cane fields, pulverizing the withered December scrub, reducing it to dust; the breeze that, come Holy Innocents, would start to smell of burnt caramel, of scorched earth, and that seemed to usher the slow roll of the last trucks loaded up with immense bales of blackened cane, which disappeared in the direction of the Mill under that grey, grey sky, when at last the boys could put away their machetes, not even rinsing them first, and rush to the highway to burn their wages, money earned with the sweat and every fibre of their aching bodies, and between great glugs of tepid beer pulled from Sarajuana's ancient fridge that rattled over the tumpa tumpa of the cumbia, *y lo primero que pensamos, ya cayó*, all of them seated around a plastic table, *sabrosa chiquitita, ya cayó*, they would go over the events of the previous weeks, and sometimes they all agreed that they'd glimpsed her from afar, or one of them might have even bumped into her on some side track, although those kids didn't know her as the Young Witch but simply as the Witch, and in their ignorance and youth they confused her with the older one, the Witch, and attributed to her, to the Girl, all those bloodcurdling stories that the townswomen used to tell them when they were kids: stories about La Llorona, the weeping woman who drowned all her offspring in a vile killing spree and was condemned for the rest of eternity to roam the earth as a ghastly apparition with the face of an angry mule and hairy spider legs, lamenting and bewailing her foul sin; or the story of La Niña de Blanco, the ghostly little girl who appears when you disobey your grandmother and slip out of the house at night, who follows you and, when you're least expecting it, calls your name, making you turn round only to die of shock on seeing her pallid, skeletal face; and in their minds the Witch was a little like that, only infinitely more exciting because she existed in real life, a real flesh and blood person who would walk around the Villa market greeting the vendors, not like that hocus-pocus bullshit their bigmouth grandmas and mothers and aunts rattled off, and all to dissuade them from going out, when those boys were only after a good time, when they only wanted to get out of the house and have a laugh, spook the pissheads and try their luck with the easy girls. Bullshit she's a witch, they all agreed, the ugly bint just wants some cock, some smart-ass would joke, if the Witch wants to suck me off she can start right here, another would say, clutching his balls, and between the wind-ups, the sniggers, the burps, the thumps on the table and the laughter, which was really more like yowling, there wasn't a thug among them who didn't sit there thinking that with all her land and all her money supposedly stashed away in chests, the sacks of gold coins, the riches, that Witch from the cane fields could well afford the luxury of paying them for what they gave away free to the girls in town, or to the odd lost sheep asking for it, right? No one knew for sure who was the first to try, the first one to pluck up the courage to head out into the darkness and all the way to that shit tip of a house, taking care not to be seen as he stood before the gate, before the kitchen door that swung open to reveal the figure of a very tall, scraggy woman, a set of keys jangling in her big hands like pale palm leaves, like lunar crabs poking out from the black sleeves of that tunic which seemed, in the darkness, to hover above the ground. And the glistering hot coals firing the cauldron gave off only the faintest of glows, but filled the kitchen with the stench of camphor, which lingered for days in the hair of the boys who were brave enough to go there, driven by either ambition or adrenaline, by morbid curiosity or necessity, to fumble with the shadow who would wait for them each night, quivering; they would get it over with as fast as they could before scampering back down the dirt track and through the fields until they reached the highway, back to the safety of Sarajuana's, where the money that the shadowy figure had slipped into their pocket when at last she'd let them leave would be spent on lukewarm beer. I didn't even have to look her in the face, one of those thugs would brag to whoever would listen; he hadn't had to do anything apart from put up with her wandering hands and let himself be licked by a mouth that was also like a shadow, poking in and out from behind the scratchy, grubby fabric that veiled her face – she only ever lifted it when strictly necessary, and even then only a fraction, never fully revealing herself, a detail for which they were grateful, just as they were grateful for the absolute silence of the whole act, no moaning or sighing, no distractions or words of any sort, just flesh on flesh and a lick of saliva in the murky gloom of that kitchen, or down one of the hallways decorated with images of naked women with their paper eyes scratched out. And once word that the Witch paid for it reached Villa and the rest of the ranches on that side of the river, it turned into quite the procession: a constant pilgrimage of boys and grown men would fight over who got to go in first; and sometimes they'd just turn up to hang out, arriving in pickups, the radio blaring and loaded with crates of beer that they took in through the kitchen before closing the door behind them, and you could hear music pumping, a raucous party, all to the horror of the locals, none more than the few decent women left in town, which by that point had been totally overrun by hookers and hussies who rolled in from God knows where, lured by the trail of banknotes that the oil trucks left in their wake as they made their way down the highway: waifs with no meat on their bones but caked in slap, and who, for the price of a beer, would allow that evening's partner to slip them a hand, full fingers even, as they danced; chubby girls who looked like they'd been smeared in lard under the clapped-out ceiling fans and who, after six straight hours of fiesta, no longer knew what was more draining: spending an hour sucking the cock of the punter who'd chosen them, or pretending that they really were listening to what the boring cunt had to say; and then the veteran girls, who danced alone when nobody picked them out, there in the middle of the dirt dance floor, drunk on cumbia and beer, lost in that amnesic tumpa tumpa; girls all washed up before their time, carried in from some far-flung dump on the same breeze that whipped up the plastic bags, leaving them wrapped around the sugar cane; women tired of life, women who, from one day to the next, would realize they no longer had it in them to reinvent themselves with every man they met, women who chuckled chipped-tooth chuckles to themselves when they recalled the dreams they'd once had; incidentally, the only women who, spurred on by the whispers and tales the older women would tell down by the river where they washed their clothes, or while they waited in line for their subsidized milk, dared to visit the Witch at home, in that hovel hidden among the crops; who dared to rap on the door until the mad shrew, dressed head to toe in black, poked her head out from a half-open door. And once there they would beg for her help to cook up one of her concoctions, the stuff that the women in town harped on about: potions to pin down the men, to really knock them off their feet, and indeed potions to ward the bastards off for good; potions that wiped their own memories, or that directed every drop of their destructive potential into the seed that those bastards had left in the women's bellies before scuttling back to their trucks; or those other tinctures, stronger still, which they say could purge hearts of the fatuous allure of suicide. Basically, those girls from the highway, not the meddlesome old bags in town, were the only ones the Witch chose to help for free, without charging a peso, which was just as well because most of them could barely earn enough to eat once a day, and plenty of them didn't own so much as the towels they used to wipe away the bodily fluids of the men who screwed them, although maybe, in the end, she helped those girls from the highway because they weren't ashamed to be seen going to her house, their tails in the air and their faces left uncovered as they called out, in their husky smoke-shot voices: Witch, Witchy, open up you silly wench, it's me again, back to bust your balls, until the Witch appeared, dressed in her black tunic and that crooked veil, which, even in the full light of day – in that bombsite of a kitchen with the kettle tipped on its side and the grimy, blood-spattered floor – couldn't hide the swollen bruising on her eyelids, the scabs where her lip and bushy eyebrows had split; the only women to whom, very occasionally, the Witch would profess her own sorrows, perhaps because they understood and knew first-hand the full, brutal force of male vice, and they would even crack jokes and try to tease a smile from her, try to take her mind off the cuts and bruises and make her open up and tell them the names of the bastards who'd attacked her, who'd got into her house and turned the place upside-down because they were on the rampage looking for money, the treasure the Witch supposedly kept stashed away in her house, the gold coins and the diamond ring that they say was the size of a fist, although the Witch swore blind that it wasn't true, that there was no treasure, that she lived off the rent from what was left of the estate, a handful of plots dotted around the house and farmed to grow sugar cane by the Mill Workers Union, and you only had to see how she lived, in a pigsty literally brimming with rubbish and mouldy cardboard boxes, bin bags full of papers and old rags and raffia and corncobs and flaky hairballs and dust and empty milk cartons and plastic bottles; crap, nothing but crap, which those thugs trampled on or smashed up in their efforts to open the door to the room upstairs, the bedroom that, for years, since back in her mother's day, had remained shut, boarded up from the inside by the Old Witch, when, in one of her raving outbursts, she propped every piece of the furniture in the room against the solid oak door so that only the full weight and force of seven uniformed police officers – who together constituted Villagarbosa's long arm of the law – including all two hundred and eighty pounds of Captain Rigorito, could finally knock it down, the very same day that the body of the poor Witch appeared floating in the Mill's irrigation canal. A horror show, people said, because by the time those kids found her, the body was already bloated and her eyes had popped out, her face had been half eaten by some animal and it looked like the crazy bitch, the poor thing, was smiling, a horror show, and, when all's said and done, a shame, goddammit, because deep down she was a good egg, always helping them out, and she never charged them or asked for more than a bit of company; and that's why they – the girls from the highway and the odd stray from the cantinas in Villa – decided to do a little collection, raise enough to give the putrid body of the Witch a worthy burial, but those fuckers from the police department – those heartless motherfuckers, may they rot in hell, every last one of them – wouldn't release the body to the women, first because it was evidence and the case was still open, and second because they didn't have the documents to prove their relation to the victim, which meant they didn't have any right to bury the body; those useless fucking pigs: what documents were the girls meant to present if no one in the village even knew that mad bitch's name, never had; if she herself refused to share it with them, said she didn't have one, that her mother only ever tutted and pssted to get her attention, or called her retard, asshole, devil child, she'd say, should've drowned you at birth, should've thrown you to the bottom of the river, damned Witch, damned fool, but it turns out she was right to hide away like she did, given what those assholes ended up doing to her; poor Witch, poor crank, let's just hope they catch the fucker or fuckers who slit her throat.

That day, Yesenia had gone down to the river early for a dip, and she was already on her way back when she spotted him: he came stumbling down the path, barefoot and shirtless, clutching a burnt tin can against his chest, his knees scraped and bloody from where he'd fallen along the way. He must have been drunk or high because he had the nerve to bounce straight up to Yesenia and ask her how the water was, to which she replied, as bluntly as possible, without so much as looking at him, deeply offended that it had even occurred to her cousin to address her, as if nothing had happened between them, as if they hadn't spent the last three years avoiding each other, that the water was crystal clear, before turning on her heel and heading home with her mind racing, going over all the things she could have said to that little shithead, all the trouble his fuckery had caused, the hell he'd put the family through: Grandma's illness, for starters, the rage that had left her paralyzed on one side and, barely a year later, the fall that broke her hip, the fall she still hadn't recovered from and perhaps never would, because it was plain to see the poor thing growing frailer and fainter by the day, at least in body, because the truth was her moods were as foul as ever and she spent her days on Yesenia's back about the boy, about when the useless prick was going to visit her and why he didn't want to introduce his new sweetheart to her. So she'd caught on to the news somehow, and given she was only deaf when it suited her, she'd almost certainly overheard those fat-mouthed Güera sisters gossiping that the kid had hooked up with a girl from out of town, and that he'd taken her to live in the hovel he'd built behind his whore of a mother's house. She was always on Yesenia's case, yapping in her

ear and asking what the girl looked like, why those two
had shacked up together so soon. There wasn't a baby on
the way, was there? Was the girl a grafter? Did she know
how to cook and do the laundry? The old woman wanted
all the details, and she wanted to hear them from her eldest granddaughter, as if Yesenia hadn't gone years
without exchanging a single word with that reprobate,
not a word since the day she caught him red-handed getting up to that sick business of his, and afterwards the
gutless prick had chosen to move out rather than having
to face Yesenia and the home truths she planned to tell
him, in front of Grandma, too, so the old bird could finally get it through her skull just what sort of monster
her grandson was: a pussy, a sneak and a fucking freeloader who never so much as thanked her for what she
did for him, for all the shit she put up with, because if it
hadn't been for Grandma, that little dipshit would be
dead: his slut of a mother abandoned him, left him
worm-ridden, half-starved and smeared in his own shit
in a wooden crate while she went whoring herself out on
the highway. It made Yesenia's blood boil whenever she
got to thinking about it, with an anger that made her guts
throb, every time she thought about that ungrateful little
prick and about what a fool Grandma had been to tell
Uncle Maurilio she'd bring him up, when she knew full
well that the slag he was seeing was a professional whore
who'd open her legs for anyone with a deep enough
pocket. Had she seriously not noticed the boy didn't
even look like Maurilio? Auntie Balbi asked when she
found out the old woman had taken that rugrat under
her wing. Had she not noticed that he didn't look like
anyone in the family? said Negra, Yesenia's mother, on
arriving at the house and finding that filthy kid hanging
like a monkey from Grandma's neck. If you ask me,

Maurilio and that rotten cow saw you coming, sweetheart; I'm surprised you don't remember the old saying, you of all people, with that dirty mind of yours, always imagining the worst of us: 'It's a wise woman who knows her grandchild.' But nothing could sway her, no amount of telling her that bringing up that kid as if he were part of the family was a mistake, that Maurilio was almost certainly not the father and that it was best for everyone to drop him off at the shelter, but no, not a chance, there wasn't a soul alive who could dissuade her. How was Doña Tina supposed to leave that poor defenceless creature, her only grandson, the son of her darling Maurilio, who was so sick himself, the poor lamb, that he could no longer care for the child! How could she say no to Maurilio, the only one who'd ever made any sacrifices for her, who'd dropped out of school when they'd first moved to La Matosa to help her set up the *fonda*, while you lot went around putting it about, throwing yourselves at the Company drivers and the labourers from the Mill, the old lady would hiss at them. Because far be it from Grandma to change a habit of a lifetime, so when she was angry she only ever remembered the bad shit, and since Maurilio was her favourite she liked to remind the rest of them that he'd given up everything for her to help get the business off the ground. But that was bullshit, total bullshit the old girl told herself because it allowed her to believe that Maurilio really loved her when he was nothing but a selfish prick who'd left school because he was thick as shit and lazy; a party boy who spent his days propping up the bar at the roadside cantinas, singing and playing a guitar some drunk left at Grandma's *fonda* one day by way of guarantee, never to come back for it; a guitar that Maurilio taught himself to play just by pressing the strings and listening to the sounds that poured out from its wooden body, all by himself, sitting beneath the mulberry tree out in the backyard – and just like that, just by watching the missionary kids play at mass in Villa, he learned to play whole songs, even composed some of his own with racy lyrics, and once he had everything tied up he went to Grandma and he said: Doña Tina, because that's what he called her, not mama or mamacita, but always by her name, always Doña Tina, the presumptuous prick; Doña Tina, he said, I'm off to work the highway, I'm a musician now, don't wait for me and don't worry, I'll send a little something the first chance I get, and with that he up and left, and he did well playing in the cantinas because he was young and likeable and the pissheads found it funny, this sombrero-clad scamp ragging them with an endless stream of filthy jokes and lewd puns, and it was around that time that the music from up north was starting to become popular, so they liked that about him too, because there was nothing Maurilio enjoyed playing more than corridos, and he even dressed like a *norteño*, that's how he appears in all the photos from that time, in his denim jeans, pointy boots, and embroidered belt, his sombrero pulled right down over his eyebrows, beer in hand and a fat cigar hanging from his mouth as girls swarm around him. The story went that women used to fall at his feet, more for his rugged, bad-boy looks than for his playing, because the truth was he was a pretty shit musician, which is why the stupid prick never played in a group or made any real money from his music; more beggar than busker, which is why he couldn't send Doña Tina the money he promised her; in fact, he continued sponging off her, and she'd help him out whenever he asked, lending money that the fucker never paid back, and on top of that she was always taking him to get cleaned up whenever he got into scuffles on nights out; and for several years she even made the quite staggering sacrifice of travelling all the way to Puerto to visit him inside, every Sunday without fail she'd visit Uncle Maurilio, who was doing time for murder, a really bright fucking idea, some guy from Matacocuite, and all because Maurilio was fucking his whore of a wife, and she'd buckled under the hiding the husband gave her and ended up spilling her guts. Uncle Maurilio was in the middle of a days-long bender when he got tipped off that someone had been asking after him in Villa, a guy going around saying he wanted to snap Maurilio Camargo's neck for dipping his wick in his wife, and Uncle Maurilio stood up from the table where he'd been drinking and said: Well, rather his funeral than mine, and he handed someone his guitar to look after and hitched a lift to Villa to confront his fate head-on, and as luck would have it he happened across the cuckold husband in the bathroom of a cantina, and so, from behind, without so much as letting him get a word in, Uncle Maurilio stabbed the stranger twice with the knife he kept in his boot, and that's how he ended up in Puerto, serving nine years for first-degree murder, nine long years, every Sunday of which Doña Tina went to see him, to bring him his Raleighs, a few centavos, his soap and some provisions that she brought all the way from Villa, always alone because she didn't want Yesenia or the other girls going, she didn't want the other inmates all over them like a pack of dogs, and since she was frightened of losing her way on the trams in Puerto she would walk from the bus station all the way to the prison to see her adored boy, her only son, taken so young, in the flower of his youth, barely a year after the asshole got out, from some calamitous bug he'd caught on the inside. Grandma always said it was nothing, that prison would do that to a man, make him weak, drag him down, and could you very well blame Maurilio for being depressed when the slag he'd been living with had run off with some other fellow? Negra and Balbi were convinced Maurilio had AIDS and they wouldn't let the girls near their uncle; they weren't about to let him infect them with his rotten bug, whatever it was, and eventually not even Grandma could deny that her son was dying, and in a last-ditch attempt to save him she decided to put him in the most expensive clinic in Villa, the one built for the oil workers, and in order to pay for all his treatments and the hospital bills she had no option but to sell the *fonda*, her holding on the highway roadside, and Negra and Balbi screamed blue murder and tore their hair out when they learned what Doña Tina had gone and done, because what was their mother thinking she was doing selling their one worldly good, which they'd worked their fingers to the bone for all those years, what were they supposed to live on now, Maurilio didn't have long anyway, even the doctors said there was no hope, that they should start making arrangements, and Grandma really blew her top when the girls came out with that suggestion, she accused them of being shit-stirring harpies, despicably greedy; the *fonda* was hers and hers alone, and if they didn't like the idea of selling it then they could go to hell, the vipers, the self-seeking, spiteful beasts, how dare they say Maurilio wasn't going to survive when, God willing, he had his whole life ahead of him, years and years to watch his son grow and have a whole brood more, and that's when Balbi and Negra said: Well, fuck this then, fuck you and your *fonda* and that gutless prick Maurilio, we're out of here, the girls too, and they rounded up the children, but Doña

Tina went after them and literally snatched them from the door and said Balbi and Negra were out of their minds if they thought she was going to let them take the girls: what, so they could end up whores like you? Negra and Balbi could go wherever the hell they liked but the girls were staying with her – little difference did the two women's ranting and raving make, Doña Tina wasn't having any of it and they were forced to head north on their own, north to the oilfields, where rumour had it there was plenty of work, and they never did return to La Matosa, not even when Uncle Maurilio finally kicked the bucket, and thank God they didn't because they would have been sick to their stomachs to see how Grandma squandered money she didn't have to give her prodigal son the send-off that, to her mind, he deserved, a funeral the likes of which no one in town had seen for years, with lamb tamales for everyone and a *norteño* band and mariachis and cases and cases of the finest aguardiente, which ensured everyone got steaming drunk and wept tears of heartfelt sadness for poor Maurilio, and on top of that she bought a gravestone, more like a chapel really, and a plot in the principal part of Villa's cemetery, the most important part, because Doña Tina couldn't very well bury her darling son in the cheap plots, now could she? Not in those plots that would be dug up ten years later and filled with other bodies. She might not even be around in ten years, and then what would become of poor Maurilio's remains? If it was left to those spiteful vixens of hers they'd end up in a mass grave, which is why she opted for one of the plots in perpetuity, a small fortune it cost her, more than the value of the house in La Matosa, an extortionate sum, and all for the honour of rubbing shoulders with the Villagarbosas, the Condes and their cousins the

Avendaños, Villa's founding fathers, lying in their fancy marble and mosaic tombs, and right there in the middle of them stood a gravestone painted canary yellow, the final resting place of that cunt Maurilio Camargo. Doña Tina spent years paying off the funeral and the burial place with the money she earned selling fresh fruit juice from a tricycle stationed on the outskirts of Villa by the petrol station. Even when she was unwell she had no choice but to get up and pedal to the market to load up the tricycle with sacks of oranges and carrots and beetroots and mandarins and mangos, depending on the season, while Yesenia stayed at home looking after the younger girls and the little tearaway destined to grow into the thorn in her side. As the eldest, it fell on her shoulders to look after the house while Grandma was out working; the house, the girls and her shit-for-brains cousin. As the eldest, she also bore the brunt of Doña Tina's towering rage and the hidings she doled out whenever things went wrong, whenever things weren't done as Grandma wanted, and it was Yesenia, too, who had to answer for her delinquent cousin's antics, when the neighbours would come over and complain that the little dipshit had stolen bottles of fizzy drinks from the shop, how he'd snuck into their houses and eaten their food and taken whatever belongings and cash he could find, or that he'd hit the smaller children, or that he'd been playing with matches and nearly set fire to the Güeras' coop, chickens and all; and it was always Yesenia who had to go over and apologize for him, pay his debts, act dumb and then watch, her blood boiling, as Grandma did absolutely nothing, didn't punish him for any of the shit he got up to while she was out. What can you do, she'd say when Yesenia reeled off the long list of trouble her grandson had caused that day; he's only a kid, he

44

doesn't mean anything by it, boys will be boys, Lagarta, let him be, the poor lamb, his father was just the same, just as cheeky, and the boy's cut from the same cloth, a chip off the old block, Grandma would say, which was a load of shit, because while she might have been happy to play dumb and pretend they were identical, the spitting image, two peas in a pod, to everyone else it was clear that the only thing those men had in common was being useless bums and a pair of ass-lickers when it came to Grandma, who let them do as they damn well pleased, and that's why the boy turned out like he did: a wild animal who bolted into the wild every time he was let loose, even in the dead of night, because according to Grandma, that was the way to raise fearless young men, but it was Yesenia who had to round him up each time to make him wash, to mend his tattered clothes, to pick off the lice and ticks that he brought back with him; and then drag him to school each morning, the whole way clipping him round the ear to get him to do as she said, although of course she never dared lay a finger on him in front of Grandma, only ever when they were alone, in the not infrequent moments when Yesenia grew tired of shouting at him and lost it, grabbing her cousin by the hair and beating his scrawny body black and blue, and even, once or twice, throwing him against the wall, hoping to kill him, hoping to split the little chickenshit's head open and stop him, once and for all, from winding her up, from hitting her, from calling her by that nickname Grandma had started, which Yesenia loathed with every fibre of her being; the name that had caught on to such an extent that the whole town knew her as Lagarta, because she was an ugly, dark-skinned, lanky thing, Grandma would say, a lizard on two feet. *Hairy bush, hairy bush,* that little shit would sing under his breath, *Lagarta's got a hairy bush*, right there on the bus headed for Villa, or queuing somewhere surrounded by people, by the stupid bigmouths who would hear him and laugh, and there was nothing she could do but slap him in the face – shut your mouth, you leprous little shit – pinch him wherever he was close enough and take immense pleasure as her nails punctured the boy's skin, a pleasure akin to the relief she felt when she scratched a mosquito bite until it bled; and maybe the boy got some kind of relief from it too, because after the beatings he always calmed down; he'd even stop winding her up, but then Grandma would notice the scratches and bruises and Yesenia would receive twice the thrashing she'd been forced to give her cousin to calm him down, and with Grandma's weapon of choice, the wet rope, which the old crone would take to their asses, their backs, and even their faces if they were dopey enough not to raise their hands in time, until Yesenia would yelp and beg her to stop, to forgive her, and sometimes little La Bola and Picapiedra were also on the receiving end, and, more rarely, sometimes even Baraja, the best behaved of them all, the one who never gave Grandma any trouble, and the boy would just stand there watching as Doña Tina flogged them and called them slackers, tarts, slobs, dogs, she should've let their whoring mothers take them, should've left them out on the street, left them to end up in the reformatory to be raped by the lesbians with brooms, how would you like that, you dirty sluts, you nasty pieces of work? she'd shout, because Grandma was prone to losing the plot from one moment to the next and confusing Yesenia with Negra, or Picapiedra with Balbi, and she'd accuse them of things that the poor girls hadn't done, like creeping out at night to turn tricks, and it was all La Bola's fault; La Bola, the moment she turned fifteen, began sneaking out to dances in Matacocuite with one of the younger Güera sisters, and in order to pay for the bus fare and entrance fee the chubby cow began stealing from Grandma's purse, that's how badly she wanted to sneak around and find a boyfriend, until one night Grandma realized La Bola wasn't in her bed with the others, and, wielding that menacing length of rope, she woke them all up and sent them out looking for the stupid girl, and I'm telling you now that if you don't bring her back you'll wish you'd never been born, you girls, and they had no choice but to traipse from door to door through La Matosa, rousing the sleeping dogs and waking the neighbours, who would spend the following day whispering to each other with a nod and a wink that La Bola was no longer a little lady, and after a while Yesenia had to pick up young Baraja and carry her, while chivvying along Picapiedra with little kicks on the backside because she was young and crying from exhaustion, and so it turned two in the morning and they still hadn't found La Bola, and since they didn't dare go home empty-handed to Grandma they snuck into the Güeras' yard, where the dogs knew them and wouldn't bite, where they could creep inside the chicken coop to rest. And imagine their surprise when they came face to face with that piece of shit La Bola, who'd hidden there when she got word that Grandma had sent out a search party. Yesenia had to drag her by the hair from the chicken coop, and the scene woke Doña Pili, the Güeras' mum, who offered to take Yesenia and the girls home to their grandmother to help calm down Doña Tina, she said, when really that two-faced harpy just liked her gossip served hot, wanted to see first-hand how La Bola went in crying and Doña Tina just stood staring at her, and how, when she saw that Doña Pili was with her, she just shook her head in disappointment and sent them all to bed, but not one of them could sleep with the anxiety of not knowing when Grandma would come into the room to thrash them, because by now they knew how the old crone worked: nothing, absolutely nothing got past her, but sometimes she pretended it had so she could catch them off guard with that rope of hers, which she used to flog their backsides once they were tucked up in bed on the sweet cusp of sleep, or fresh out of the bath, which is how she finally caught up with La Bola two days later. Remember, Bola chubs? You were naked and glistening wet, singing in the bath, and on top of the whipping she gave you, Grandma said that from then on you could forget about school because you were going to sell juice with her, learn how to earn a living, and that cut deeper than all the floggings she'd ever given you put together, right? Poor chubs. She'd always dreamed of finishing school and becoming a teacher, but none of that happened because, even though she swore blind that one day she'd go back and finish school, within a year of Grandma pulling her out the stupid cow had gone and got herself knocked up, a baby girl, Vanessa, and any hope of her finishing her studies went down the drain. Who knows how the old bitch always knew if you'd been up to no good, with nothing but a look, as if her eyes were two beams that could pierce right through your skull and see everything going on in there, everything you were thinking in that very moment. And who knows how she always knew the right punishment, exactly where to hit you where it hurt most. Lagarta would never forget the night Grandma hacked off all her hair with the poultry shears, after discovering that she'd also snuck out at night, but not to go dancing or fooling around with the boys like that strumpet La Bola, no, just to follow the kid, to see where he went each night and to catch him red-handed, since everyone in town knew he was up to no good; she longed to open Grandma's eyes and finally make her see the kid for the degenerate he was, see how he spent his life getting drunk and high, stumbling around town, exactly as Yesenia found him that day down by the river, the day she woke up early to go and have a dip in the early dawn light and she saw him reeling in the direction of the beach, barefoot and shirtless, his hair a tangled viper's nest, eyes dilated and bloodshot from the drugs, and his gaze distant, lost in who knows what visions. There he was, jabbering like one of those loons you see on the highway, drifting aimlessly with that burnt tin can in his sooty hands, his big lips broadening into an idiotic grin as he asked Yesenia how the water was, and, without so much as looking at him, stunned with rage that the little shit had dared address her, she replied that it was crystal clear, before scuttling away with a dull ache in her guts and spending the whole journey home thinking about all the things she could have said, all the insults that, for three long years, Yesenia had been storing up for her stupid son-of-a-bitch cousin, if only he hadn't caught her off guard. That was the first time she'd bumped into that pussy around town because he usually steered clear of her, and he only went out at night, after dark, like some sort of fucking vampire, to meet up with those wasters who spent their lives getting shitfaced on booze and drugs, mugging unsuspecting locals in Villa's park under the cover of darkness and coming to blows with, sometimes even bottling the other hooligans who hung out at the cantinas in the centre of town, or smashing the bulbs on the streetlamps and pissing against the walls and shutters of the shops around the park; useless, spineless shirkers, every single one of them, a bunch of pathetic, sponging, fucked-up junkies. They should be locked up and ass-fucked and then disappeared. She'd like to see how big and tough they'd be then, as big and tough as when they went around molesting the local girls, and even the boys, the guys who dared walk through the park when they were hanging out there. As if the police didn't know, for Christ's sake, as if they didn't know about the sordid set-up between those punks and the owner of the Hotel Marbella, about how they make their drug money right there in the park, in the shadows, or if not there then in the public of the cantinas and highway dives, or behind the derelict warehouse down by the railway tracks, where everyone knows the rent-boy homos get up to their filth, like dogs, in broad daylight. Yesenia could vouch for it, she'd seen it with her own eyes and there weren't enough fingers on her hands to count the number of times she'd had to haul the kid out of those places, because the stupid prick hadn't come home for days and Yesenia had run out of excuses, and in the end those fucking bigmouth Güera sisters would always turn up to tell Grandma what people in town were saying about the boy, even though Grandma always denied it, dismissed it as rumour, her grandson wasn't involved in anything of the kind, he was in Gutiérrez de la Torre for the lemon harvest, all that talk about how he spent his days in the Witch's house was a load of rubbish, hot air from bitter neighbours who had nothing better to do than go around spinning yarns, and back then Yesenia would keep quiet, she wouldn't dare tell Grandma the truth: what she'd seen with her own eyes and what the Güeras went around telling anyone who'd listen; but also what Aunty Balbi had predicted all along, ever since Grandma took that filthy runt in; he'll

50

turn out like Maurilio, or worse, because people said some pretty nasty shit about Uncle Maurilio: that he was a pisshead, that he was a dumb shit who sponged off his missus, and that later in life he fell into drugs, and they even said that's how he caught the disease that ended up sucking the life out of him, but at least he never earned a name for himself among the local rent boys, nor did he spend every waking hour at the Witch's house, at the orgies that went on there, which Yesenia had seen with her own eyes one night, *that* night, the night Grandma took the poultry shears to her hair and sent her out to sleep in the yard, like the mongrel bitch that she was, Grandma told her. Yesenia didn't need the Güeras to bring her up to speed; she'd seen it all with her own eyes and had run back home to wake Doña Tina and tell her of the nasty shit her darling innocent grandson was up to that very moment, to see if Grandma would finally stop kidding herself and recognize just what kind of vermin she'd allowed to live under her roof; to see if she would finally stop blaming Yesenia for everything because she was the eldest, because it was her job to watch her cousin and not to go around telling tales that the Güeras could later spread, terrible accusations that these lazy lowlives in town would then go around repeating. Grandma hadn't believed a word Yesenia said; Grandma had simply glowered at her and said: Lagarta, you little shit-stirrer, you're sick in the head, only you could come out with such a rotten, disgraceful pack of lies, aren't you ashamed of yourself, whoring around and then pointing the finger at your cousin? There's only one thing'll stop you wanting to leave the house, you wicked little tramp. Grandma had cut off all her hair with the poultry shears while Yesenia sat motionless, as still as a possum in the headlights, terrified of being slashed by those icy blades,

51

and afterwards she'd spent the whole night out in the yard, like the mongrel bitch that she was, and Grandma had said: a stinking animal that didn't deserve so much as a flee-ridden mattress beneath its fetid coat. She spent a long time shaking off the hairs that had stuck to her clothes, wiping away her tears, and when at last her eyes adjusted to the darkness, she untied the washing line, took it down and used it to flog the back wall of the house, to flog it until the blisters of plaster from the humidity flaked off, then she went at the bushes that grew beneath the kitchen window, whipping them until they'd been thrashed bare, and it was just as well that they didn't happen to be keeping any lambs just then because that night she could have flogged one to death, to death or until one of her cousins rushed out to stop her, and it was a good thing too that her cunt of a cousin didn't show his face again at Grandma's, because Yesenia had made up her mind to kill him. She spent the whole night waiting in the darkness of the hallway, a blunt machete in hand, ready to pounce on that fucker the moment he came tumbling down the path with a shit-eating grin on his face, because everything was a joke to that kid, even the beatings Yesenia gave him, even Grandma's pleas and sobs, he didn't give a shit about any of it, he only thought about himself, and who knows, maybe not even that, because the drugs probably dulled his ability to think straight, he probably didn't think about anything at all or understand the suffering he inflicted on everybody around him, just like that bastard father of his, you'll see, Balbi said, the apple never falls far from the tree, like father like son. You mean like mother like son, Negra cut in, that little prick'll turn out just like his whore of a mother, about whom far worse stories circulated in the village, with some even going as far as to say

that she was the reason seven men had died, seven truckers, all from the same transport company, and all from
AIDS, seven dead men, or eight if you counted Uncle
Maurilio, if you paid any mind to the rumours, and the
worst thing about it: the old wench herself was still in
one piece, she showed no signs of how sick, how rotten
she was on the inside; she looked right as rain, with as
much meat as ever on her bones, still flaunting the
curves for which she was known in the rat hole she ran
on the highway, employed by her lover, the *güero* sent
down from the north by the Grupo Sombra to push
drugs in the area, the one who prowls the highway in a
pimped-up, blacked-out pickup; the one from the video
– you know, the famous video that everyone keeps shar-
ing on their phones, a video of him doing horrific things
to some girl, barely more than a child, all skin and bones,
barely able to hold up her head she was so doped, or so
ill, because they say that's what those fuckers do to the
poor girls they abduct on their way to the border: they're
put to work in the knocking shops like slaves and when
they're no longer ripe for the picking, they slaughter
them like lambs, exactly like in the video, they chop
them up into pieces and sell their meat to the roadside
food stands as if it were a prime cut, perfect for the region's legendary tamales, the same tamales Grandma
sold in the *fonda*, only hers were made with actual lamb,
not girl; one hundred per cent lamb, which Grandma
butchered herself out in the yard, or bought from Don
Chuy in the market in Villa; lamb, not dog meat, as
those gossips in town would have it, a spiteful bunch
with nothing better to do than go around making up
stories, those goddamn Güeras sisters, for instance,
always sticking their noses in where they weren't wel-
come, the bitches: really it was their fault that Grandma

was always on Yesenia's case, asking about the boy and the girl he'd shacked up with, as if Yesenia didn't have better things to do than chase after that prick; as if her days weren't already busy enough taking care of Grandma and the meals and the laundry and those lazy brat cousins of hers who never do as they're told, or only after a good clip round the ear. If it hadn't been for the Güeras running their mouths, everything would've been fine, everything would've turned out exactly as Yesenia planned on that Monday, the first of May, after overhearing Mary, the owner of the haberdashery, tell another lady how that very morning, barely a couple of hours earlier, they'd found the body of the Witch in one of the irrigation canals near the Mill, with her throat slit and her flesh all rotten and pecked at by the buzzards, so repugnant that Police Chief Rigorito hadn't been able to contain his nausea; and Yesenia, who was in Villa with Vanessa, stopped dead when she heard this, and she couldn't help thinking about what she'd seen on Friday, the same day she went early for a dip in the river and bumped into her cousin, barefoot and shirtless, stumbling down the path. The brazen little fuck even had the cheek to ask her how the water was and Yesenia had replied that it was crystal clear and then turned on her heel and headed home, even though she'd have liked to smash his stupid face in and tell him all the trouble he'd caused. She hadn't told anyone she'd seen him that morning down by the river, and of course she hadn't dared tell Grandma or her cousins that, a few hours later, she'd spotted him out and about again, that same Friday but this time gone noon, at around two or three, while she was standing at the laundry sink out in the yard, scrubbing the knickers and nightie her grandma had just pissed herself in, when she heard the sound of a car rolling slowly down the dirt track towards the house and she poked her head out just in time to see a blue or perhaps grey van – it was hard to know for sure because it was covered in dust and dirt – which belonged to that guy everyone called Munra, who happened to be the husband of the skanky bitch who bore her cousin. A useless bum was Munra, and lame in one leg; a drunk, a kept one at that, who did nothing but drive around in his van with the kid. Of course she recognized Munra; no one else in town had a ride like that, and besides, the windows were down, although at that point she couldn't make out if there was anyone else in there, if the kid had come along with a mind to turn up at Grandma's. Yesenia even raised a wet hand to her forehead like a visor to see if she could make him out inside the van, but no such luck. Her heart started pounding from the fear and rage that hadn't abated since that morning; fear that her cousin was going to show up and upset Grandma, and rage at all the pain the prick had caused the old girl by leaving. She left the clothes in the sink and headed out towards the dirt track, her eyes glued to the van, and to her horror she saw that it came to a stop two hundred yards up the way, almost directly in front of the Witch's house. Her eyes were watering in the blazing sun but Yesenia didn't look away from the van for a second, convinced that at any moment she'd see her asshole of a cousin step out of the vehicle, but after barely a few minutes Grandma began moaning from her room and, since no one else was in, Yesenia had to go to her side; the girls would be home from school soon enough, provided those idiots didn't stop to fuck around on the way, as usual. That's why she took so long to get back out into the yard, where she found the van still parked in the same place, and, a little calmer now, she began rinsing and wringing out the clothes she'd left soaking, glancing furtively up the dirt track every now and then. She was just about to carry the clothes over to the washing line when she saw the door to the Witch's house burst open and two young men emerge carrying a third person, holding them by the arms and legs as if they were unconscious or dead drunk. One of those guys was her cousin, Maurilio Camargo Cruz, otherwise known as El Luis Miguel, or Luismi – Yesenia would've bet her life on it, she'd brought up the little shit: she could spot that mop of wild curls from ten miles off. She was also certain that the person they were carrying was the Witch, from the size of the body, and also because of her clothes, all black, the only colour the Witch had dressed in for as long as Yesenia could remember. She also recognized the other kid with her cousin, one of the wasters from the park; she didn't know his name or nickname, but he was roughly the same height as her cousin, about five foot five, and similarly thin and scrawny, although his hair was black and he wore it very short and sort of brushed up at the front, the fashion among the kids. She recounted all of this to the policemen who attended to her grudgingly that Monday first of May, only to repeat it all again for the district attorney's secretary: her cousin's name, where he lived and what she'd seen with her own eyes the night she'd secretly followed him to the Witch's house; the nasty filth that Grandma didn't want to believe when Yesenia woke her up to tell her, to finally make her see what kind of scumbag her grandson really was, but Grandma hadn't wanted to believe any of it; Grandma said that Yesenia was making it up because she had a dirty rotten mind and that the only one who snuck out at night to get up to that kind of filth was Yesenia, and she dragged her by her hair to the kitchen

56

where she grabbed the enormous poultry shears, and for a moment Yesenia thought Grandma was going to stab her in the throat, she closed her eyes to avoid watching her own blood spurt across the kitchen floor, but then she felt the rasping edge of the blade against her skull and heard the dull crunch of the blades as they cut through thick locks of her hair, the hair she kept so beautifully, her one lovely feature: that thick, very straight black hair, the envy of all her cousins because it was shiny and smooth like the hair of the actresses from their favourite soaps, not wiry and frizzy like theirs, like Grandma's, sheep's hair she called it, fuzzy black-girl hair, and not even Balbi, who had green eyes and claimed to have Italian blood, not even she'd been spared the family gene, only Yesenia, the ugliest, swarthiest and scrawniest of the lot, but the only one with exquisite hair that tumbled over her shoulders and down her back like silk curtains, a cascade of bluish-black velvet which Grandma hacked away that night until Yesenia was left looking like someone out of a madhouse, to teach her a lesson, to see how she'd prowl around looking for men now; the hair Yesenia cried over as she brushed great clumps of it from her clothes, snatched the washing line and lashed the walls of the house and the bushes beneath the window until they were left as bald as she was. There were no more tears to cry now, of either sadness or rage, she only listened in silence to Grandma as she wept over her grandson in her room, and every sob, every wail from the old bird was like an icy dagger plunged into Yesenia's heart. It was all that prick's fault, she thought – that little shit will be the death of Grandma, who, for better or worse, was like a mother to Yesenia now that Negra and Balbi had left them high and dry – no more calls, no more money. That fucker had to die, and

Yesenia was prepared to beat the life out of him. She'd stay up and wait in the darkness, ready to pounce on him the moment he tried to sneak into the house like he always did, in the middle of the night, and with the rusty machete she found under the laundry sink, with that blunt blade that stank of copper, of coins, she'd slash his face and slit his neck and the game's up, you little prick, fun's over, I'm not going to watch you take the piss out of my grandma any longer, and, having killed him, she'd dig a hole at the bottom of the yard to bury him in, and if Grandma wanted to turn her over to the police, well, she'd go quietly, happy in the knowledge that she'd accomplished her mission to rid Grandma of that son-of-a-bitch leech once and for all. But the prick never did show his face that night, nor the following day, week or month. He never went back to Grandma's house, not even to collect his clothes or belongings, and certainly not to say goodbye to the old girl or thank her for everything she'd done for him – it had to have been those stupid fucking Güeras who went and blabbed to Grandma that the boy had gone to live with his mother, a blow to the old crone who couldn't believe he'd chosen that slut over his own grandmother, all because the whore was prepared to turn a blind eye to the shit he got up to, when Grandma had brought him up as if he were her own, and in the end she was so distraught that two weeks later she suffered the stroke that paralyzed her all the way down one side, just like that, and then, a year later, the fall in the bathroom from which she never got up, and so God only knew how Grandma would take the news that the little prick was a murderer, that they were putting him behind bars; she'd probably still visit him, the fool, take him money and food and even smokes, just like she did for Uncle Maurilio when he was inside; she'd tell Yesenia to get her dressed and order her a taxi down to the station in Villa, as if the taxis there came cheap, as if the poor old girl still believed she had it in her to go anywhere when she hadn't left her bed for two years and had the ulcers to prove it. No, Grandma mustn't find out that the kid was a murderer, and under no circumstances could she know that it was Yesenia who snitched on him to the police, the one who went down to the station that Monday, the first of May, and told them everything, his full name and address, so they could go and arrest him, right after she overheard the lady who runs the haberdashery in the market, where she'd stood rooted to the spot, thinking about what would happen if she dared tell the authorities what she'd seen that Friday morning, and then again at noon, thinking about what Grandma would say if she found out, but thinking, too, about how much she hated that useless prick and wanted to see him put away, and all while Vanessa stood gawping at her like the dopey cow that she was, frightened by how tense her aunt had suddenly become. Go home, she ordered the girl finally. Run as fast as you can, now, and tell your mum and your aunts to stay indoors and not to let anyone in the house, no one, do you hear? Especially not the goddamn Güeras. How did they always get wind of everything? It was as if they had antennae, or maybe the shameless bitches were part-witch too. How could they go blabbing to Grandma when they knew full well how badly the old crone took it every time she heard anything about the kid; how could they bring themselves to tell her the boy was inside, that they'd charged him with killing the Witch? They had no way of knowing Yesenia snitched on him, right? So how the fuck did Grandma know? She only had to catch Yesenia's tear-filled eye as the girl leaned over to check on her grandma, later than usual because the bastard police had taken her to the Public Prosecutor's office to repeat her whole story, and the retard of a secretary had taken forever typing Yesenia's statement on to the computer for her to sign, so it was already dark when at last she got back to La Matosa, back to the house where all the lights were on, and that was enough for her to know that something terrible had happened, and she ran inside, straight to Grandma's room and found her doubled over on the bed, her mouth open as if frozen in a scream and her wide eyes staring at the ceiling, and it was that ratface La Bola who told Yesenia what had happened: Grandma had another fit, just a few hours earlier, from crying so hard after what the Güeras had come over earlier that evening to tell her, the word going around that the police had arrested the kid on suspicion of killing the Witch and throwing her body in the irrigation canal, and Yesenia wanted to slap La Bola, to tear into her for being so careless. Why on earth had she let those fucking Güeras in when she'd explicitly told Vanessa that everyone was to stay inside the house and not to open the door to anyone, especially not those dumb bitches? And that was when she realized, looking one by one at the sullen faces around Grandma's bed, that the rotten dog Vanessa wasn't there, because the little tart had clearly made the most of the fact that her aunt had let her go home alone to run off and see her boyfriend, that ratty pothead who was always lurking around at the end of school, and so Yesenia had no choice but to leave the bedroom, leave the house and walk down the dirt track to the Güeras' house, kicking and pounding on the door and screaming at those nosey cows, asking those gobshites what the big idea was winding up Grandma with their bullshit lies, because it was either that or knocking the shit out of

60

La Bola for having given birth to that goddamn numb-skull Vanessa, who was incapable of following the simplest orders. The Güeras didn't open the door, of course; they didn't even dare poke their heads out the window because they knew if they gave Yesenia the slightest backchat she was more than capable of kicking down the wall, so of course they didn't light the candles on the Virgin's altar either, not even after Yesenia had shouted herself hoarse and stomped back home, where she waited, surrounded by her cousins and nieces, for Picapiedra to arrive from Villa with the doctor, and for Vanessa, too, and Yesenia planned to give her a severe whipping with the wet rope the moment the little slut came through the door, while Grandma wheezed with the effort of staying alive, no longer capable of speech, only peeling her eyes from the ceiling for one terrifying moment, when Yesenia rested her grandmother's head on her lap to caress the old girl's coarse white hair, tell-ing her that it was okay, everything was going to be okay, the doctor was on his way to make her better, she must hold on a little longer and be strong for her, for them, for her granddaughters who adored her, but the words stuck in her throat when the old woman dropped her gaze and locked eyes with Yesenia, and who knows how, who knows how Yesenia could tell, but she'd have sworn on the Holy Cross that Grandma looked at her as if she knew what she'd done, as if she could read her mind and knew that it was Yesenia who ratted out the kid, who told the police in Villa where the little shit lived so they could go and arrest him. And Yesenia also knew, as she drowned in the old woman's furious eyes, that Grandma despised her with every ounce of her being and in that very moment she was putting a curse on Yesenia, and in the faintest of voices Yesenia begged for forgiveness and explained that it had all been for her, but it was too late: once again, Grandma hit Yesenia where it hurt most, dying right there, trembling with hate in the arms of her eldest granddaughter.

Honest, honest, honest to God, he didn't see a thing, on his mother's soul, may she rest in peace, he didn't see a thing; didn't even know what those fuckers had done to her, without his crutch he was as good as stuck in the van, and besides, the kid had told him to stay put behind the wheel with the engine running, they'd be in and out in a matter of minutes, or that's what Munra had taken him to mean, and that was as much as he knew, he didn't get out for a better view or turn to look out of the open side door, and although, truth be told, he was tempted, he even resisted the urge to watch through the rearview mirror. Too spooked, because suddenly the sky turned black and a great gust of wind swept those banks of clouds across the neighbouring hills, flogging the cane against the ground, and he said to himself the rain wouldn't be too far behind, and right before his eyes a soundless bolt of lightning burst from the murky sky and landed on a tree, burning it to a crisp in perfect silence, a silence so thick that for a moment he thought he'd gone deaf, because the only thing he could make out a sharp ringing in his head and the guys had to shake him to snap him out of it, and only then did he realize he wasn't deaf and that he could, after all, hear those fuckers screaming at him to step on it, step on it, come on, you cripple fuck, put your foot down, the engine's already running, get the hell out of there, hit the dirt track leading down to the river, skirt round Playa de Vacas and head into Villa up near the cemetery, cut across town along the main drag, past its sole set of lights and the park, till they were back on the highway bound for La Matosa, Munra thinking the whole time how sweet it'd be to get home, slip into bed with a bottle of aguardiente and drink himself into oblivion, forget about everything, forget even that Chabela hadn't been home for days, forget the way the van's headlights seemed to intensify the darkness around them as they raced at breakneck speed along that dirt track, forget the laughter coming from those dipshits cracking jokes that went straight over his head, and finally, when at last he was stretched out on his bed, Munra even entertained the idea of popping a couple of Luismi's pills, because every time he closed his eyes and tried to fall asleep his body started shaking and his stomach churned and the bed disappeared beneath him, as if he was teetering on the edge of a cliff, about to fall into the abyss, and then he'd open his eyes, toss and turn on the bed and try to drift off again when that same lightheaded feeling would return and he'd call Chabela but her phone was still off, and that's how he spent the whole night, to the point where he even considered crossing the yard to ask Luismi for one of his pills, to see if he could finally nod off and sleep till noon, but deep down he knew that without his crutch he wouldn't make it over to the kid's room, so he resigned himself to shifting restlessly on his bed until he finally did slip into a kind of fitful slumber, which only the roosters crowing in the distance and the sun rising through his window could eventually break. He didn't feel like getting up, but he couldn't stand the heat of that room or the reek of his own body or the empty space beside him on the bed where Chabela should have been, so he struggled to his feet, holding on to the furniture and even the walls, and he hobbled out into the yard to take a piss and wash, and God only knew what time it was but the kid still hadn't shown any sign of life, and nor was he about to, by the looks of things, because from the yard Munra glimpsed him spread-eagled across the mattress that covered practically the whole floor of his tiny room – his *casita*, he called it – with his mouth parted and his puffy, almost purple eyes half-shut. Judging by the amount of pills he'd polished off the night before, Luismi wouldn't be up till the following day, and, lo and behold, that's exactly when he crawled out of his hole, Sunday night, when Munra spotted him lurching across the yard and heading off up the dirt track towards the highway, no doubt to wangle more cash for his filthy rotten pills. What the kid got out of that shit Munra would never understand: why would anyone want to go around like a space cadet all goddamn day, tongue stuck to the roof of your mouth and your mind as blank as a TV with no signal; at least with booze the good things in life got better and the bad shit a little easier to stomach, and the same was more or less true of weed, Munra thought; but those pills, which Luismi guzzled like sweets, had only ever given Munra a terrible urge to lie down, to do sweet fuck-all and sleep, you don't even dream of crazy shit or hallucinate like people say you do on opium, no, they just sent you headlong into a deep, deep, lazy-ass sleep from which you woke up gasping, head pounding and eyes so swollen you could hardly open them, with no idea how you got to bed or why you were covered in dirt or even shit, or who it was that smashed your face in. That prick Luismi said they made him feel dope, chilled out, sort of normal, not anxious or shaky, and they got rid of that fucked-up itch of his to click his fingers, the tic he'd had since he was a boy, the one that also made him whip his neck to one side and that, according to him, only stopped when he took those pills, because when he didn't take them the shakes and the tics came back, along with all those other fucked-up feelings, like when the walls moved as if they were about to cave in on him, or when his smokes didn't taste of anything at all, or when his chest went tight and he couldn't breathe, anyway, nothing but excuses on the kid's part so he didn't have to give up that shit. Not even when he invited Norma to move in to his *casita*, not even then could he really quit, even though he'd sworn he'd stop, just beer and weed, he'd said, no more pills, but his good intentions didn't last three weeks before fucking Norma sold out to the police and landed the poor kid in jail for something he didn't even do, his only crime was to help the little mare, Miss Butter-Wouldn't-Melt, who turned out to be nothing but trouble, nothing but strife. Munra had never liked that little scamp, never trusted her, with her wouldn't-hurt-a-fly act and her dumb prissy voice that put everyone under her spell, even Chabela, who'd have thought it, Chabela, the woman who claimed to know every trick the girls down at Excalibur's had or were likely ever to pull, even she was powerless to young Norma's charms: two days was all it took, two days in the house and Chabela was already going around saying that the girl was like the daughter she'd always wanted, such a good girl, a grafter, so accommodating, so this, so that, so the other, it was like a fucking campaign, the silly cow, and Munra would just suck it up and click his tongue, genuinely sickened by the treacle pouring from his wife's mouth. It pissed him off seeing the girl in the house, at the stove, washing plates or even just sniffing around Chabela with her phoney grin, her rosy native Indian cheeks and look of feigned innocence, nodding along to whatever Chabela said. His wife was so far up the girl's ass, so flattered by her attentions that she seemed to have forgotten they were now supporting not one but two spongers, and frankly, Munra didn't trust all that domestic bliss, and he couldn't help wondering what the girl was up to, where the hell she'd come from and what the fuck she saw in the kid; because he wasn't swallowing any of that bullshit about how they were made for each other: what woman in her right mind would choose to live in a filthy hovel with that half-starved fleabag? Munra was sure there was something shady going on, but he decided to keep quiet because that shithead Luismi always did as he pleased anyway, so why waste his breath? Besides, he'd already tried to warn him once, the night Luismi came and asked for a ride to the pharmacy in Villa to buy some medicine for Norma, who was bleeding and in pain, and the first thing Munra thought was that the little diva was putting it on, trying to get them to waste their money and petrol like a pair of cunts, and he even had words with the kid that night about not letting her take him for a ride. Didn't he know all that was normal, that women bled from their bits each month and that they didn't need any medicine, at a push some of those towels which Luismi could buy off Doña Concha right there in La Matosa, but there was no need to go all the way to Villa. Was he seriously that clueless? But the kid was having none of it. He went on and on about how this was different and Norma was in a lot of pain and her whole body was burning up. In the end, though, Munra managed to convince him that everything was normal and the kid slunk back to his *casita*. And Munra could see the two of them lying on that stinking mattress, Luismi holding her as if she were at death's door. Quite the actress, Munra said to himself, although, in the end, who'd have thought, it turned out to be pretty serious and in the middle of the night he got the fright of his life when the kid almost kicked the front door down trying to get him to open up because he was holding Norma in his arms and her skin was green and her lips white and her eyes were sort of rolling back like she was possessed, her thighs streaked with trickles of blood, still wet and dripping on the floor, and the kid was out of his mind going on and on about the stain she'd left on the mattress, about the amount of blood Norma was losing, and please, please, he had to drive them to the hospital in Villa that minute, and Munra told Luismi that he'd take them but only on the condition that he lay something under Norma, a rag or a blanket or something, because he didn't want her staining the seats, and Luismi did as he asked, but so shoddily that the upholstery did end up soaked in her bloody mess, and Munra didn't even get the chance to give the little prick what for or make him scrub it clean, not after everything that happened, after they took Norma to the hospital and hung around outside like a pair of dickheads waiting for someone to come out and tell them how the girl was doing, sitting on the edge of a raised flowerbed until noon, when Luismi couldn't take it any more and he marched into the hospital to ask what was happening because no one had told them anything; and about a quarter of an hour after going in the kid was back again with a face like a slapped ass, sounding off about how some social worker had called the police on them, but he didn't want to tell Munra anything on the way back to La Matosa, not even once they were in Sarajuana's, where Munra took the boy for a beer, which Sara's halfwit granddaughter served them lukewarm. *No quiero que regreses nunca más*, went the radio, *prefiero la derrota entre mis manos*, tuned to the station that played nonstop rancheras, the songs that did Munra's head in, *si ayer tu nombre tanto pronuncié*, what was wrong with a bit of salsa? *hoy mírame rompiéndome los labios*, but the kid, who'd have thought it, looked

like he was about to start blubbing, his eyes all glassy
and bloodshot, and it even occurred to Munra that
Norma might have died, or that she was in really bad
shape and needed a big, expensive operation, but three
beers later the kid still hadn't spilled the beans and he
didn't give anything away that day, not even after Munra
agreed to take him to Villa to look for Willy in the cantinas to buy a strip of those stupid fucking pills that he
hadn't touched for three weeks, and God knows how
many he popped but by closing time Luismi was already
on the floor, high as a fucking kite, and Munra had to ask
some guys to help get him in the van, which is where the
kid ended up sleeping that night because by the time
they finally reached La Matosa, Munra couldn't wake
him up and there was no way Munra could carry him on
his own. And Munra had no idea what time it was when
he came to the next day, because his phone was dead,
clean out of juice, Chabela still wasn't back from work,
and that worried Munra a little because lately Chabela
had been staying out for two or three days in a row, supposedly keeping her clients entertained, but the bitch
didn't even let him know. He went to plug in his phone to
call his wife and tell her what he really thought about the
way she treated him, but when he bent over the side of
the bed to look for his charger a wave of nausea sent him
reeling to the floor, so he decided to lie back down for a
while on the sheets steeped in his wife's scent, as if the
mad bitch had snuck back in the dead of the night to
spray it with her perfume before heading back out onto
the streets, back to her partying, or as if she'd come back
as he stirred and was now standing there, watching him
from the doorway, a shadow plunged in deafening silence, the silence Munra had always found more
disturbing than any shouting or screaming, which is

why, there and then, he began telling her what had happened the previous night: baby, the fucking kid had to carry Norma in his arms, she was bleeding all over the place; the little bitch looked dead, and those cunts in the hospital nearly called the pigs on us, but Munra soon realized he was talking to himself, that there was no one else in the room, that the shadow he'd mistaken for Chabela had faded, and once he'd plugged in his phone and waited for it to turn on, he found that Chabela hadn't sent him a single message, nothing, no explanation, not so much as a fuck you, the selfish bitch. He tried calling; five times he pressed the call button and five times the phone sent him to voicemail. He put on a shirt and a pair of trousers that he found on the floor, looked for his crutch, which had somehow ended up under the bed, and headed out to check that the kid was still alive and hadn't spewed his guts all over the van, and there he was, curled up like a snail in the passenger seat, his fat lips slightly parted, his eyes flickering, and his hair pasted to the window. Oi, he said, banging on the glass with the palm of his hand to wake the kid up, before opening the door. Inside it was roasting. How could that numbskull stand the heat and all that sweat drenching his clothes and pouring down his face? We're off: hair of the dog, Munra said, starting the van, and the kid nodded without so much as looking at him. Munra didn't even ask the boy if he had any money – of course the kid didn't have any – but he was in serious need of a pick-me-up, some broth and a cold beer to cure the pounding headache that had begun to hammer away at his brain, and he also wanted the kid to tell him what had really happened with Norma, although he soon regretted it because the cheeky fuck began ordering beers as if they were at Sarajuana's, where a *caguama* cost thirty pesos, while here, at Lupe la Carera's, even a regular size bottle set you back twenty-five, but it was worth it because everyone knew that at Lupe la Carera's they served the best dog-meat 'lamb' consommé around, and if you asked Munra it made no difference whether those juicy strips that he chewed patiently with the few teeth he had left were lamb, dog, or human, the main event was Lupe la Carera's special sauce, made from scratch, one of God's gifts to man: so damn tasty and full of curative properties it immediately made him feel human again, and in his head he even said to himself how nice it would be if Chabela came home now; she was probably just with clients, and there was no need for him to make a scene or go around imagining that the silly cow had finally made up her mind to leave him, right? And he even got the itch to drive to Villa and hit up La Concha Dorada, to see the gang and do something with his day. The kid, on the other hand, looked miserable, sitting there with his head cocked and his arms dangling down, his bowl of broth untouched, the spoon still laid on the wooden table, which was specked with pieces of onion and coriander. Oi, Munra began, feeling the anger rising in his belly, as it did whenever he saw the kid in that state, totally baked, totally braindead, and these days he couldn't even put it down to the kid being off his skull with the gang in the park or the cantinas, no, it was just to avoid having to speak or listen to anyone, just so he could curl up in his own head, shut himself off from the world, and Munra wanted to slap him sometimes, slap some sense into him, or any reaction at all, but he knew there was no use, that the prick was old enough to know what he was doing when he got himself into fixes like that business with Norma. Oi, he said, what's the deal with your woman, then? Lusimi's shoulders slumped even lower, he rested his elbows on the table and began to pull at his scruffy mane, and Munra asked again: Come on, fucker! What happened, what's the deal, and the kid, as melodramatic as his goddamn mother, a chip off the goddamn block, took a deep breath, shook his head and then downed his beer in one go and gestured at Lupe la Carera to bring him a third – son-of-a-bitch, twenty-five fucking pesos a pop – and waited for her to open the bottle to start telling Munra what had happened when he went to ask after Norma in the emergency room, and the nurses all played dumb and ended up leading him to some office with piles of paper all over the place, where a woman with bleach-blonde hair introduced herself as the hospital's social worker and asked him for Norma's documents, her birth certificate and also the certificate that proved that he and Norma were legally married, and of course he didn't have any of that, so the bitch told him the police were on their way to arrest him, for corruption of a minor, this being the case, because who knows how the hospital found out that Norma was underage, that she was only thirteen and... Munra's beer went down the wrong way and he gasped, scandalized by what the kid was telling him, because swear to God he had no idea Norma was so young, practically a child, for Christ's sake, you couldn't tell at all, fuck me, such a big, stocky girl. This has got to be a fucking wind-up, he managed to croak when at last he stopped spluttering: you stupid, stupid prick, what the fuck were you thinking getting involved with a thirteen-year-old, it's a fucking miracle they haven't put you away, you know full well you can't marry a girl that young, dumb fuck, and the kid swearing blind that he could, because Norma wasn't a kid, she was a woman and mature enough to make up her own mind who she

wanted to be with, and besides, at thirteen his grandma
was already married to his aunt Negra's dad, and Munra,
tugging at his moustache, said: Kid, that doesn't mean
shit; that was then and this is now, the law's changed, you
animal, you can't do those things now, you can't marry a
girl that young even with her parents' consent, so sort
your fucking shit out, the party's over, forget that tod-
dler, she's nothing but trouble; it was probably her who
snitched on you to the social worker, just to fuck you
over, that's what these goddamn bitches are like, he said.
But the kid wasn't listening to him, he just shook his
head, arguing the toss without actually stopping to
think: No, he said, I can't just leave her, I have to get her
out of there, I have to rescue her, because I'm all she's
got; he couldn't let her down, and especially not now
they were expecting, and he still had no idea how he was
going to get her out of that hospital so they could be together again, and while he mumbled all this shit Munra
just stared at him in silence, thinking about the blood
running down Norma's thighs and the stain she'd left in
the van, and he seriously doubted that the little scamp
was still pregnant, if she ever had been, if that pot belly
she'd been carrying around wasn't just full of worms;
fucking women, there isn't a single one who doesn't love
cooking up this kind of drama to pin you down and fuck
you right up the ass, although Munra was mindful to
keep his thoughts to himself, because at the end of the
day, what did any of it matter to him? Norma, Luismi,
their alleged kid... not his problem; that dipshit Luismi
was big enough to wipe his own ass, it wasn't Munra's job
to watch his back, to tell him what he should and
shouldn't do, and besides, the little prick had only ever
turned his nose up at Munra's advice, which he offered
out of the goodness of his heart; in the end, instead of

listening to his stepfather's words of wisdom, he always did whatever the fuck he liked. He was just like Chabela. Just as pigheaded as his mother. As stubborn as fucking mules and proud to boot: you couldn't tell those two anything without asking for a fight, and you were always the one who had to back down, smile like a prick and even apologize for having offended them. Like the time last year when Munra got that job promoting the mayoral candidate for Villagarbosa, when the Party, the government that is, paid Munra hard cash for every person he got to join the campaign, and he'd even made friends with people in politics, important people who would acknowledge him in the street and wave and call him Don Isaías, not Munra like those over-familiar assholes in town, and for a while he became sort of famous because one day Adolfo Pérez Prieto himself, then candidate for mayor of Villagarbosa, asked him for a photograph, together with Munra, who happened to be wearing his T-shirt with the Party's logo on it and his Pérez Prieto cap, and someone had even pulled out a wheelchair, God knows where from, which they sat him in so that Pérez Prieto appeared pushing him in the photo, both of them smiling, and Munra had never seen a photo of his face as big as the one on the enormous billboard on the highway, just as you entered Villa coming from Matacocuite, which said something like 'Pérez Prieto – a man of his word', which as a matter of fact was true, because they did actually give him the wheelchair after taking the photo, even though Munra wasn't one for chairs, he thought they made him look like a fucking cripple, a decrepit creature who couldn't fend for himself, when the truth was he could get around just fine, even without his crutches, goddamn it, he didn't need any help, there were his two legs and both in one piece,

the left one just a little bent, that was all, right? A little
shorter than the other one and sort of wedged up inside,
but alive and kicking, goddamn it, well and truly at-
tached, no? Did it look like he needed a wheelchair?
And so he'd sold it; he had things covered with his
crutch and the van, which got him from A to B, got him
wherever he wanted, and all in all it was a shame that gig
had only lasted six months, because it was a nice little
earner, and just for hanging out at the odd rally applaud-
ing everything Pérez Prieto said, all clackers and
whooping and 'Pérez Prieto, he's our man, if he can't do
it, no one can,' hoo, hoo, and seriously: just for doing
that the Party paid him two hundred pesos a day and
two hundred more for every person he brought to sign
up, plus food by the pound that they gave out each week,
plus farming tools and even construction material, and
to think that Munra had never voted in his life; and
maybe that's why he assumed it'd be easy to convince
Chabela that she should jump on the bandwagon too and
reel in some voters, because at Excalibur's, between the
girls and the clients, she could get a shitload of registra-
tions and make herself a little extra pocket money, which
was never a bad thing, right? But Chabela took it the
wrong way; she reacted as if Munra, instead of giving
her a tip, had said go fuck yourself, Chabela; she got the
hump so badly she started shouting at him right there in
the street, calling him a dickhead, a complete fucking
imbecile, he must have half his brain missing if he
thought that she, *she*, was going to sniff around those
mongrels from the Party like a beggar, like you, fucking
Munra, you've got no pride, no shame, you old git, the
only thing you make me feel these days is pity; fuck you
if you think I've got time to go around kissing that cunt
Pérez Poofter's ass, and she said all this right there, right

outside La Concha Dorada, with people walking past laughing their heads off at Chabela's effing and blinding, and Munra had to keep his cool, because he knew it was pointless, or rather suicidal, arguing with his wife in public: a bit like swallowing a grenade with the pin pulled. So he didn't say a word but he did promise himself not to buy her any more shit with his honest earnings from the campaigns; she could go fuck herself, fucking Chabela, fucking dick-eating Chabela. But he didn't expect Luismi to get all high and mighty and come out with the same shit as his mother, because, surprise surprise, the prick was out of work, he didn't have a clue what he was doing with his life, and Chabela spent the best part of hers giving him grief because he never had two pesos to rub together, never gave her any rent or upkeep for the house when he was the one who'd decided to move in right next door, at the hardly tender age of eighteen, when he should have been looking after her, his mother who gave birth to him, who went through all that pain and sacrifice, he should let her stop working instead of spending his days holed up with the Witch, or in the cantinas, or in that park in Villa with his slacker friends, spending what little money that fell into his hands on booze and drugs and God knows what else. That's why Munra thought to invite the kid onto the campaign: Come on, look, he said, it makes sense, just till the elections, you don't even have to vote for that prick Pérez Prieto if you don't want to, you just have to be seen at the rallies with the crowd, just hang around waiting for whatever goes down, and the stubborn prick was all fuck that shit, politics was for mugs and there was no way he going to crawl around on all fours for three measly pesos, he'd rather hold out for the gig he'd been promised with the Company: the famous gig with the

Company, a goddamn pipe dream which the kid had pulled out of his ass, something about being hired to work down in the Palogacho in the oilfields, a technician's role, he said, with all the perks that came with working under the union, and it didn't matter how hard Munra tried to make him see straight, to make him see that it was never going to happen because the Oil Company never hired anybody who wasn't an immediate relative or recommended by those at the top, not to mention the fact that the stupid prick knew nothing about the wells or petrochemistry, he hadn't even finished school, and to top it all off he was as skinny as a salamander and weighed less than half of what the barrels he'd have to lug around weighed, but it was no use, there was nothing Munra could say to make him see that the promise of that job was a scam, a dream he was a fool to hold on to, and all because his mate the engineer told him he was a surefire shoo-in at the Company. A load of bullshit that the kid had swallowed whole; real pie-in-the-sky stuff that would cost him dearly, because while he hung around for years waiting for the engineer to make good on his promise, the stupid prick let a string of perfectly good opportunities go by, like the offer one of Chabela's clients made him, some fellow who, according to her, had his own fleet of trucks and who, one day, overheard Chabela bitching about what a lazy good-for-nothing leech her son was because he couldn't find work, and this gentleman told Chabela that he just happened to have lost his assistant for the trip to the border that he was about to make, and why didn't she tell the kid to go with him the next day, at the crack of dawn, to see if he liked the job and if he had what it took, and this fellow said he could even help him get a licence so he could start working for him as a driver, and that morning

Chabela came home full of beans, happy as a clam, the poor love, because she thought she'd finally found the way to get rid of her bum of a son, but the little fucker said no, no fucking way, he wasn't interested in becoming anyone's lackey, he wasn't going to be a shitty driver, he'd rather wait for his friend the engineer to get him a job at the Company, and, boy oh boy, did Chabela give him hell: she even ripped his T-shirt while pulling and hitting him as she screamed that he was just like his waster of a father, a bastard just like him, a fucking scrounger who was more use dead than alive, and things got so ugly that for a moment Munra thought the kid was going to hit Chabela back, from the crazed look in his eyes and the way he raised his fists to defend himself, but nothing came of it, and thank God, because the last thing Munra wanted was to have to pull those two apart, he'd long since learned to leave them to it: there's no reasoning with dogs, two ferocious dogs who refuse to let go of their prey until they've been torn to shreds. No fucking way was he getting involved and risking that pair of animals sinking their teeth into him, nope, no fucking way; they could go fuck themselves, they never listened to him anyway; why should he waste his time telling the kid how good the pay was as a driver and all the places he'd see and the women he could have, and how those lucky bastards were never in the same place long, how they were always on the move, all over the country, not trapped in the ass end of nowhere dying in the heat – what was the point in painting the whole pretty picture when that prick always came out with the same old shit about how he couldn't go because he was still waiting for the gig at the Company to fall from the heavens into his lap, and Munra couldn't believe the kid could be so stupid, so goddamn stupid to believe this was ever going to happen, to have that much blind faith in a stranger's promise, because really, who was this engineer he called his friend anyway? Why would some top-dog big-cheese cunt want to help out a bum who wasn't even family? More than once he'd almost asked the kid what exactly that engineer would get in return, how the kid intended to repay such a huge favour, but since he had a feeling he already knew the answer he preferred to play dumb. What did he care? To be honest, he'd had just about enough of the whole thing. It was Luismi's funeral if he wanted to swallow that story, Luismi's problem if he didn't want to accept that it was all a pack of lies made up by his so-called friend the engineer, who, to top it all off, had stopped answering the kid's calls months ago, Luismi's problem if he wanted to keep believing in Santa Claus and the Three Kings, because at the end of the day, you do what you like and what you can in this life, right? And what business did Munra have sticking his oar in the kid's affairs? None, right? Let him do what he wanted, to hell with it, he was a big boy, too big to go around thinking life was like a TV show, a fairy tale, and sooner or later he'd figure out that the job with the Oil Company wasn't real, just like in the end he'd also have to accept that he and Norma were well and truly over: the little diva was the hospital's problem now, handed over to the authorities, and Luismi should really just stop fucking around and find himself a real woman: a *woman*, not a pain-in-the-ass baby like fucking Norma, a rat who fed her man to the lions the moment things got a little heavy; this is bullshit, kid, first-class bullshit from some little tramp playing at houses. Look: go find yourself a real woman, one who knows how to look after you, a working girl, like Chabela. And Luismi, welling up right there by Lupe la Carera's stand, in full view of everyone, replied, almost shouting, that he'd never leave Norma, not ever, and that he'd rather die than end things with her, and even Lupe herself looked up from the grill and rolled her eyes at the kid, thinking, what the fuck is his problem? Easy kid, easy, Munra mumbled, taken aback. For as long as he'd known that little prick, Luismi hadn't given two shits about anyone; nothing on God's earth could make him care about anything other than his pills and partying. Easy now, easy, he repeated, and then the penny dropped and he wagged his finger at his stepson with a big smirk on his face: Looks to me, he said, and Luismi jumped straight on the defensive: What? What does it look like to you, dickhead? Looks to me like our Norma's slipped you a little love potion. Your mum, Luismi mumbled. Don't give me that, Munra teased him, you know exactly what I'm talking about. You know what these vipers are like when they want to tie you down: they take a few drops of their skanky blood and slip it in your drink or your broth when you're not looking, or they put a drop on your heel when you're sleeping, and then you're well and truly cuntstruck, putty in their hands, just like you're putty in Norma's hands, don't you see? And there are bitches who go even further, they head into the hills in the rainy season to pick a wildflower shaped like a trumpet, angel trumpets they call them, and they take their angel trumpets and they brew them into a tea that turns you into a real prick, a real soft touch, brings you to your knees, cowering at their feet like a slave, and you don't have the first fucking clue what's going on. Don't act like you don't know what I'm talking about when your own mother goes around telling anyone who'll listen about the black magic the girls from Excalibur's perform on the punters, to make them go soft in head so they can rob them or get them all het up pining for the girls and even put a roof over their heads, make honest women of them. But the kid, who'd finally begun listening to Munra with something bordering on attention, just shook his head saying no, Norma wasn't like that, Norma would never be capable of any of that, and Munra laughed at how naïve the kid was: They're all the same, dipshit, all up to the same tricks, all capable of untold fuckery just to hold on to you, and he went on like this until eventually the kid had enough and retreated into the surly, silent shell from which Munra had no chance of retrieving him, not even after they moved on to Sarajuana's, not even after he'd paid for another round of that warm fucking beer, which you'd be forgiven for thinking was the house speciality but was actually down to the fact that the old fridge hadn't been replaced in donkey's years, not since Sarajuana was crowned Carnival Queen, you know, back in the dark ages. Sugartits, Munra repeated for the umpteenth time to Sara's granddaughter, does it never occur to you to make some ice and pop the beers in there first thing, get them nice and cold for when I get here? The girl was no stranger to Munra and she just tutted, put her hand on her jutting hip and snapped back: For an ugly fuck like you? Dream on. If you don't like it, you know where the door is, and Munra gestured with his arm for her to go fuck herself, but neither of them took the other's snub too seriously, they both knew Munra would be back, and not because the girl pulled any hocus-pocus shit on him, but because it was the closest cantina to his house: five hundred yards straight down the dirt track; at the end of the night he could just hop in his van, drive for a few seconds and there he was, right back at his place, without even having to take the highway, without having to risk another accident like the one that almost cost him his leg, in 2004, 16 February 2004, how could he forget: the truck making a U-turn without its lights on at the San Pedro exit, that son of a motherfucking bitch; Munra was so wasted he hadn't seen it coming and it rammed right up his ass, grinding every last bone in his leg to dust. The doctors told him they were going to cut it off, and he said no, no fucking way, he didn't give a shit if it was bent or missing bits of bone, it was his leg and no one was lopping it off, and the doctors said nope, no can do, that leg was as good as gone and, besides, the risk of infection was too high, but Munra dug his heels in and with Chabela's help he escaped from the hospital the day before they were due to hack it off, and in the end he made those quack cunts eat their words because his leg never did get infected and it never died on him either, it just wound up a little bit wedged out of place, right? Sort of bent away from the foot, but even so he could still walk, even without his crutches he could manage a good few steps, right? It wasn't like he had no choice but to be chained to some fucking wheelchair, right? And besides, he had the van; the van he'd bought off some old codger in Matacocuite who'd brought it all the way from Texas – an absolute bargain, thirty big ones, half of what the truck company paid him as compensation for the accident. That van had been a good buy and whenever he was cruising along the highway, pushing one hundred an hour, windows down, watching everything from above, the dog's fucking bollocks, it was almost as if the accident had never happened, as if he were still the same guy who rode the coast on his motorbike, couriering export request forms between the customs agencies, the slick dick who danced salsa till the sun came up and swept Chabela off her feet and flung her over his shoulder, showered her with kisses to shut her up, pinned her against the wall and made her come her tits off, the silly cow, where the hell was she? Why the hell hadn't she call him yet? No client stayed three days at Excalibur's, she could spare him the bullshit; for starters, there weren't enough girls working there, and the ones who did weren't all that. Had she fucked off to Puerto with some cunt without telling him? It wouldn't be the first time; the previous Christmas she'd ended up in Guadalajara, the filthy tart, working, she called it, work's work, she'd say, and usually Munra agreed, but this was too much, this smacked of that bitch holed up in the Motel Paradiso drinking straight from a bottle of whisky and sniffing blow like it was going out of fashion with that sick cunt Barrabás, sucking his cock for the pure pleasure of it, and that was why each time he called her mobile he heard a message telling him that the number he'd dialled was not in service, or that the phone was off, and it was already dark and Munra was drunk enough to even consider taking the van and driving past the Paradiso to see if he could see that prick Barrabás's Lobo parked there, even if he got torn apart by the ruffians who followed him around like a shadow, half a dozen sombrero-clad thugs with wonky jaws and assassin eyes, and when he came back to his senses he was already in the van halfway home. Fuck Chabela, he said to himself, nearly tumbling out of the driver's seat, and he didn't even take his clothes off before getting into bed; he just flopped facedown onto the mattress, on top of the rumpled sheets and Chabela's bra and hair combs, and he slept, and in his dream he was a ghost haunting the streets in town trying to talk to people, but nobody paid him any attention, or perhaps they didn't even know he was there because they couldn't see him, he was a ghost, and nobody but the small children could see him and they wept in fear when he spoke to them and Munra felt sad; and then suddenly all the streets disappeared and he was walking in the wilderness, and he crossed mountains and forests and grasslands and fields and deserted ranches until, out of nowhere, he came to another town; he wandered through those streets and came across a house he recognized, the house of his darling Nana Mircea, and he went through the kitchen door, which was always open, into the living room, and there was his nan sitting on her rocking chair, just as he always remembered her, as if she hadn't been dead for twenty years, because in his dream he was the dead one and his nan was alive, and even though she couldn't see him either, she could sense and even hear him, very faintly, as if from very far away, and Munra was distressed because he had something really important to tell her, something he couldn't remember when he woke up but which in his dream had been truly urgent, something he had to warn his nan about at all costs but that he wasn't able to get across to her because he could only speak in the language of the dead, a language she didn't understand, not even while he was screaming at the top of his lungs, and his nan, who in life truly was a saint, always so insightful, such a ray of sunshine, Doña Mircea Bautista, God rest her soul, she smiled at him and told him to calm down, not to worry, that he'd better be a good, kind boy if he wanted to get into heaven, and she spoke in a serene voice that made Munra so sad when he finally woke up, the smell of Nana Mircea's hand cream still lingering in the air even though he understood perfectly that he was on his bed, in the bedroom he shared with his wife, and that his back was drenched in sweat, which felt cold despite the sweltering heat of that room. He wanted to go on sleeping but the stifling air and a

pounding headache soon drove him from his bed. He
stripped down to his underpants and, using his crutch
for support, made his way to the toilet and then out into
the yard to give himself a quick wash by the fresh water
barrel. He was just rinsing off the soap when the kid
walked past, barefoot and shirtless, filthy like he'd been
rolling around on the dirt track, and then he staggered
to the far end of the yard, to the other side of his *casita*
where Munra couldn't see him; he was back there for a
good long while because Munra had time to rinse himself, go back into the house, dry off, put on a pair of clean
pants and even to go back out, all the way across the
yard, to see what the kid was doing standing there behind his little shack, staring into an open hole in the
ground, a hole about a foot and a half deep, which the kid
was gawping at, oblivious even to Munra's presence beside him, because when at last Munra said: Whassat? the
kid jumped, spun round and looked at him as if he'd
seen a ghost, as if Munra had caught him red-handed
getting up to no good, but that expression on his face
only lasted one or two seconds before he recovered his
senses and opened his mouth to reply: Nothing, and
Munra glanced at the hole and then back at the kid's
arms, elbow deep in muck, his nails black with dirt.
What had that urchin just dug up? Munra wondered,
and perhaps it was the memory of his dream, still lingering in his head, but he remembered how once, years ago,
when he was still a boy, living with his mother in his
Nana Mircea's place in Gutiérrez de la Torre, a neighbour, an elderly thing who lived right next door to them,
was replumbing the house and the men who dug up the
front garden found something that his nan had called a
'work', a work of witchcraft: one of those extra-large
mayonnaise jars with an immense toad floating inside, a

dead, decomposed toad swimming in a murky liquid along with a couple of garlic heads, a few bunches of weeds and who knows what other shit that Munra never got to see because his mother covered his eyes and led him away from there, but even so he began to feel a sharp pain in his head and his nan had to cleanse him with a few bunches of basil and an egg that she ran across his brow and later cracked, and inside it was all rotten, and she explained to him that the thing the men had dug up was a work that an evil person had put there to do witch-craft on the neighbours; she said a powerful evil force would make the toad enter the body of whoever had the misfortune of walking over the spot where the work was buried, and that once it had found its way inside that un-lucky person, the toad would begin to eat away their vital organs and fill them with all kinds of nasty things until the person dropped dead, and Munra, who back then was just five or six, couldn't quite remember how, but later on he discovered that the neighbour's husband had died on her just months later from a disease that no-body could put their finger on, something to do with his liver, they said, and young Munra kept getting those headaches for a while, and his nan healed them by brush-ing bunches of basil over his body and rubbing his temples with alcohol, and sometimes he struggled to sleep because he couldn't help thinking that he might have stepped on the buried work while out playing or running some errand, and that maybe, in that very mo-ment, the horrible animal was eating away at his brain, slowly killing him, although with time his fears abated, to the point that he'd almost forgotten about it altogether until he saw the hole that the kid had clearly dug with his bare hands, and, overwhelmed by the sensation that he was still asleep, that he was still trapped inside the strange dream in which he was dead, a lost soul in purgatory, he asked the kid again what it was, not because he was interested in the answer – Munra was now convinced that it was a work of witchcraft, there was no other explanation – but to assure himself that the kid could hear him, to check he wasn't still trapped in that horrible dream, but since Luismi just stood there staring at him blankly like a limp dick, as if he didn't recognize him, Munra had to raise a hand to his ear and pinch himself to make sure that he wasn't dreaming, that he wasn't dead, and then he felt a little better. Burn it, he told the kid. Whatever you found in there, burn it. And the kid pointed to a burnt tin can at the base of a nearby palm tree and said, his voice squeaky and his tongue lazy from the pills, that yeah, he'd already burned it, inside that can, and that he'd just come from throwing the ashes in the river, because earlier that night he'd heard sounds coming from behind his *casita* and when he went out to see what it was he'd found a dog outside, a huge white wolf-like beast scraping away at the spot where the hole was, and that's how he'd found it, and Munra took a step back because, although he felt a little better now he knew he wasn't trapped inside his dream and there was no longer any bewitched toad in that hole, all the same it felt like some dark force from the spell was lingering in the air: he'd always been sensitive to these things and he could feel its weight pressing against his temples. Shouldn't touch it with your bare hands, he told the kid, you'd better have a wash now. Come on, let's get out of here until the air clears, he said, better safe than sorry. And besides, Munra was in a hurry to go out and see if his suspicions were right, to see if Chabela really was shacked up in the Motel Paradiso with that prick Barrabás, and that's why he told the kid to get ready while he went back into the house to finish getting dressed and grabbed the keys to the van, his phone and what little money he had left. But when he reached the dirt track he realized that the kid hadn't listened to him: he was standing next to the van, all set to leave, he claimed, but still covered in muck and stinking like a goat, barefoot and with his face caked in soot. Munra had to tell him: I'm not taking you anywhere like that, you smell like shit, fuck me, go and splash some water under your pits at least. And the kid went over to the barrel and plunged his big head into the fresh water like a horse, he stayed under for a while, until most of the dirt ran off him, and then Munra had to lend him a T-shirt because the dipshit didn't have any clean clothes, but all in the name of getting out of that house for a while, of staying on the move, Munra thought, and also so he could look for Chabela, but not without first having a beer with clamato at Sarajuana's, which as it turned out was closed because, as Sara's granddaughter told them when she opened the door in her nightie, it wasn't even nine in the morning, you've got to be kidding me, you absolute pissheads; so they had no choice but to cross the highway and go to El Metedero, where the crab empanadas that came free with your drinks were stale and greasy but the beer was ice-cold and the sound of the music calmed Munra down because it stopped his mind from racing, although who knows what was up with the kid, who after the first round sort of revved up and even leaned in closer to Munra to rattle on above the noise of the speakers about how fucking rotten he'd felt lately, with all the fucked-up shit that kept happening to him; all totally out of character because the kid never opened up to Munra, but there he was, whining in his earhole with his vinegary breath about how much pain he was in, how shitty, how jinxed he felt because nothing ever worked out for him and now this stuff with Norma: he was sure they were going to take her away without telling him how the poor girl was or what would become of her and the baby, where they'd take them or whether one day he'd be allowed to go and see them; the final straw was that business with the job at the Company and his friend the engineer who'd disappeared months ago and no longer answered his calls, and all this had happened right after he'd fought with the Witch, earlier that year, over some money the crazy bitch claimed he'd robbed off her, but it wasn't true, someone else had robbed it off *him*, or in all the madness he'd lost it, but the Witch wasn't having any of it and she'd sent him packing, and now she was probably putting all kinds of hexes on him, on him and Norma, to break them up, and Munra just threw nervy glances at his phone and turned to face the dance floor, not because the loose old birds dancing cheek-to-cheek over there were doing it for him, but because the mere mention of the Witch put him on edge, got his back up, and that stupid prick knew Munra hated hearing about the shit the kids in town got up to with that damn queen. What did he need to hear all that for? Why should he have that shit clogging up his head, right? It was just like he was always telling Chabela: Sugar, that's nice your clients are such a refined bunch, such gentlemen, all of them, but I don't want to hear it, don't come chewing my ear off with the details, I don't want to know what they're called or where they're from, or if they've got a thin one or a thick one or if it's bent or multi-fucking-coloured, because fucking Chabela was always trying to give him the gossip from work, telling him all about the cunts she got with and her fights with the other girls from Excalibur's, but Munra didn't like it; all he wanted was to be left in peace; she could do whatever she had to do and good for her, but I don't want to hear it, Chabela, he had to tell her constantly, and with the kid he'd never had to ask him to keep his business to himself because his stepson was generally reserved, but that day, with all his weird pent-up energy, he wouldn't shut up, and Munra, wanting to change the subject, wanting to erase the images that had begun to form in his head, stood up suddenly and pressed his phone to his ear as if it had rung: Just a sec, he told Luismi, and he grabbed his crutch and left El Metedero, apparently to be able to hear better, and once outside, leaning against his van, he took the opportunity to call his wife but her number still wasn't going through. Fucking Chabela, she was with that punk Barrabás, no two ways about it. At that very moment those two were getting their rocks off in the Paradiso or some other rat hole on the highway, or maybe even right there in Barrabás's pickup, that son of a bitch, and her too, the slag, what did she think, that Munra was some kind of a cunt? That he didn't know what was going on? That she could just swan back to the house after three days and say she'd been working and that the shit wouldn't hit the fan? And without a second thought he climbed into the van, put his foot flat out on the accelerator and drove the six or so miles to the Motel Paradiso, which was deserted, completely deserted – strange for the weekend after payday – and without stopping to ask any questions he kept driving for several miles until he reached the exit for Matacocuite, with the Mexican pink concrete block of Excalibur's Gentleman's Club, outside of which Barrabás's notorious pickup was nowhere to be seen, nor was there any sign of the reprobates in sombreros who were always hanging around that *norteño* fucker, nothing, even the metal shutter was drawn, without the padlock, though, and Munra breathed a sigh of relief because deep down he doubted he had the balls to drag Chabela kicking and screaming from the marathon coke session she was almost certainly in the middle of, not without her scratching his eyes out and kicking his nuts, or, worse, having to face up to Barrabás's armed thugs. He drove on without stopping, made a U-turn, pulled up at the petrol station and took out his phone to type as vulgar, scathing, hate-filled and vindictive a message as any man ever wrote his wife, a truly terrible message that would make her shit herself, piss herself, weep with regret for having treated him that way, but before he could send it, the phone buzzed unexpectedly in his hands, nearly making him drop it on the floor of the van, and for a second he thought it must be Chabela, but it was just the kid, a message that went: anuther round come on, to which Munra replied: where are you, and the kid: villa park. Munra looked at the fuel gauge and thought that the most sensible thing would be to drive back to La Matosa and ask Doña Concha to put a litre of aguardiente on his tab and drink the whole thing in bed while he waited for Chabela to get home, and drink until he passed out or died, whichever happened first, and just then his telephone buzzed again and, once again, it was the kid, now telling him that he'd got hold of some cash, that he'd spot Munra's petrol if he did him this one solid of taking him to a job, by which the witness understood that his stepson had required the services of taking him to a specified location where he could obtain the money to continue drinking, a proposal the witness accepted, meaning that inside his closed-top Lumina van (colour grey-blue, model 1991, with vehicle registration plates from the State of Texas roger, golf, X-ray, 511), he drove

to the agreed-upon meeting point, namely, a row of
benches in the park facing the Palacio Municipal de
Villa, where he met his stepson, who was accompanied
by two subjects, one of whom was known by the nickname of Willy, occupation VHS retailer in Villa market,
roughly thirty-five to forty years of age, long black
greying hair, dressed in his customary rock band T-shirt
and black combat boots, often referred to as toe-capped
boots; and the other person was a young man about
whom the witness knew nothing, apart from that he went
by the name of Brando, although he was unsure if that
was his surname or given name, roughly eighteen years
of age, a slim build, black eyes, short black spiky hair,
light-skinned, wearing brown shorts and a Manchester
United shirt bearing Chicharito's number on the back;
and finally there was his stepson. The witness spent ap-
proximately two hours in the company of these three
men in the aforementioned public space, during which
time they imbibed several litres of an orange-flavoured
drink with aguardiente that the young man nicknamed
Brando had brought with him pre-mixed in a gallon
plastic tankard, in addition to a marijuana cigarette; and
together they – namely, Luismi, Brando and Willy –
also consumed psychotropic pills – the make or type of
which the witness does not know – until two in the afternoon, at which point his stepson asked if he was gonna
do him that solid, and I told him I was out of petrol, that
he had to give me the money first, and that's when I
twigged that the one with the ready was Brando, because
he handed me a fifty and said: Take us to La Matosa, and
I said: One hundred and you've got yourself a deal, and
Brando said: Fifty now and fifty later, and I agreed and
we left, everyone except Willy, who'd passed out on the
park bench and didn't see us pile into the van and head

for the petrol station, where I put the fifty pesos' worth in, and then drove towards La Matosa along the main drag, on Brando's instructions, before taking a right down the track that leads to the Mill. Only then did I realize that the boys were leading me to the house of the person known as the Witch, and I wasn't happy about this because I don't like hanging around those parts, mainly because of the things people say about that place and the things that go on in there, but I kept my mouth shut because I knew that they were just going to ask for money and wouldn't stay long, it was an in-and-out job, and I could wait in the van and then we'd all be able to carry on drinking, or that's what Brando said, immediately after ordering him to park next to a post in the ground sixty feet or so from the Witch's house, where he told him not to move, not to even think about getting out or shutting the door, that they wouldn't be long, and Luismi didn't say a word but I noticed he was really edgy, that both of them were on edge and hardly even seemed drunk now, and I thought that was pretty weird but I didn't say anything, and so basically they left, and it was a while before Munra noticed that one of them had taken his crutch, and when he looked in the rearview mirror the two kids had already gone round the side of the house to enter by the kitchen door, this being the same entrance the witness had once used, the one and only time in his life, over eight years ago, back when Munra still had his motorbike, before the accident. Chabela had taken him for a spiritual cleansing, but when the door opened and Munra saw the putrid state of that house, crap spread all over the place and the kitchen stinking of rotten food, and the opposite wall, the one that led out into the hallway, plastered in scratched-out porno images and spray paint and some mysterious symbols saying who knows what, well, he knew something was up, because what's more he wasn't from those parts, he was originally from Gutiérrez de la Torre, and up until that point nobody had told him that the Witch they all went on about was in fact a man, a fellow of about forty, forty-five back then, dressed in black clothing, in ladies clothing, and with long, black painted nails: a horror show. And even though he had something, a sort of veil, covering his face, you only had to hear his voice and see his hands to know that he was a homosexual, and Munra told Chabela that he'd changed his mind, he didn't want his spirit cleansing anymore, because the very thought of that poof's hands on him creeped him out, and Chabela got the real hump and for ages afterwards she'd bang on about how Munra's accident was what he got for not having gone through with the cleansing, that God had punished him for being so proud, although Munra suspected that it was the Witch herself who cursed him for snubbing her that day, and that was the one and only time he'd entered the kitchen in that house, and not because I had anything to do with that person, but for the reasons I've explained, which is that her lifestyle and appearance disgusted me, but at no point did I ever display any desire to harm that person, I didn't see a thing, I already told you, not a thing, and I didn't have a clue what had gone on, what they'd done to her, I didn't see them kill her because, well, look at me, officer, I can't even walk, I've been disabled since 2004; I don't know what money you're talking about, I swear to you those little shits didn't tell me anything about their plan, they just handed me fifty for the petrol and promised me another, which, by the way, I never saw. I thought they were going in for a fumble with the Witch, how was I supposed to know they wanted to kill her, I didn't even

94

leave the van, didn't move from behind the wheel the whole time, sat waiting for them to come out of the house, because those pricks were taking their time and Munra was already feeling uneasy and was just about to hit the road when at last he heard Luismi calling out and he turned round to see the pair of them at the sliding door, half-carrying, half-dragging a limp body that they lifted into the back of the van and dropped onto the floor, and his stepson and the other kid shouted put your foot down, go, go, and Munra stepped on the pedal and the van went tearing along the dirt track towards the Mill, but instead of heading straight, in the direction of the river, the boys told him to take the other track, the one that led to the fields behind the facility complex, which of course wasn't unfamiliar to Munra, it's where he'd go some nights with Luismi and their other friends to relax in the cool shade of a grove beside the irrigation canal, to smoke marijuana while they looked out over the vast sea of green crops in the waning glow of sundown, and since the van radio didn't work someone always played music on their phone, the volume as high as it would go, and they'd just hang out there, taking it easy, and they were almost at the first bend when the Witch began gasping and whimpering and those pricks shouted at her to shut the fuck up, kicking and stamping on her, and once they reached the canal they told Munra: Stop here, stop, and Munra did as he was told and the boys carried the Witch out, or rather they yanked her hair and clothes until she was on the ground, and Munra noticed then that her hair was all matted and wet, completely soaked with what he later discovered was blood, because the van floor was covered in it, although at that point he neither knew nor made any attempt to find out what it was. He just sat behind the wheel with his hands on his thighs and his eyes locked on the low rows of sugar cane, parched cane awaiting the rainy season, field after field of cane that grew all the way up to the riverbank and beyond, right up to the blue hillsides, and honestly? He did want to look, because he was convinced those guys were going to strip the Witch naked and throw her into the water for a joke, like he'd seen the gang do before, just fucking around, that's all, for shits and giggles, but something stopped him from turning round, something rooted him to the spot, as if paralyzed, to the extent that he didn't even dare look in the mirror, and he sensed that he wasn't alone, that there was someone there with him in the van, someone creeping forward from the back to where Munra was sitting, and he could even hear the noise that the springs in the seat made under the weight of that person or thing or whatever it was, and Munra remembered his dream and thought about his Nana Mircea and about the words she'd always spoken whenever someone mentioned the devil: Lord, I put my trust in you, deliver me from evil, Munra whispered; Protect me, God, for in you I take refuge. I say to the Lord, You are my Lord, and a sudden gust of almost wet wind blew in through the driver's window, an unrelenting wind – like the imminent rains – that lashed the scorched shrubs against the ground, and in the distance, high in the sky, a great cloud veiled the sun and a lightning bolt struck the outlying mountains without a sound, not even a snap as it parted that tree clean in half, burning it to a crisp, and for a moment Munra thought he'd gone deaf, because those pricks had to shout right into his ear and shake him into a reaction, into turning the ignition – even though the engine was already running – releasing the handbrake and tearing off, not even processing what the other two in the back were saying, because as he drove, with both eyes fixed on the dirt track ahead, they shouted and whooped and even punched each other, by the sounds of it, and when the penny finally dropped it was already dark and they'd passed Playa de Vacas and were driving into Villa along the main drag, past the park in front of the Town Hall, which, at that time of day, was packed with people strolling or simply sitting on benches enjoying the relative cool of the evening, and some schoolkids from the marching band were practising for the May Day parade on Monday, and it all felt so normal and peaceful because the two boys had calmed down at last, and a few streets down Brando asked to be dropped off on the next corner and Munra pulled up and Brando got out, and only when the kid ran off did Munra notice he wasn't wearing his Man U shirt anymore, but a black top, and then Luismi hopped into the front seat and began singing to himself, like he sometimes did when he was alone in his *casita* and he thought no one was listening, and as Munra drove towards La Matosa it occurred to him that the whole thing must have been a joke, that those dipshits had just been clowning around because they'd had enough of the Witch and wanted to ruffle her feathers, right? Give her a bit of a fright. How was he to know that in that very moment she was dead or dying down by the canal, when he never saw what they did to her, they just used him, those sons of bitches, they offered him money for a lift, which he gave them, but he didn't know what they were planning, you should be asking them about the money, they actually went inside the house, and besides, they're the ones who were always holed up in there, everyone in town knew that the Witch and Luismi had been lovers for years and that they'd fallen out over some shit to do with money – ask Luismi, ask Brando; that nasty prick lives three streets up from the park, pretty much right in front of the games machines outside Don Roque's, a yellow house with a white door, ask that bastard what he did with the money, and while you're at it ask him about the other fifty he owes me, the fifty pesos that Munra, in his shock, completely forgot about until he was in his bed, tossing and turning on his sweat-drenched sheets because he wanted to sleep but every time he closed his eyes he felt himself plummet into an abyss, and he didn't want to be awake anymore but at the same time he couldn't take his mind off Chabela, he spent a while calling her again and again but her phone was still going straight to voicemail, and at some point in the early hours he even thought about asking the kid for one of those shitty pills, but he didn't dare cross the yard in the dark and that junkie prick would have popped them all by now anyway; one of these days he'd take so many he wouldn't wake up, Munra thought, before slipping into a fevered slumber.

A miracle, my baby boy is nothing short of a miracle, the woman in the pink dressing gown was saying, living proof that God exists and that nothing's beyond St Jude, not even the hopeless cases, look. And she looked down, beaming at the child suckling at her left breast: my year of prayers really paid off, a full year, not a day missed, not even when I couldn't get out of bed, when I thought I was dying of sadness, even then I said my prayers to dear St Jude and asked him for my boy to live, for my womb to hold him, protect him, for it not to happen again like with the others, when I'd been so careful and taken all my vitamins, only for the babies to fall out of me, that blood I'd find on my clothes in the toilet, and I'd just break down and cry; I even dreamed of blood, dreamed I was drowning in it, after years of rushing to the bathroom only to realize I'd lost another one: eight times in a row, my friend, eight times in the last three years, God's honest truth. My own doctor started coming down on me: Your womb won't hold it, you're lacking in this, you're lacking in that, you need surgery and who knows what'll become of you, best not to try again, best give up, she told me, the stupid bitch – no man, no kids, probably barren herself – because this, because that, because my organism had been compromised, and why didn't we adopt, that's what the cow said to me; it was her fault my husband gave up hope, and I'd got to the point where I was sure it was only a matter of time before he divorced me, when some people we knew, friends of my sister's best friend told me: Why don't you try praying to St Jude? But properly, mind you. I was to get myself a little votive statue and take it to be blessed, then decorate it with twigs and light a sandalwood candle and pray to it every day, with devotion, with humility, and I said to myself: There's no harm in trying, and just look, my friend, St Jude's performed a miracle, he's given me my little angel: Ángel de Jesús Tadeo, that's what we're calling him, to thank the Lord and our blessed saint for this miracle, because that's what this is, isn't it? A miracle. And Ángel de Jesús Tadeo, all of six hours old, punched his tiny fists into the air and whimpered, overwhelmed by the heat on the ward. There was something in that little boy's bleating that made Norma's hair stand on end, and if it weren't for the fact that she was tied to the bed guard with those rough bandages that had already rubbed the skin on her wrists red raw, she would have raised her hands to her ears to block out the boy and the sickly coos from the mothers in the ward. In fact, if she weren't tied to that stupid bed she'd already be out of there, as far as possible from that hospital, from that rotten town, it didn't even matter that she was barefoot and wearing the weird gown that left her back and bum exposed, with nothing underneath but her own tumescent flesh, anything to get the hell away from those women, from their tired eyes and their stretch marks and their groaning, from the frog-lipped scraggy runts sucking on their black nipples, and above all from the suffocating smell on that ward: the smell of whey, of rancid sweat, a sweet smell that reminded her of all those afternoons spent shut up in Ciudad del Valle rocking Patricio in her arms, pacing from one side of the room to the other to prevent him from suffocating; rubbing his tiny chest with the palm of her hand to warm up the air inside, the air that escaped from her brother's mouth in a muffled sigh, an asthmatic wheeze that made Norma think dear Patricio's lungs were rotting. That poor creature, doomed to be born in the month of January, in the biting cold of Ciudad del Valle, and, worse still, in that room where they lived back then, a stone's throw from the bus station: a single room with no partition walls, a concrete block and cement box in the shadow of a five-storey building that robbed them of every last drop of the sun's warmth, which explained why there were mornings when they'd wake up and see their own breath, lying there under the covers with every item of clothing they owned draped across them, Patricio's Moses basket hanging overhead almost touching the light bulb that they left on all day to provide even the feeblest dose of warmth, to stop the poor thing from freezing up there where none of them could crush or suffocate him, her mother's great fear. Because she knew Patricio was gasping for air, Norma had already told her about the whistle in his throat, as if he'd swallowed a whistle in fact, which the little man tried to bring up by coughing and panting, always in vain, his tiny fists flapping wildly in the biting air while Norma sang lullabies and jiggled him, and sometimes, in her eagerness to help, she even put her finger in his tiny mouth to try to feel whatever was choking him, which Norma imagined as a marble of hard green phlegm, but always in vain. Her mother knew, Norma had told her, and perhaps that's why she didn't shout at her or smack her or call her a waste of space the morning Patricio woke up blue and stiff in the Moses basket that hung above the bed where the rest of them slept packed like sardines: Norma at one end of the mattress, their mother at the other and the three younger siblings between them, because I'm hardly going to let one of them roll off the bed and crack their skull on the concrete floor, am I? her mother would say, and Norma would just nod, and that's why she wouldn't move from her edge of the bed all night, even when she was so desperate to pee that she couldn't get back to sleep, and she would lie there perfectly still under the blankets and clothes, clenching her sphincter and holding her breath to try to distinguish her mother's breathing from the snores and sighs of her brothers and sister, containing the urge, too, to lean over them to touch her mother's chest and check that she was still breathing and that her heart was still beating and that she wasn't stiff or frozen like poor Patricio, while she held in her pee in the same way she held it in lying there in that hospital bed, surrounded by women losing their shit and all those grizzly babies and the relatives with their incessant chitchat: clamping her thighs together and gritting her teeth and tensing her aching abdominal muscles to hold in the warm urine that trickled out regardless in a slow, painful stream, and Norma closed her eyes in shame, so as not to see the dark stain that appeared suddenly on her gown, soaking through the bed sheets, so as not to see the other patients scrunch their noses in disgust, or the nurses' reproachful looks when at last they came to change her, all without untying her from the bed for one second because those were the social worker's orders: to hold her prisoner there until the police arrived, or until Norma confessed or told them what had happened, because even after they'd administered the anaesthetic, just before the doctor went in with his metal spoons, the social worker wasn't able to get any information out of Norma, not even her name or her real age or what it was she'd taken or who'd given it to her or where she'd dumped what she'd had inside her, and least of all her reasons; they hadn't got a word out of Norma, not even after screaming at her, telling her not to be an idiot, asking repeatedly for her boyfriend's name, the little bastard who'd done this and where he lived so that the police could go and arrest him, because the shameless boy had just dropped her off at the hospital and bolted. Wasn't she angry? Didn't she want him to pay too? And Norma, who'd only just begun to realize that all this was really happening, that it wasn't just a terrible dream, clamped her mouth shut and shook her head and didn't say a word, not even when the nurses undressed her there in front of everyone waiting their turn in the emergency room corridor; not even when the bald doctor stuck his head between her thighs and began to poke around the sex that Norma no longer recognized as her own, not only because she couldn't feel a thing from the ribs down, but because when at last she was able to lift her head and focus her gaze, what she saw was a red, scalped pubis which didn't remotely resemble her own, and she couldn't believe that all that flesh down there belonged to her, all that yellowish, pimply flesh that resembled the skin of the dead, gutted chickens in the market, and that was the moment they decided to tie her up, supposedly to hold her still while they inserted the metal spoons, so she wouldn't do herself any harm, but Norma knew that really it was so she couldn't escape, because it wasn't a lack of will that stopped her from flying out of the room at the first opportunity, even if she was butt naked, and even if the breeze wafting in through the door made her shiver and set her teeth chattering, a breeze that was warm, sticky even, but to Norma – who was running a temperature of forty plus – seemed as glacial as the wind that came down at night from the mountains surrounding Ciudad del Valle, the bluish rock mass covered in pines and chestnut trees, which, one February fourteenth, a few years earlier, Pepe had taken them to see, because how the hell had Norma, her brothers, sister and mother been living all that time in

Ciudad del Valle without ever going to see the forests; they were really missing out on something special, one of the wonders of the world, Mother Nature in all her glory, that clown Pepe had said. Snow! We're going to see the snow! her siblings sang as they trundled along the path winding its way through those giant trees, and at first Norma had skipped along beside them, delighted with the walk and the view of the city at her feet and the clouds, so close, and the frost dusting the lichen- and pine-needle-capped ground, but who knows what must have been going through her head when she got dressed that morning because she'd forgotten to put on any socks, and the damp from the forest floor soon seeped in through the broken soles of her shoes and Norma's feet ended up frozen, as cold and stiff as poor Patricio, and the pain became pretty unbearable and Pepe had to cancel the walk and carry her down the mountainside and all the way to the bus stop that would take them back to the city, without having reached the summit, without having touched the snow or thrown snowballs or made snowmen like on the TV, her siblings whined, and all because she was such an idiot, such a ridiculous fucking fool, her mother had said, because Norma was always screwing everything up, and Norma had wept in silence the whole way home while Pepe tried to cheer her up by cracking jokes about how their mother was permanently stressed out, but her mother had scowled at her the whole way back with the same accusatory eyes and pursed lips as the nurses when they found out why Norma was tied to the bed, the same look that the social worker had given her the night they hospitalized her: They're barely old enough to wipe their own asses, these tarts, and yet off they go, legs akimbo. I'm going to tell the doctor to scrape you out with no anaesthesia, that'll teach you.

How do you suppose you'll pay the hospital bill, eh? Who's going to look after you? Whoever he is, he just took what he wanted and tossed you out, left you high and dry, and here you are trying to protect him, like a fool. Who did this to you? Tell me his name or you'll be the one who ends up inside, you'll be an accessory, don't be silly now, girly, and Norma, on the brink of passing out from the icy breeze whistling in from the open door leading to the corridor, closed her eyes and clamped her mouth shut and imagined Luismi's smiling face, his ruffled hair, his brown, almost auburn hair in the sunlight, one of the first things she'd noticed when he'd approached her in the park; poor Luismi, who had no idea what Norma had done, what the Witch had done, what Chabela had convinced her to do, because at first the Witch had said no, no, no and Chabela was the one who begged her: Oh, be a doll, she needs help, poor girl; don't be an ass, come on, Witchy, don't get on your high horse now, how many times have you sorted me out, me and my girls, is it such a big ask, how much do you want, and the Witch just shook her head, paying no attention to Chabela, busying herself moving trinkets from one side of that grimy kitchen to the other, that low-ceilinged kitchen with walls posted in smut and shelves holding dusty jars, sketches depicting dark arts, little religious images of saints with their eyes scored out and cuttings of busty old bitches flashing their wide open bits. Oh, come on, Witchy, even the boy knows, he's on board, right, mamacita? she asked Norma, and Norma said nothing for a moment but when she felt Chabela kick her shin under the table she nodded strenuously, and the Witch looked her directly in the eyes and Norma felt a shiver run down her spine but managed to keep holding her gaze, and who knows what the Witch read there in

Norma's eyes, because after stoking the coals glowing in the stove she said fine, she'd do it, she'd prepare Norma her famous potion, that thick, salty concoction, ferociously hot from all the alcohol the Witch poured in with the bunches of herbs and powders from grubby containers – the potion she finally decanted into a glass jar and placed on the table in front of Norma, next to what was left of a rotten apple sitting on a plate of sea salt, an apple with a fillet knife struck all the way through and dead petals scattered around it. The Witch hadn't wanted any money and she looked at the two hundred pesos that Chabela put on the table with such disgust that Norma was sure she would burn it the moment they left the house, which they did immediately after the Witch handed them the potion, to Norma's great relief. But once outside, on the dirt track that led back to Chabela's, they heard the Witch calling after them from the kitchen door in that strange voice of hers, somehow both gruff and high-pitched at once, and Norma spun round and understood that the Witch was calling her, even though she'd already pulled her veil back down over her face: You have to drink it all! she shouted. You'll retch but you have to drink it all! It'll feel like your insides are being torn out, but hang in there...! Don't be afraid! You just push and push until...! And then bury it! Chabela was pulling her by the wrist, digging her nails in ever so slightly. Does that freak think I was born yesterday? she muttered, picking up the pace and pretending not to hear the Witch's shouts. Better still, stay here to take it...! the Witch cried in one final plea, but her voice was already faint. Norma could no longer hear what the old sorceress was trying to tell her, she was panting from the effort of keeping up with Chabela and holding on to the jar with her free hand so that it didn't fall and smash to

pieces. Stupid Witch, Chabela went on, she's going soft
in the head; what a scene, as if I didn't know everything
there was to know about these things, for fuck's sake,
when I was the first one to realize you had a bun in the
oven, wasn't I? I saw the line, the tell-tale line when you
took your clothes off to try on my dress, the one I gave
you because yours was in tatters, remember, mamacita?
And Norma remembered only too well; barely three
weeks had passed since Luismi took her home to his,
three weeks since that first night they'd spent together,
barely sleeping at all, inventing all kinds of lies because
they didn't know each other, which meant they couldn't
tell what was true from what wasn't, whispering their life
stories to one another on that bare mattress and in almost total darkness because the light bulb in Luismi's
casita had blown and the only thing they could make out
was the gleam of their teeth each time they laughed. That
night they'd ended up fucking, or something like it, in
part because Norma had spent the whole time waiting
for the moment he'd claim what she owed him for his
hospitality, and she was scared that when he did he'd notice, that he'd figure it out from her round belly, or from
the taste in her mouth, but she was in luck because
Luismi didn't kiss her that night, and when he touched
her it was only with the very tips of his fingers, shy caresses, which every now and then she mistook for the
wings of the hovering insects that flew in through the
open gap in the doorway, no doubt attracted to the sweat
on their bodies. They'd undressed slowly, to cope with
the heat, a sweltering heat that felt to Norma as if it were
coming from within her, from inside that stupid swollen
belly that would end up betraying her the moment
Luismi reached out his hand to touch her, but he didn't
even try; in fact, he didn't do anything that night, or

nothing more than just lie there next to Norma and sigh whenever her hands, restless from all the uncertainty, from the wait, took the initiative and started playing with Luismi's dick, tugging on it in the same way that, years before, those hands had tugged Gustavo or Manolo's willies when they were in the bath, because it used to make her laugh to watch their little sausages grow harder and bigger the more she touched them. And Luismi, just like her brothers, stayed very still while she stroked him, and he barely let out a moan when she straddled his bony hips and started rocking back and forth and up and down with that energetic pace that Pepe liked so much, but this seemed to leave Luismi indifferent, for at no point did Norma hear him groan with pleasure, nor did he try to touch her breasts or clasp her ass, nothing; he was so quiet and so still that Norma, who couldn't see his face clearly, began to suspect he'd fallen asleep under her, and, feeling humiliated, with tears welling in the corners of her eyes, she moved off him and lay back down on the mattress with her back to him, completely soaked in sweat from that pointless workout, her eyes fixed on the strip of velvety night that she could just make out above the board Luismi had propped up across the entrance as if it were a door, and she was just nodding off when she felt Luismi shuffle up behind her, rest his hand timidly on her naked hip and kiss her between her shoulder blades with his dry lips. Norma felt a shiver run through her and once again she searched for him with her hand, but this time it was he who took the initiative and, without removing his lips from her back, thrust inside her with surprising ease given that he'd used a new hole, the only orifice on Norma's body that Pepe hadn't been able to claim for himself, because that business made Norma feel gross, and she'd always suspected that it would hurt like mad, but with Lusimi it turned out to be pleasurable, maybe because Luismi didn't try to crush her under his weight, or maybe because he moved in a different way than Pepe, in and out of her in a peculiar motion, which, all at once, made Norma groan with pleasure, unable to contain herself, a muffled groan that made Luismi lie perfectly still again as if suddenly petrified, and it was Norma who had to keep things going, eager to bring him to climax, to feel him come inside her, desperate to be done with the whole thing, but after what felt like an interminably long time of frantic wiggling, of driving herself down onto him as far as her body would permit, Luismi, without a word, placed his hand back on Norma's hip and with great delicacy, almost excusing himself in silence, pulled out of her completely flaccid. Who knows what time it was when Norma finally managed to fall asleep, but when she opened her eyes again, panicked by a sharp jabbing in her painfully full bladder, she saw that it was already day. She tried to wake up Luismi so he could tell her where the bathroom was but he didn't react, not even when she shook his shoulders: he remained curled up in a ball on the mattress, his spine painfully visible beneath his brown skin. He was so thin it occurred to Norma that he might even be younger than her, with his bony sides and skinny penis like a timorous snail hiding in the little forest of hairs that grew between his legs, his arms skeletal and his full lips closed around the thumb he sucked in his dreams. Norma sat on the mattress and put on the same dress she'd worn the day before, thinking maybe Luismi would wake up when he heard her moving around, but he just went on sleeping with his thumb in his mouth, even when she got up and pulled aside the makeshift door and went down to the end of the yard to squat for a pee. Once she'd finished relieving herself and wiggled her backside to shake off the final drops that threatened to run down her leg, she stood up, arranged her dress, and looked over at the cement block house at the other end of the plot, where to her surprise she saw a woman with long, curly hair waving her over from one of the open windows. Norma looked around to check there wasn't anyone else in the yard and that the woman really was talking to her. Don't be scuzzy, mamacita, was the first thing the woman said to her when Norma finally reached the window. The woman smiled with thick, deep red lips. Her shoulders were bare and her loose hair was frizzy in the morning humidity, like an auburn halo around her face, which itself was powdered and lined with dark ruts where her make-up had run. This must be Luismi's mum, Norma thought on seeing that hair, so similar to the boy's, and she felt her face flush with shame. The woman lit a cigarette. We've got a toilet in here, she said, blowing her first puff over Norma's head. She pointed inside the house with the lit tip. You wanna use it, just come in. Don't worry, I don't bite. Norma nodded and gawped at the two rows of perfect albeit yellowish teeth that appeared from behind those painted, almost clown-like lips. I'm Chabela, she said. And who are you? Norma, the girl replied after what she considered to be a prudent pause. Norma, Chabela repeated, Norma... You know what? You're the spitting image of my sister Clarita, the littlest. I haven't seen her for donkey's years but fuck me if you aren't her absolute double. And a little goer like her, too, I'm guessing? Because you came to screw that little fucker in there, right? she said, arching her thin, black-pencilled eyebrows while with the tip of her cigarette she pointed in the direction of the scrappy tin house

110

where Luismi lay sleeping. Norma bit her lips and couldn't stop herself from blushing again while Chabela read between the lines of her silence and let out a shrill cackle, followed by a bellow that must have been heard all the way on the highway, and which cut through the hazy morning air: You've gone too far, fucker! She's barely out of nappies! And then to Norma, with a different smile, more strained than kindly: You really are the spit of our Clarita, mamacita; only you need a good scrub, you reek of rotten fish and those fucking rags are filthy. It's the only dress I've got, Norma admitted in a whisper, and Chabela rolled her eyes impatiently. She took one last hasty drag on her cigarette and flicked what was left of it out into the yard. With a subtle roll of her shoulder she told Norma to follow her inside, but the girl hesitated. Come on, don't be a dummy, Chabela shouted before disappearing from the window. Norma walked around the outside of the house and went in through an open door leading into a room that seemed to serve as a lounge, diner and kitchen all in one, a room with walls painted various shades of green, and smelling of cigarette ash, cooking grease and metabolized liquor. In the middle of the room there was a man slouched on an armchair with his legs spread and his interlocking hands resting on his belly. He had dark glasses and a thin, greying moustache; he was watching a game show on TV with the volume turned way down. Norma hesitated in the doorway then muttered hello and bowed her head as she hurried past the television screen, trying not to disturb the gentleman, although seconds later, when the man opened his mouth and produced a long, honking snore, she realized he was fast asleep. Letting herself be guided by the smell of cigarette and Chabela's husky voice, which hadn't paused for one second, Norma continued down a short hallway and poked her head round the only door she found open. This is my room, Chabela greeted her. Nice, eh? But before Norma could mutter a reply, the woman went on: Chose the colours myself. Wanted it to look like a geisha's room, see? I've got a few dresses in here I hardly wear. I was thinking of giving them to the girls at Excalibur's, but they're a bunch of thankless bitches, only out for themselves, fuck 'em. Norma gazed at the red and black walls, the chiffon curtains that must've once been white but were now tinged yellow from all the smoke and nicotine, the enormous bed that took up almost the entire room and on which lay a towering pile of clothes and shoes and pots of creams and make-up and hangers and bras. Here, try this, Chabela said, holding out a red Lycra dress covered in blue polka dots. Well, come on then, chop chop, I already told you I don't bite. Don't just stand there like a dummy, mamacita. What did you say your name was? Norma opened her mouth to answer but Chabela didn't pause to listen: Got to keep your wits about you in this world, she pontificated. You drop your guard for a second and they'll crush you, Clarita, so you better just tell that fuckwit out there to buy you some clothes. Don't you be anyone's fool, that's what men are like: a bunch of lazy spongers who you have to keep rounding up to squeeze any use out of them, and that kid's no different; either you tell the little shit what's what or he'll spend all the money on drugs, and before you know it you're the cunt providing for him, Clarita. I'm telling you because I know the little prick, I know him and his tricks alright... I pushed him out! So don't you go losing your head on me, you hear? You've gotta tell him, you tell him to buy you clothes, give you spending money and take you out in Villa, you've gotta keep men like that on

112

a tight leash, keep them busy to stop them coming out with all their shit. Norma nodded, but she had to raise a hand to her mouth to hide her smile when Chabela stopped talking for a second and the pair of them heard thundering snores coming from the man sleeping in the living room. Fucking Clarita, I see you pissing yourself laughing, you silly bitch, Chabela said, although she was also smiling, baring her big yellow teeth. To see him now you wouldn't believe that dead weight used to be a real man, a real handsome fucker, before the accident. They well and truly fucked up my man, Clarita; turned him into a waste of space, a fucking piss artist who can't so much as make me a coffee when I come home dead on my feet from work. I should've sent him packing, right? Upgraded to the latest model, got myself a real man; because I'm not short of offers, eh? Old maid that I am, I can still turn heads when I roll up in Villa, and I'd only have to snap my fingers and a queue of bastards would be fighting over who could have me, who could win me over. Well, come here then, Clarita, don't just stand there like a dodo, mamacita. And Norma walked to the middle of the room with the dress in her hand, overcome by Chabela's verbal onslaught and by the haze from the cigarettes that the woman chain-smoked even as she talked, never once coughing or spluttering, even when she bit the cigarette between her teeth as she bent down to pick things off the floor and toss them onto the bed, or as she took items of clothing piled on top of the bed-spread and discarded them on the floor. What do you reckon, Clarita? Shall I send him packing or keep supporting the lame old bum? It is my house, after all, I fucking sweated my tits off to build it, and don't think for one second that cunt raised a finger to help me do any of this. Chabela raised her hands with her palms facing up and turned from side to side pointing out the furniture and everything in the room, from the walls to the curtains, and apparently the whole house and the land it was built on, and maybe even the entire village. Norma chewed her bottom lip, terrified by the responsibility of replying, but fortunately Chabela kept bleating on without any need for a response from Norma. And that's precisely why you have to keep your wits about you, Clarita. You're just a baby, mamacita, you've got plenty of time to find someone better than that shithead in there. I'm sorry to put it like that, but I'm speaking from the heart: I don't know what the hell you see in him but I'm telling you, you can do better, because you and I both know that cunt's going nowhere. I tell you what, I'll shout you the bus fare, mamacita, back to your own town or wherever the fuck you came from, because I'd bet my balls that you're not from La Matosa... Am I right or am I right? I bet you're not even from Villa... Oh, for Christ's sake, Clarita! Don't just stand there stiff as a dick! Take that filthy dress off, girl. Don't tell me you're embarrassed, because at the end of the day, you don't have anything I don't have. Chop chop, get a wriggle on! And Norma was left with no choice but to take off the cotton dress she was wearing and let it fall to the floor, and then slip her head and arms into the dress that Luismi's mother had given her. The material was very soft and it stretched to adjust to the curves of her body. She looked in the mirror hanging on the black wall: she was horrified to see that she was showing more than ever. Oh, Clarita, you silly cow, Chabela said from behind her, why didn't you tell me you're that far gone? Luismi's mother's face appeared in the mirror, just above Norma's shoulder. Those deep-red lips curled into a malicious smile. Let's have a look, show me, she ordered, and Norma, thrown by the woman's proximity and the determination in her voice, bent down gently to take the hem of the dress and lift it up. Chabela ignored Norma's hairy legs and her naked sex and stared avidly at the roundness of her belly. With one nail, painted radioactive green, she traced the purple line that ran up the middle of Norma's stomach, from the point where her pubic hair began right up to her belly button. More than a tickling sensation, what the girl felt was a kind of vertigo, a shudder. The tell-tale line, Chabela said. Norma let the fabric of the dress drop again, turned her head towards the window and stared out at the row of palm trees swaying in the breeze in the distance, partly because she was too embarrassed to look at Chabela, and partly to avoid breathing in the smoke from yet another cigarette. Is it Luismi's? the woman asked. No, Norma replied. And does he know you're in this state? The girl shrugged her shoulders, but then shook her head. No, she repeated. She looked at Chabela in the mirror. The woman looked pensively at her belly with her eyes screwed up. She folded her arms and flicked cigarette ash in the air. Right, she said at last, after exhaling a great puff of smoke from one side of her mouth, let's not tell him anything for now, okay? Norma stood staring at the woman's reflection. Because you don't want it, right? Or do you? Norma felt her ears begin to prickle; once again her cheeks burned up. Because if you don't want it, I know someone who can help you, someone who knows how to fix these things. She's half gone in the head, the poor mare, and between us she gives me the creeps, but deep down she's a good egg, and you'll see how at the last minute she won't even take any money. You've no idea how many fixes she's got me and the Excalibur girls out of. We can tell her to sort you out if

115

you don't want it. Or do you want it? You'd best make your mind up, mamacita, and pronto, because that bump's not getting any smaller. Norma couldn't look Chabela in the eyes, not even in the mirror, so instead she looked at her own body. Not only was her belly fatter than ever, but now her boobs hung heavy, a whole cup size bigger, or maybe even two, she wasn't completely sure. A week earlier she'd stopped using the only bra she owned and of course she hadn't been wearing it the day she decided to run away from home: it didn't even fit anymore. Only that dress fitted, the cotton dress that Chabela scooped up off the floor with two fingers and a grimace; the dress she'd been wearing when she decided to run away from Ciudad del Valle, together with her open-toed sandals and a jumper that quickly stopped serving any purpose as the bus made its way down to the coast and headlong into the stifling heat; the jumper that, by all accounts, Norma had left somewhere along the way. Probably on the bus seat when the driver woke her up to tell her to get off. Or maybe she left it in the reed bed where she'd had to hide when those men in the pick-up began hassling her. For a second, prompted by Chabela's conspicuous silence, she was about to open her mouth and tell her everything – everything, sparing no detail – but a voice shouting her name from the yard stopped her. It was Luismi from the other side of the window, Luismi in his underpants, his eyes squinting in the midday sun – or in anger? – and his hair all over the place. What are you doing in there? he asked Norma, when at last his eyes adjusted to the dim room and he was able to see her. What the fuck's it to you, you prying little shit? Chabela snapped back, a fresh cigarette dangling from her lips. Luismi gave his mother a death stare, pursed his lips into a grimace, turned on his heel and stormed off back to the rickety fleapit he called his *casita*. Norma decided to follow him. She thanked Chabela for the dress and ran back through the living room where the man was still sleeping in front of the TV. I don't want you talking to her, was the first thing Luismi told Norma when they entered the *casita*. I don't want you talking to her and I don't want to see you in that house again, understood? He didn't raise his voice, but he did grip Norma's arm so tightly that he left finger marks on her skin. If you need to pee, go back there, he went on, but I don't want to see you in that house, I don't want you to become one of her whores, understood? Norma had told him yes, she understood, and she'd even apologized, although she wasn't altogether sure what she was apologizing for. Over the following days, whenever Luismi lay snoring on his mattress, sometimes well into the afternoon, Norma, unable to bear the infernal heat under the tin roof of that shack, would get up silently and sneak into the cement block house on the other side of the property, to Chabela's kitchen, entering through the door that was always open, and make coffee and eggs and refried beans or rice with plantains or *chilaquiles* or whatever she could rustle up with what she found in the cupboards, before even Munra, Chabela's husband, woke up. And by that time Chabela would be home from work, tottering around the house in her high heels, her curls unkempt and her eyes bloodshot from cigarette smoke and lack of sleep, and Chabela would take one look at the food on the table and a wild grin would spread across her face: Clarita, you angel, you're twice the woman I am, you are. Look at those eggs, Jesus, tell me again why I didn't get a daughter like you instead of that ungrateful fuck out there, and once Chabela had eaten, once she'd smoked one last cigarette before staggering to her room to lie down, the fan blowing over the foot of her bed at full speed, Norma would dish up a mountain of food onto another plate, cross the yard, wake up Luismi and force him to eat. The poor love was so thin Norma could almost wrap one of her hands around his biceps; so thin she could count his ribs, and without him even having to breathe in. So thin and, truth be told, so ugly, with his spotty cheeks and wonky teeth, his black man's nose and that coarse, frizzy hair, which, by the looks of things, was the norm in La Matosa. Maybe that's why it pulled on Norma's heartstrings to see him happy: to see him smile at some silly thing she said, when his eyes would light up for a second and all that sadness he wore on his shoulders would disappear, and for the briefest of moments he would go back to being the kid who approached her in the park in Villa, where she was crying on a bench because she was really hungry and really thirsty and she'd run out of money and because the bus driver who'd brought her all the way from Ciudad del Valle had woken her up suddenly, kicking her off there, at a petrol station in the middle of nowhere, in the middle of miles and miles of sugar cane fields, and what's more, her face and arms were sunburnt and her feet were swollen and scorched from having walked from the petrol station into the centre of town along the furrows dividing the fields, and by the time Luismi approached her to ask why she was crying, Norma had all but made up her mind to cross the road and walk into the small hotel overlooking the park – Hotel Marbella, said a sign on one of the walls, painted in blood-like high-gloss red – where she would beg the receptionist to let her make a call, just one, and then she'd speak to her mother up in Ciudad del Valle and she'd tell her where she was and why she'd run away, she'd tell her everything and her mother would of course scream at her and hang up the phone, and Norma would be left with no option but to walk to the highway and hitch a ride to Puerto, to go through with her original plan. Of course, with a bit of luck, she might not even have to go all the way to Puerto. With a bit of luck she might find some nearby stretch of coast, and maybe there'd be an outcrop to throw herself off and into the sea. To make matters worse, those guys from the pickup, the ones who'd harassed her on the way into town, appeared now on the other side of the park, and Norma was just about to stand up from the bench to run into the hotel when the boy with tawny hair, the skinny kid who'd spent the whole afternoon glancing at Norma from the benches at the furthermost end of the park while his friends smoked marijuana and giggled uncontrollably, crossed the plaza grinning, sat down next to Norma and asked her what was up, why was she crying. And Norma looked into the boy's eyes and saw that they were pitch black, but sweet, capped with long, long lashes that lent him a dreamy look, even if the rest of his face was ugly as a pig's, from his grubby cheeks to his big nose and thick lips, and Norma didn't have the heart to lie to him, but neither did she dare confess the whole truth, so she decided to tell him something in between: she told him she was crying because she was really hungry and really thirsty and because she was lost and she didn't have a peso to her name and because she couldn't go home because of something really bad that she'd done. She didn't tell him that, until that very morning, until the moment the bus driver dumped her on the side of the highway once she'd ridden as far as her money would take her, her plan had been to go to Puerto because she remembered having gone there once with her mother, when Norma was so young that none of her brothers or her sister had been born yet; in other words, she must have been about three or four, or, doing the maths, maybe her mother was already pregnant with Manolo by then, but Norma hadn't known. That trip to Puerto was the last time she could remember being alone with her mother, just the two of them, looking out over the Gulf from their tent, swimming each day in the warm sea, trying *mojarra frita* and crab empanadas, which to Norma were beyond delicious. Nor did she tell the boy what she'd planned to do on arriving in Puerto: walk along the same beaches she'd visited with her mother until she found the enormous outcrop to the south of the city, and then climb to the top of that great rock to dive into the dark, choppy waters down below to bring an end to it all, to her life and the life of that thing growing inside of her. She didn't tell him any of that; she only told him that she was really hungry and really thirsty and that she was dead tired and scared, because she didn't know anyone in town, but also because some guys had followed her in a pickup as she'd walked into the centre of Villa and she'd had to leave the roadside to hide in the reed beds because the men riding on the back of the pickup were shouting at her, calling her names, clicking their tongues as if she were a dog, and the man driving, a blond fellow in dark glasses and a cowboy hat, turned down the blaring music, *me haré pasar por un hombre normal*, and told Norma to get into the pickup, *que pueda estar sin ti, que no se sienta mal*, but she was terrified and instead ran as fast as she could into a field and crouched down among the sugar cane until the men grew bored of looking for her and drove off; the same men who, right in that very moment, Norma whimpered, were parked on the other side of the park, outside that cantina next to the church, and Norma pointed to the pickup, and Luismi, with a nervous smile, a grimace that revealed his wonky teeth, took her hand and wrapped it in his fist and whispered to her not to point, she must never, ever point at those men; she'd been very wise to run away from them, because everyone knew that the blond one in the hat was a narco; his name was Cuco Barrabás and he regularly abducted girls just to hurt them, and then, with his eyes boring into the ground and his voice trembling slightly, as if he were embarrassed, Luismi told Norma that he had no money to help her but that if she could wait for him a while he might be able to scrape a little together, and then they could go and grab a couple of *tortas* over there in front of the park; and if Norma wanted she could spend the night with him, at his place, only he didn't live in Villa but in a town called La Matosa, some eight miles from there; if she wanted, of course, because it was all he could offer to help her, to stop her spoiling those pretty eyes of hers with those tears, but, look, if she didn't want to it was no big deal... She only had to promise him that under absolutely no circumstances would she get into Cuco's pickup, because everyone in town knew that *güero* was a son of a bitch and that he did evil, evil things to the girls, sick things that the boy didn't want to go into then, but the important thing was that Norma understood that she must never, ever get into that pickup, or go asking the police for help, because those fuckers worked for the same boss, and at the end of the day they were basically the same thing. And Norma, welling up in gratitude, her throat raw from thirst, promised him she'd do exactly that, she'd wait for him, and so Luismi went off to find some cash and she stayed there on that bench with her hands clasped together on her lap, her eyes screwed up and her mouth clamped shut as if she were praying, although really what she was trying to do was ignore the little voice inside her telling her she was an idiot for trusting a man she didn't even know, a man who probably just wanted to take advantage of her, to reel her in with his empty promises and sweet talk, because that's what they were all like, wasn't it? A bunch of assholes with all the lines but zero intention of keeping their word. But Luismi had come good; Luismi had proved that little voice wrong; it had taken a couple of hours but he had come back, when the park was already dark and there was nobody left but the stoners, and he showed her the money he'd got and took her to eat in the *tortería* in front of the park, and after that he led her by the hand through the winding streets of that town: dusty, silent streets patrolled by squadrons of stray mongrels that stared at them warily. From there they crossed a vast mango grove with trees laden with still-green fruit and, further along, a hanging bridge suspended over a river, which, at that hour, in the prevailing darkness, was already completely invisible, before coming to a dirt track that ran right into the heart of the whispering grasslands. The night had grown so thick that Norma couldn't even see well enough to put one foot in front of the other; the path ran up and down, tapering one minute and widening the next, and all the while Norma wondered how Luismi could make out anything at all in that pitch darkness; it seemed to her that at any given moment the path would vanish beneath their feet and the two of them would go tumbling over a cliff edge, which is why she squeezed Luismi's hand and, every so often, asked him not to go so fast, and when they had to walk along a narrow pass buzzing with menacing-sounding insects, Luismi put an arm around her shoulders and began to sing very softly. He had a sweet voice – the voice of a man, unlike his body, which was still very much a child's – and in the ominous darkness that seemed to be swallowing them, his song calmed Norma's nerves, relieved her aching, blistered feet and her muddled head, still confused by the voice inside insisting she must walk away from that kid, walk back to the highway and use any means possible to reach Puerto, climb to the top of that rock and dive into the water, let herself be smashed to pieces and end it all. And after a really long time, that path – flanked on either side by living, breathing brushwood – finally opened out onto a tiny village with no roads, no park, no church, just a handful of houses illuminated by dim light bulbs. They half-tumbled down a dip in the path that led to a small cement block house, also lit by a single bare light bulb hanging above the porch. But instead of going into the house or knocking on the door, the boy led her to the end of the property and to a little wooden shack with a tin roof that he boasted he'd built with his own hands, a den that seemed just perfect to Norma, who was exhausted, and without waiting for Luismi to tell her to, she lay down on the mattress and began to whisper her story, or rather part of her story, the parts she was less ashamed of; he listened to her, lying on his side, and at no point did he try to touch anything besides her face and her hands, he didn't even tell her to lie on her back and spread her legs or to bend down to suck his cock, as Pepe did every time they went to bed together. Suck me off, he'd say; and my balls, hard, baby girl, like you want to, that's it, all the way down, don't pretend you think it's gross when I know you like it, even though that wasn't true, even though Norma didn't like it at all, but that's what he would say and she never corrected him; because the truth was that at first she had liked it; the truth was that at the beginning she had even begun to think of Pepe as good looking, and she was truly happy when her mother brought him home to live with them, to be Norma and her siblings' stepfather, because when Pepe was around everything was better: her brothers and sister gave her less shit and her mother didn't lock herself in the bathroom to scream that she wanted to die because she was so alone, and nor did she lock them in the house at night and go out drinking. But Norma wasn't ready to tell Luismi about Pepe; she didn't even want to think about him and the things they'd been getting up to, because if she told Luismi what had really happened, he'd realize what a terrible person Norma was and he'd wish he hadn't helped her and he'd throw her out of his house and send her back out into the darkness, so she simply told him about Ciudad del Valle, and how ugly and cold and sad it was, like the building block where she'd lived with her mother and her mother's husband and the pack of wild animals she called her siblings who made her life hell, and how her mother was always telling her off for things they'd done. She even made up that she had a boyfriend: some kid supposedly at the same middle school as her, but in the third year, not the first, a really good looking guy, a real rebel with long hair and ripped denim jeans who her family did everything they could to keep her away from, anything so she didn't have to confess to Luismi that in fact the only man she'd ever kissed was Pepe, her stepfather, her mother's husband, when she was twelve and he twenty-nine, that time they'd been watching a film on the TV, curled up under a blanket on the sofa, and he'd teased her because she'd never kissed anyone, and then Norma, totally joking, obviously messing around, put her hands on either side of his face and smacked a big kiss on him, a wet raspberry against his lips and the moustache that Pepe was trying to grow back then, with little success; a kiss he celebrated with a hearty laugh and a tickling session that her siblings came rushing in to join. Pepe liked to tease her, to set her little challenges; he would place his hand palm up in the exact spot where she was going to sit and then pinch her bottom and pretend it wasn't him, and all of this was funny, or it had been funny at the start because the attention made Norma feel important, since Pepe insisted on sitting next to her whenever they watched cartoons and he would put his arm around her shoulders and stroke her back, her shoulders and her hair, but only when Norma's mother was at the factory, only when her siblings were out playing with the other kids in the communal yard of their building, and always under that blanket so that no one could see what Pepe's hands were doing while they watched the screen, the way his fingers slid across Norma's skin and traced the curves of her body, caresses that nobody, not even her mother, had ever given her, not even back in the good old days when it was just the two of them and Norma didn't have to vie for her attention and love. Tickles, which, truth be told, didn't actually tickle, but left her sort of quivering, all sticky inside, embarrassed about the sighs that would escape from her mouth suddenly, moans that she had to cover up at all costs because she was scared her siblings would hear them, that her mother would find out, that Pepe – who in those moments would seem livid with her because he'd scowl and his breathing would grow heavy and deep – would leave her and stop doing any of that if he discovered how much she liked it, and that's why she would stare at the TV screen and smile at all the funny parts of the cartoons and make out that she couldn't feel anything, as if she were completely impervious to Pepe's caresses, until he'd grow bored of her or simply tired, at which point he would get up from the sofa and lock himself in the bathroom, and when he came back he'd hold his open palm under Norma's nose and make her smell the pong left on his hands after peeing, and then Norma would giggle, because it was all just silly and fun again and Pepe had only been joking, and Pepe had only been trying to show his affection for her, a love far deeper than the love he felt for her siblings, even Pepito, the baby he'd had with her mother just a couple of months earlier. And at night, when they were all meant to be sleeping, Norma would strain to hear what he and her mother talked about, especially when it was about her, about her mother's growing concern about how quickly Norma was growing up, how weirdly she'd been behaving recently and how much it got to her that Pepe showered the girl with attention, and he'd tell her not to be stupid, the only thing he was trying to do was show the poor kid the love she'd never felt from a father – it was normal that the girl should feel a bit confused by Pepe's genuine and entirely innocent affections, and even that she should start to get a little crush on him, come on, she's at that awkward age, hormones raging, poor girl, she might even imagine I love her in another way, because she's too young to know how to express all the unsettling emotions she's beginning to feel in her heart, and he had a real way with words, Pepe; sometimes you'd have never guessed he hadn't finished elementary school; sometimes it was as if he'd studied law or journalism, as if he was a teacher or university graduate, because he had an answer for everything and he used words no one else knew, and Norma's mother would just listen, rapt and placated, and the next day she'd be back on her old drum before heading out to work and leaving Norma at home to take the others to school and get lunch ready: Norma, you're not a little girl anymore, you'll soon be a young lady so you better start acting like one, accept your responsibilities in this house and set a good example for your siblings. God help you if I find out you still hang out with Tere and those other little tarts down there; and God help you if anyone comes around here telling me they've seen you go into that pool hall with the older boys. You must think I was born yesterday, that I don't know what goes on in there; I've heard all about the dropouts who hang out waiting to get their hands on the first floozy who'll give it up and then leave the girl with her Sunday seven. And Norma would shake her head and say: No, mama, I don't go to those places, stop worrying, you'll drive yourself mad, I always come straight home, although later, when she was alone, she thought about her mother's words and realized she hadn't understood the part about the Sunday seven, or what it had to do with her neighbours or the pool hall on the corner, or with anyone getting their hands on anyone else, and around that time she began to worry because Pepe had become totally obsessed with putting his finger inside her and how his whole middle finger had to go inside, even if it jabbed her, even if she ended up feeling little punches in her lower tummy. And she worried even more, to the point of not being able to sleep, when one afternoon she went to the girls bathroom at school with stomach cramps and when she sat on the toilet she discovered her knickers were stained with blood, a maroon, putrid blood that came out of precisely the same hole Pepe had been poking around in lately. So it had finally happened, she thought, horrified: the fateful Sunday seven that would ruin her life and the lives of her entire family; her punishment for having let Pepe put his hands between her legs, and probably also for having carried on all that touching by herself, at night, when nobody could see or hear her, while her siblings slept soundly on their side of the bed and Pepe and her mother were too busy making the bed springs creak to turn round and see what she was up to: touching that hole of hers thinking of Pepe, Pepe's fingers, Pepe's tongue. That's why she decided not to say a word to anybody about that blood: she was scared her mother would work out what had been going on, what Norma had done, what Pepe still, to that day, would do while her mother was at work. Norma was terrified her mother would kick her out, because she was always telling Norma what happened to the stupid girls who wound up with their Sunday seven; how they were thrown out onto the streets and left to fend for themselves, completely stranded, and all for having let some guy take advantage of them, for not having demanded some respect, because everyone knows men will take whatever the woman lets them. And the truth is that by then Norma had let her stepfather take a lot, too much, and worst of all, she wanted to give him more, wanted to let him do whatever he wanted, the things he was always whispering in her ear, the things the boys in school would scrawl and doodle on the walls in the toilets, things that old men would mutter at her in the street and that she wanted them to do to her. Pepe or the boys or the old men or whoever wanted to, in truth: anything to keep her from thinking about the gaping void that for months had made her weep silently into her pillow, in the dead of night, before her mother's alarm went off, before the first trucks filled the glacial greyish morning air of Ciudad del Valle with their smog; tears that came from deep inside her, tears she didn't understand but hid from the others all the same, because she was ashamed: to sob like that, for no reason, at her age, as if she were still a little girl. Because that's what her mother was always telling her: she wasn't a little girl anymore, she'd soon be a young lady and she'd have to start demanding some respect and setting a good example for her siblings, stop being such a lazybones at school, stop squandering the small fortune they paid Doña Lucita from the seventh floor to watch little Pepito in the afternoons while she studied, start appreciating the superhuman effort that she and Pepe made so that Norma could finish school and make something of herself, and above all, Norma must see herself through her mother's eyes, a phrase her mother used to mean that Norma must always remember her mother's mistakes and avoid repeating them, but it took Norma a long time to work out what her mother really meant by 'her mistakes': Norma and her siblings, of course; but above all Norma, the firstborn, the first of five children, six if you counted poor Patricio, rest in peace; six mistakes that her mother made one after the other, each in a desperate attempt to hold on to a man who in almost every case wouldn't even admit to being the father; men who, for Norma, were mere shadows that her mother cloaked herself in on nights out drinking, her bare legs showing under her sheer tights and her feet in the high heels that she never let Norma try on. Don't be an idiot, she said, the one time she caught Norma clattering about in her shoes and putting on make-up with Natalia in front of the mirror shard hanging on the wall. So you want men to look at you, do you? What, for them to put their paws all over you? It's in one ear and out the other with you, isn't it? Learn from my mistakes, Norma. Wash your face and take those off and God help you if I ever find you dressed up like that in the street, God help you if I hear the neighbours saying they saw you in my clothes and lipstick. And Norma nodded and apologized and washed her blood-soaked knickers in secret so that her mother wouldn't throw her out, so that she wouldn't discover that her worst fear had come true, until finally one day Norma realized she'd been wrong all that time: the Sunday seven wasn't the blood that stained her underwear but what happened to your body when that blood stopped flowing. Because one day, on her way home from school, Norma found a little paperback book with a ripped cover and *Fairy Tales for Children of All Ages* written across it, and on opening it at random the first thing she saw was a black-and-white illustration of a little hunchback crying terrified while a coven of witches with bat wings stabbed the hunch on his back, and the illustration was so strange that, ignoring the time and the ominous rain clouds, ignoring the dishes waiting to be washed and her siblings who needed feeding before their mother got home from the factory, Norma sat down at the bus stop to read the whole story, because at home there was never time to read anything, and even if there were she wouldn't be able to, with her siblings' racket, the blare of the TV and her mother's constant yelling, not to mention Pepe's fooling around or the piles of homework that awaited her each night after washing the pots, which she herself had used at noon before leaving for school; and so she pulled the hood of her coat over her head and folded her legs under her skirt and she read the whole story from start to finish, the tale of the two hunchbacks, that's what the fairy tale was called, and it was about a hunchback who lost his way one evening in the woods close to his home, dark and sinister woods where witches were said to meet to do their evil deeds, and that was why the little fellow was so frightened to find himself lost there, unable to find his way home, wandering blindly as night fell, until suddenly he spied a fire in the distance, and thinking it might be a campfire he ran towards it, convinced that he'd been saved. So imagine his surprise when he arrived at the clearing with the gigantic fire only to realize it was a Witches' Sabbath: a coven of horrifying witches with bat wings and claws instead of hands, all dancing around the blazing fire in the most macabre fashion while they sang: *Monday and Tuesday and Wednesday, three; Monday and Tuesday and Wednesday, three; Monday and Tuesday and Wednesday, three,* and they were cackling their terrible witchy cackles and howling up at the full moon, and the hunchback, who, still unseen, had taken cover behind an enormous rock not far from the fire, listened to that cyclic chant and, unable to explain how, unable to explain the overwhelming urge that came over him, took a deep breath as the witches sang their next *Monday and Tuesday and Wednesday, three,* jumped onto the rock and shouted at the top of his lungs: *Thursday and Friday and Saturday, six!* His cry resounded with surprising force in that clearing, and on hearing him the witches froze where they were, petrified around the fire that was casting horrible shadows on their beastly faces. And seconds later they were all running around, hovering between the trees, shrieking and hollering that they had to find the human who'd said that, and the poor hunchback, once again crouched behind the rock, trembled at the thought of the fate awaiting him, but when at last the witches found him they didn't hurt him as he'd imagined, nor did they turn him into a frog or a worm, or much less eat him. Instead, they took the man and cast spells to conjure enormous magical knives, which they used to cut off his hunch, all without spilling a drop of blood or hurting him at all, because the witches were pleased that the little fellow had improved their song, which, truth be told, they were beginning to find a little boring, and when the hunchback saw that he no longer had a hump, that his back was completely flat and that he didn't have to walk hunched over, he was happy, enormously happy and contented, and as well as curing his hump the witches also gave him a pot of gold and thanked him for having improved their song, and before resuming their Witches' Sabbath they showed him the way out of that enchanted part of the woods, and the little man ran all the way home and straight to his neighbour, who was also a hunchback, to show him his back and the riches he'd received from the witches, and his neighbour, who was a mean, jealous man, believed that he deserved those gifts more, because he was more important and more intelligent and those witches must be real fools to go around giving away gold just like that, and by the following Friday the jealous hunchback had convinced himself that he should copy his neighbour, and as night fell he entered the woods in search of that coven of cretinous hags and he walked for hours in the darkness until he, too, lost his way, and just as he was about to collapse against a tree and cry out in fear and desperation he glimpsed, in the distance, in the thickest, gloomiest part of the woods, a fire surrounded by witches dancing and singing: *Monday and Tuesday and Wednesday, three; Thursday and Friday and Saturday, six; Monday and Tuesday and Wednesday, three; Thursday and Friday and Saturday, six*, and with that the jealous neighbour scurried towards them and hid behind the same enormous rock, and at the next round of *Monday and Tuesday and Wednesday, three; Thursday and Friday and Saturday, six*, the vile little man

– who, despite believing himself more intelligent than his neighbour, was not the smartest of fellows – opened his mouth, took the deepest breath he could, cupped his hands around his lips and shouted: *SUNDAY SEVEN!* with all his might. And when the witches heard him they froze on the spot, petrified in the middle of their dance, and that dimwit of a hunchback emerged from his hiding place and opened his arms to reveal himself, thinking they'd all flock to him to fix his hunchback and hand him a pot of gold even bigger than the one they'd given his neighbour, but instead he saw that the witches were furious, clawing at their chests and yanking out great clumps of flesh with their own nails, scratching their cheeks and pulling the flowing hair that crowned their horrific heads, roaring like wild beasts and screaming: Who's the fool who said Sunday? Who's the wretch who ruined our song? And then they caught sight of the mean little man and zoomed towards him, and with hexes and jinxes they conjured the hump they'd removed from the first man and put it on him, and as a punishment for his imprudence and greed they placed it on his front, and instead of a pot of gold they pulled out a pot of warts that hopped out of the container and immediately stuck to the body of that despicable man, who was left with no choice but to return to the town like that, with two humps instead of one and warts all over his face and body, and all for having come out with his Sunday seven, the book explained – and in the final illustration of the story the jealous neighbour appeared with those two humps, one deforming his back and the other making him look pregnant, and that was the moment Norma finally understood how silly she'd been to think that the fateful Sunday seven was the blood that stained her knickers each month, because clearly what it referred to was what happened when that blood stopped flowing; what happened to her mother after a spell of going out at night in her flesh-coloured tights and her high heels, when from one day to the next her belly would start to swell, reaching grotesque proportions before finally expelling a new child, a new sibling for Norma, a new mistake that generated a new set of problems for her mother, but, above all, for Norma: sleepless nights, crushing tiredness, reeking nappies, mountains of sicky clothes, and crying, unbroken, ceaseless crying. Yet another open mouth demanding food and whingeing; yet another body to keep an eye on and care for and discipline when her mother returned to work, exhausted and as hungry, cranky and grubby as the youngest of Norma's siblings; her mother, just a child herself, who Norma had to feed and stroke and comfort, massaging baby oil into her calloused feet and her aching muscles, stiff from all the hours spent on her feet performing the same movements over and over again at her sewing machines. And above all Norma had to listen, yes, above all that: listen to her mother's woes, her grumbling and griping, the same admonishments as always, and she had to nod and agree and look her mother in the eyes with a smile on her face and kiss her forehead and pat her back when she wept, because if Norma could just help calm her down, if Norma could help her unburden her chest, perhaps her mother wouldn't feel compelled to lock herself in the bathroom and scream that she wanted to die, perhaps she wouldn't go out and get drunk looking for affection in the caresses of strange men or let herself get hurt by those bastards who were all the same, bastards who'll pluck the moon and the stars from the sky for you but then, when push comes to shove, toss you out like a filthy old rag. So don't you believe them, Norma, don't let them fool you: don't expect them to look after you, don't expect anything from those assholes; you've got to be smarter than them, you've got to demand respect because you give them an inch and they'll take a mile, so you better keep your wits about you, use your head, save yourself for a decent man, an honest, hardworking man who keeps his word, a decent man like Pepe who won't desert you with your Sunday seven, and Norma would nod and say yes, that's what she'd do, she'd never take any man at his word, she'd never let those bastards get their filthy way with her or do the nasty things they do to women only to ruin them, and in the early hours, as she wept in silence on the bed, she thought there must truly be something evil inside of her, something rotten and foul that made her take so much pleasure from the things she and Pepe did together, when he worked the night shift at the factory and would come home at the crack of dawn, just after Norma's mother left, walk into the kitchen and drag Norma from whatever chore she was doing, carry her to the foot of the big bed, the one that he and her mother shared, and undress her, even if she hadn't washed yet, then lie her down on the icy sheets, trembling with anticipation and cold, and cover her with his own naked body, squeeze her hard against his muscly chest and kiss her on the mouth with a rapaciousness that Norma found delicious at times, and repugnant at others, but the trick was not to think; not to think about anything as he squeezed and sucked on her breasts; not to think about anything as Pepe climbed on top of her and with his saliva-slick cock made her hole bigger and wider; the hole that he'd first unlocked with his fingers one time when they'd been watching TV under the covers. Because before Pepe there'd been nothing there at all, nothing but folds of skin from which a stream of pee would flow when she sat on the toilet, and that other hole where her poo came out, of course, so who knows by what trick Pepe made another hole appear, a hole that, with time and Pepe's rough fingers and the tip of his tongue, grew and grew until it could take in her stepfather's entire cock, right down to the base, he'd say, till it hit the back, like it should, like Norma deserved, like she'd been pleading for it in silence all those years, right? Because there was that kiss she'd given him: proof that she'd started the whole thing, that she was the one who seduced him, begging for it with her eyes; and she was the one who, in bed, wiggled and swayed so nice, and slid down right onto his hard cock, gagging for it, almost possessed, desperate for his cream. That's why he almost never lasted more than a minute inside her: she was that good, that tight still, that soft in his arms. Christ, you could tell she was hot for it even when she was a kid; ever since she was a little girl you could see she'd be a goer, a regular fuck machine, from the way she moved her ass as she walked and from the way she looked at him, and because she never left his side, she was always all over him, always spying on him when he did his exercises or took off his clothes for the shower, with that sly smile of hers, not the smile of a little girl, but of a woman, the horny woman who'd one day be his, sooner or later she'd be his, although first he had to prepare her, right? Educate her, show her, get her slowly used to it so he didn't hurt her; because he was no brute, far from it; he only gave her what she'd asked for: a gentle caress, a little rub, a massage of those breasts that grew with each day from the touch of his fingers, those nipples all juicy and plump after a couple of good sucks, and the little triangle between her legs nice and wet from having rubbed her little bell, the little oyster which he

136

liked to lick with his mouth in such a way that when the time came his cock slipped in by itself, without hurting her one bit. Quite the opposite: it's Norma herself who asks for it, her body that needs it. Because if you didn't ask for it, Norma, my cock wouldn't fit, you see? If you didn't like what I do to you, you wouldn't get so nice and wet. And as her stepfather said all of this into her ear Norma bit her lips and focused all her energies into keeping up the furious pace at which she jerked her hips, because the faster she swayed, the quicker Pepe came, and then she could curl up into his armpit while he held her and rocked her and kissed her hairline in the time it took for his cock to prick up again. That was the moment Norma always waited for: when she could close her eyes and feel her naked body pressed tight against Pepe's, and forget for a minute that it never lasted long enough, that there was something evil and terrible inside her for wanting that contact, that crude embrace, and for wanting it to last forever even if that meant betraying her mother, betraying her in spite of everything she did for Norma and her siblings. Because Norma always ended up feeling disgusted with herself, an obstinate self-loathing for having destroyed her mother's one chance at happiness with a man by her side, with a father to her children, someone to make the bed springs creak with on Saturday nights, and in among all the disgust and the pleasure, the shame and the agony, Norma didn't know how it happened, how she fell pregnant, because in her mind Pepe took care of everything, Pepe sorted all that out with his whole thing about keeping an eye on her cycle and being constantly on top of when her period came, and supposedly he knew when he could and couldn't put it in her, and for a while he'd even given her those little pills that meant that he could come inside her

137

whenever he wanted, but later he got spooked that Norma's mother would find them and he stopped giving them to her. Norma didn't know when it had happened, but suddenly it seemed life had become even greyer and colder than usual; she found it harder and harder to get up at five to make her mother's coffee, to pack her lunch for the factory; at school she spent the whole time yawning, the cold was torturous and she was constantly hungry even though food suddenly tasted horrible and the only thing she felt like eating was bread, sweet or savoury, freshly baked, stale or even mouldy; she could eat bread all day long, and every other kind of food, the smell of cooked tomato, for example, made her gag; the same as the smell of grease coming from the people she had to sit next to on the bus, and the sour pong of her siblings, above all Gustavo, who still hadn't learned how to clean his backside properly and always insisted on sleeping next to Norma, and that stench of sweaty shit followed him everywhere and would stick to Norma's nostrils and prevent her from sleeping, which made her want to kick the kid out of bed, to punch him and yank his hair until he learned how to wipe his ass properly, the dirty pig: one day I'm going to leave you out in the street for you to go missing and for someone to come and take you; I'm going to take each one of you by the scruff and let the child snatcher come and get you, let's see how you like that, maybe then you'll stop giving me shit, maybe that way things would go back to how they used to be when Norma and her mother lived alone, before moving to Ciudad del Valle, to those dingy rooms her mother rented by the day and where they couldn't make their own food and had to live on sliced bread, bananas, and condensed milk, and even then her mother still managed to grow bigger and bigger, so big she couldn't

138

even bend over to tie the straps on her *huarache* sandals, until one night Norma woke from the cold and saw that she was alone in the bed because her mother had left without saying anything, leaving her locked in, and it didn't matter how long or hard Norma cried – for what seemed to her to be days and days – her mother didn't return until two nights later, pale and haggard and holding a bundle in her arms: her brother Manolo, a whiny, wrinkly, magical creature who spent his life hanging off her mother's breasts and who bawled nonstop every time Norma looked after him while their mother went out looking for work. And after Manolo came Natalia, and after Natalia, Gustavo, and then Patricio, poor Patricio, and each rented room was damper and more freezing than the last, and Norma never saw her mother because in the end she found a job in a clothing factory making coats, and sometimes she'd work two shifts back-to-back just to make ends meet, and Norma missed her but she soon learned that if she cried when she got home from work, if she moaned about her siblings or the mischief they'd been up to, her mother would get so depressed that she'd throw on her heels and go out looking for someone to buy her a drink, so Norma didn't say a word. She couldn't let her mother down, she had to help her; alone, without Norma, and surrounded by those squealing little runts her mother would surely go mad; that's what she was always telling Norma, that she couldn't live without her, without her by her side, without her help. That's why she'd get angry that Norma was so stupid and ignored all her advice, which went in one ear and out the other; that's why it made her so mad that Norma came home later and later from school, for fuck's sake, your place is here at home, Norma. Where the hell did you go? What took you so long? What the hell do you mean, you were reading in the street? Do you think I'm stupid? Do you think I was born yesterday, that I don't know when you go fooling around with those boys? Aren't you embarrassed to leave your brothers and sister on their own? Does it really not make you ashamed to keep failing your exams, over and over? Just look at the bags under your eyes, look at that pot belly, you look like a whale, probably full of worms, you little pig; you've eaten all the bread, what are we going to give your brothers and sister for tea now? You have no shame, I swear to God. A real piece of work, this one. And Pepe: Alright, woman, don't get your knickers in a twist, what's the problem? This little bitch is the problem. What are we going to do when all her fucking around catches up with her, when she comes out with her Sunday seven? What'll we do then? Well, nothing, woman. Why get all bent out of shape when that's just the way the world works. That's what makes us a family, isn't it? We support each other, pull together, isn't that right? And even then he dared to wink at Norma behind her mother's back. If Norma has a kid, we'll give him my surname and look after him between us, right? And her mother: If I find out you've been fooling around with those older boys you'll be out on your ass, do you hear me? Pepe and I don't work like dogs for you to go fucking around. And Norma would bite her lip, bite her tongue to stop herself from answering back; rather dead than tell her mother the truth, tell her what she and Pepe did right there in her own bed, because Norma was convinced that it would destroy her mother, although perhaps what really terrified her was the possibility that her mother wouldn't even believe her. What if Norma told her the truth and Pepe convinced her it was a pack of lies? Or what if she believed her but decided to stay

140

with him all the same and kick Norma out, sending her packing without a second thought? Maybe it would be better to leave now, leave before it became even more obvious, run away from home, from Ciudad del Valle, from that cold, which, even in May, chilled her to the bone each morning; go back to Puerto, back to the time when she and her mother would go on their trips, climb that rock again and throw herself into the sea, herself and that thing growing inside her guts. Her mother would never find her; she'd think that Norma had run off with some boy and she'd be so furious she might not even bother looking for her or cry at night thinking about what a good girl she'd been really, how helpful, and how empty the house was without her. Better to make a run for it now, before her mother stopped needing her – better to die than to lose her. That's why she'd said yes to Chabela. She'd been in La Matosa for three weeks by then, and Luismi had begun to throw doting looks at her belly, even though she didn't dare tell him anything. That's how things were with Luismi: they barely spoke. He would wake up after midday when the heat in that room had become infernal, then head straight down to the river to wash after eating whatever Norma gave him, never once complaining, but not praising her either, because he knew full well that Chabela was the one who paid for that food. Luismi never gave Norma any money. He didn't give her an allowance like her mother used to each day before leaving for the factory. He didn't give her a thing, well, nothing beyond that roof over her head and, occasionally, in the middle of the night, and only if she asked, he offered her his droopy cock, and Norma, more as a means to repay his kindness than out of any desire, would climb on top of him and lean down to kiss his half-open mouth, that mouth which

141

almost always smelled of rancid beer and someone else's saliva, that mouth that never rejected her but also never searched her out, unless it was to lay sweet, gentle kisses on her belly. Who knows what Luismi must have thought about the thing growing inside her; who knows if he held out some hope that it was his, even with Norma's whole story about the imaginary boyfriend who'd won her over with his cheating ways. Who knows what went through his head when he woke up at noon to sit comatose on the mattress and stare blankly at the dirt floor, cracked from years of ruthless sun, lost in the din of the rooks and magpies nesting in the nearby trees, his hair all over the place and his mouth hanging open. So ugly, Norma would think as she stood watching him, and so tender at once; so easy to love but so hard to understand, to reach: why did he insist on telling Norma and anyone who'd listen that he worked as a security guard in a warehouse in Villa, when Norma had never once seem him in a uniform, when he never came or went at the same time, never seemed to follow any kind of normal working schedule. Why didn't he ever have any money but always come home smelling of beer, and sometimes even carrying a new item of clothing for her or some useless gift: a wilted rose wrapped in cellophane, a painted paper fan, a fake plastic tiara, the kind people gave away at parties, gifts for a little girl, not for a wife. Why did he tell Norma that she was the best thing that had ever happened to him, the purest, most special and genuine thing that he'd ever felt, but then hardly touch her or even talk to her? Why did Norma feel that the love he claimed to feel for her was so fragile that the slightest puff of wind could whip it away at any moment? He's as much of a prick as his father was, Chabela would say, waving a forkful of cold food around, but I was an even bigger prick for letting him get me up the duff. Oh yeah, a real sucker I was, honest to God, a real fucking prick; because Maurilio had me wrapped around his finger with his sweet talk and his stupid fucking love songs, but above all with that cock of his, because I was fourteen when I met him, I'd just landed up in Villa, sick to death of picking lemons over on the ranch while my dad pissed away all our money betting on cockfights, until, one day, I learned they were building a new highway to connect the oil wells with Puerto, and people said it was going to be a real gravy train, bring in a load of work, and all I knew how to do was pick lemons, but I came down anyway, and, what do you know? What did I find when I got here? An even bigger shithole than Matadepita, fuck me, and the only place they'd give me work was at the *fonda*, at Doña Tina's: what a bitch, what a stingy cow, tighter than a nun's cunt. I almost had to beg her to pay me, the black bitch, and she'd say I stole the tips, but what tips, when not so much as a fly ever landed in that shit shack? Ah, but then, the old cow fancied herself as influential, well-to-do and honourable, as if her pack of kids had been fathered by the Holy fucking Spirit himself; as if she hadn't bought that shack and the land with the money she'd earned riding the food vendors and other workers who'd set up by the side of the highway before her. So now the old half-breed wants to play the saint, the decent sort, but those two daughters of hers turned out even blacker and looser than her, and don't even get me started on the granddaughters. They've always been wary of me, the lot of them, treating me like dirt since my first day at the *fonda*, and even worse when they found out I was seeing Maurilio; from the start they came out with some bullshit about how I had the bug and how I'd killed off God knows how many drivers from

some transport company, those rotten jealous bitches, nothing better to do than to go around making up stories. And that Maurilio never once stood up for me, the gutless prick. I swear it's beyond me how I could have been so stupid as to let that leech give me a child. I was a sight for sore eyes before I got pregnant. I'll show you the photos one of these days: I stopped traffic with my leg stuck out in the road, mamacita, and if I'd gone to the capital, like every fucker I spoke to told me to, I'd have been snapped up for the TV, or at the very least for magazine work. I was that gorgeous, hot fucking stuff, mamacita. That's right, I charged what I wanted in those days, before I fell pregnant. I could even play hard to get and still I'd rake the clients in: I only had to pull down my top or flash my ass and those bastards would be hard as rods. That's right, my big mistake was falling for Maurilio. He was my downfall. I didn't even charge him – can you imagine? That's how tight he had me wrapped around his finger. People used to say he forced me into the work, like a pimp, but that's bullshit, he didn't have the nous for that; he was no entrepreneur. I started turning tricks off my own back, thank you very much; and why not, when it comes so natural? And I think you know exactly what I'm saying, Clarita, because you might like to play all dumb and meek, but you wouldn't be in this fix if you didn't like a bit of anaconda action yourself, you dirty cow. Didn't you always feel a sort of tingling down there, even when you were young? Didn't you have your little boyfriends who you'd play soldiers with, to make them stand to attention? I'd sneak out past my dad and down to the empty lots to spy on the couples getting off, and then I'd copy what I'd seen with the boys back home, I'd take them off somewhere secluded, and there, hidden in the bushes, I'd pull down my knickers,

144

spread my legs and fuck them all, and I'd literally be trembling with excitement when those boys climbed on top of me with their rock-hard little boners; they'd line up to screw me! And don't forget, all this was before any of us even had hair down there. And precisely because I was always so up for it I went and let that useless prick knock me up, because I loved fucking Maurilio so much. Not the others; I got no kicks with anyone but him. But Jesus, was that pleasure short-lived, Clarita. We'd only been living together six months when they put him away for killing some poor fucker from Matacocuite, and I wound up on my lonesome and got on the game so I didn't starve to death, and so I could slip Maurilio a bit of cash and carry on banging him there, inside. And you wouldn't believe it, but I made a small fortune during that period. Don't get me wrong, I really fucking missed that shithead Maurilio, but at the same time I was freer than ever, with no one getting in my way or wasting my time, and I worked morning, noon and night and didn't turn down a single punter, not even the ugly fat fucks: if they had the cash, I gave them the goodies. Anyway, I was saying, all men are the same, same shit, they all want the same thing, they all dream of showing you their little love muscle and you saying: Oh, papacito, what a beast, hmm it tastes so good, put it in slowly or you'll hurt me, even if in their heart of hearts they know it's part of the game, right? Because all of them, every last one is the same. Alright, they might have their personal preferences and you've got to know how to find the way, because it's not the same thing, some spotty teenager nestling his pecker into you, as a whole pack of nameless stinking fat truckers pounding away down there, pounding, pounding, am I right? And that's the hardest part, at first: learning how to handle all those cunts, to humour them, to put up with the drunks, but you soon find your feet, and the truth is your body even starts taking pleasure from that shit, and the best thing of all is that the older you get, the less of a sucker you are, you start seeing that there's money to be made in this game, I mean real money, all you need is a tidy ass. Or you know what, mamacita? Even better, some other bitch's tidy ass, a piece of fresh meat with the same swagger you had when you started out: that's where the real money's at. And that's why I don't give it away cheap anymore. How else do you think I stay looking like this? I should be a wrinkly old maid by now but look, just look at this ass, look how perfect it is; and look, not a single stretchmark on my belly. And I can still clench it like the best of those girls. Because these days I only screw someone if he takes my fancy, and still I earn enough to support my husband, who might look like a hobbling cunt, but between us he can do things with his tongue you wouldn't believe, Clarita; I just sit on his face and I don't get up till I've come at least five times, bam, bam, bam, bam, bam; it's unholy what my Munra can do. And that's the only reason I don't send him packing, the only reason I've put up with the useless cripple all these years. And, my God, if you'd seen the figure he cut when he was young, what a stud he was on his bike, before that fuckwit trucker well and truly fucked him up. And Norma would turn to look at Munra sitting in his armchair in front of the TV, using the nail on his forefinger to pop a giant spot on his neck, and she couldn't help but shudder at the thought of that man's face between her legs. At least Pepe was actually good-looking; at least Pepe had biceps that he could flex until the stitching on his T-shirt almost burst. Pepe did a hundred push-ups, a hundred squats and a hundred crunches every morning, as soon as he got up, and he was so strong that once he carried her for miles down a mountainside, on their daytrip to the forests surrounding Ciudad del Valle, when Norma's feet had frozen because she'd forgotten to put on socks. Oh no, Chabela went on, by the time Munra turned up I'd seen it all, and that's why I told him if he wanted to be with me he had to have the snip, because I sure as hell wasn't having any more kids, wasn't up for any more little surprises, no sir. I was traumatized enough when that prick came along, thank you very much. And I don't even mean labour – it was after he came out that the real problems began: I felt like shit, I couldn't work, and with Maurilio doing time and me sick and without a bean, I almost starved. Although now that I think of it, it was also around then that I finally woke up and smelled the coffee, realized what a prick I'd been, and I told myself: That's it, Maurilio has to go; I'm not visiting him inside again and I'm not giving him a peso; let his bitch of a mother and his son support him. But it wasn't an easy decision to make, because the truth is I was still under Maurilio's spell. He was the only one I could get my kicks with – not with the clients, no, with them it was just work, just talk, but with Maurilio it was different. And that fucker had a shlong like this, mamacita, and it didn't even matter that he didn't know how to use it, I only had to turn up, push him onto the bed, climb on top and sink down onto his cock till there was nothing left of it to see. I rode him like a fairground ride, mamacita, like a bucking bull. Because I'm telling you, I was a real blockhead back then; I had no idea that when you take pleasure with a man your womb warms up and it makes it easier for the cum to stick. I didn't know anything. I was fifteen, for fuck's sake. I had no idea anything was up till it was too late to get rid of him. Because I never wanted kids, and your boyfriend in there knows it only too well because you've got to be open about these things, why go around playing the martyr, better to be open and say it how it is and for everyone to be on the same page: this children business is bullshit, bull-fucking-shit; there's no way of dressing it up: in the end, all kids are a burden, spongers, parasites who suck the life and all your blood from you. And to top it off they don't appreciate any of the sacrifices you've got no choice but to make for them. You know what I'm talking about, Clarita, you watched your mum clock up the kids, one after the other like a fucking curse, and all because she couldn't get enough, don't try and tell me otherwise; all because she was a horny bitch, and a dumb one at that, for believing those assholes were going to help her, because when push comes to shove it's you who has to bust your balls and squeeze the little fuckers out, then bust your balls to look after them, then bust them some more to pay for them while your fuckwit husband hits up the bars and rolls in when it fucking well suits him. Or you really think Luismi will change if you have that kid? No sir! I know him! And don't tell me, he's already told you that you should keep it, that he'll support you, that he'll be the father, and who knows what other crap, am I right? But you just listen to what I'm about to tell you, mama-cita, and don't take it the wrong way because I know what that little dick's like; I didn't push him out for noth-ing. So let me tell you that he's just as useless as his father, and he'll never change, he'll never keep his word because the only thing that asshole thinks about is drugs. Drugs and whoring. And even if he tells you he's stopped all that; even if he promises and swears blind that he's only going for a couple of beers, it's only a mat-ter of time before he falls off the wagon, back to his pills,

148

back to the highway dives. Jesus, if only he'd snort a little coke at least then he'd perk up enough to get with it,
but that's not his thing, is it? His thing's going around
like a brain-dead dipstick, and you know full well I'm
telling the truth because you're no fool, Clarita, it's not
your fault some opportunist fuck took you for a ride, but
you have to understand that the prick out there isn't ever
going to change, no matter what he says or what he
promises. You think I don't know the shit he's got himself into? You think one day he's going to give up the
game and fuck you the way you want, the way you deserve? The best advice I can give you is this: let me take
you to see my friend, let me at least help you out there.
That way you can have a long hard think about what you
want to do without the added pressure of having a bun in
the oven, because you're only young, Clarita, too young
to know what the fuck you want in life, and when I look
at you it's like I'm looking at me as a girl and I think: if
only I'd had someone to help me get rid of that useless
thing inside me before it was too late, someone who'd
taken me to see the Witch. And you'll see, Clarita, when
it comes to it she won't even take any money; she's that
minted she doesn't need it, a millionaire, although you'd
never guess it to see her in that shithole, dressed in rags.
You'll see, you'll see how she helps you out, just let me
do the talking: Oh, go on, hon, we've gotta help her, poor
thing, can't you see she's just a helpless kid? Tell her how
old you are, mamacita. And Norma: Thirteen. You see?
Don't mug me off, Witchy, don't get on your high horse
now – the kid's on board, eh? Can't you see these two
numbskulls can't even feed themselves? And the baby's
not even Luismi's – tell her, Clarita, tell her all about
how you gave it away to some creep from Ciudad del
Valle, tell her there's no problem, that you want it out.

149

And the Witch, who throughout this whole exchange just carried on tinkering about in that noxious kitchen with her back to them, turned and stared at Norma, her eyes sparkling behind her veil, and after a long silence she said that before doing anything she had to examine Norma, to see how far gone she was; and right there on the kitchen table they laid her on her back and hitched up her dress and the Witch pressed her hands all over Norma's stomach, roughly, almost angrily, perhaps enviously, and after a few minutes of groping around the Witch told them it was going to be tricky, that she was already really far gone, and Chabela: Fuck me, I'll pay you whatever you want to take it out, and the Witch: It's not about the money, it's about her, and Chabela: It's Luismi who wanted us to ask you, only you know how proud he is; he's saving face, he's embarrassed to ask you after your little bust-up, and all the while Norma lay there on her back with her dress hitched up to her breasts and her head next to the rotten apple driven through with a razor-sharp knife, and when at last she lifted her head the Witch was shuffling around the room looking for things, moving pots, taking the lids off jars and bottles and muttering who knows what prayers or diabolical spells with her fluty, raspy voice, and all that time Chabela continued to fill the unbreathable air in the kitchen with the smoke from her cigarettes and to yak on to the Witch about her new lover, a certain Cuco Barrabás, the guy Luismi had warned her about, the guy from the black pickup that had followed Norma on her first afternoon in Villa, after she'd ridden as far as her money would stretch and the bus driver threw her off by the petrol station, where she sat for several hours without knowing what to do or where to go, and unsure even which way it was to Puerto, or whether to hitch a lift with

150

one of the truckers who drove past the bus stop every few minutes, eyeing her up. And part of her was scared that they might do something to her, but another part said it didn't even matter anymore, since she was going to throw herself into the sea to drown, and to drown the thing floating inside her: something Norma didn't picture as a tiny baby but as a hunk of meat, pink and shapeless like a chewed piece of gum. And that's why it no longer mattered what happened to her along the way. And she spent hours arguing with herself at the bus stop by the side of the highway until the blond guy in the black pickup stopped and smiled at her, staring, music blaring out from the windows: *me haré pasar, por un hombre normal, que pueda estar sin ti, que no se sienta mal, y voy a sonreír;* the same song that began to play on Chabela's telephone as they made their way back home in the darkness that was growing thicker by the minute, swallowing all the colours around them, transforming the crowns of the trees and the shrubs in the cane fields and the canvas of the night into one solid mass of schist, against which the bare bulbs from the houses in town shone like tiny red carbuncles in the distance. Chabela was dragging her by the wrist while Norma did her best to keep up, clinging with her free hand to the jar containing the life-saving potion, her one hope, but with the mounting fear that at any moment the path would open up before her and she'd go hurtling over a precipice and break every bone in her body, or that the jar would break and the potion would spill out onto the parched earth, or worse still that she'd come face to face with one of those evil beings from fairy tale forests, a wizened, thin-haired *chaneque* who would emerge out of the darkness and cast a spell on them, making them go mad or condemning them to walk in circles along that ominous path for all eternity, to the maddening drone of the cicadas and the occasional squawk from a bright-eyed pauraque. Chabela's phone rang: *me haré pasar por un hombre normal*, and Norma very nearly let out a cry, *que pueda estar sin ti, que no se sienta mal*, as she walked into the back of Chabela, who'd let go of her hand to look for her phone and then answered it, gushing: Baby...? How are you, baby? I was just thinking... Of course, absolutely, right away... No, no, but I'm not far, I was just out... No, don't you worry, in fifteen tops, yeah. And she hung up with a sigh and snapped at Norma: Move it, mamacita, we've got to get back before those cunts arrive; I'm going to have to leave you to it, but don't you worry; take that and you're all set. Tomorrow morning you'll be like new, you'll see, I've done it a hundred times and it's no big deal, but don't drag your heels, mamacita, Jesus, I had no idea of the time! I haven't even had a wash yet. Shit! Shake a leg, Clarita, fuck me! Norma tried to keep up with Chabela but she began to get the feeling that the woman's voice was coming from further and further away and that if she didn't hurry up she'd be left alone in the darkness clutching her jar, the foul contents of which, every last drop, she was supposed to drink. And the Witch had been right: Norma could barely contain the heaving waves of nausea brought on by that gunk, but harder still was holding back her screams of agony when the pain finally hit her: at times it felt like someone was ripping out her insides, stretching and stretching them until the flesh tore away, and who knows where she found the strength to crawl off the mattress and out into the yard, turn her back on the *casita* and dig a hole in the dirt with her fingers and her nails and with the little rocks that she dug up as she went; a hole she climbed into, squatting through the pain that had turned her sex into a great sickled gash, and then pushing until she felt something inside of her burst, and still she felt the need to put her fingers up there to make sure there was nothing left inside, before covering the hole, patting down the earth with her bloody hands and then dragging herself back to the unmade mattress, curling up into a ball and waiting for the pain to pass, waiting for Luismi to come back from work, completely steaming, and hug her from behind without realizing that she was bleeding profusely, that she was burning up – hug her until the following day at noon, when, forced by the infernal heat in that squalid room, Norma tried to get off the mattress and couldn't, and the only thing she managed to say to Luismi was it hurts, it hurts, and water, water, and when her lips touched the liquid from the bottle Luismi brought to her, Norma drank until she passed out and dreamed about the hole she'd dug behind the *casita*; she dreamed that a little live fish leaped out from the hole, swam through the air, and started chasing her down the path, trying to get under her dress, to get back inside her, and Norma was screaming, terrified, but not a sound came from her mouth, and when she woke up again she wasn't on the mattress in the *casita* anymore, she was lying on her back on a hospital bed with her legs open and the bald head of some man stuck between her legs, and the blood was still flowing and she didn't know how much more there could possibly be left inside her body, how long before she died there under the sickened gaze of the social worker and the echo of her questions: Who are you, what's your name, what did you take, where did you leave it, how could you do it? And then nothing, a black silence shot through with screams, the cry of newborns calling her, calling out her name, and she woke up to find herself naked under the rough fabric of her

153

hospital gown, fastened to the bed with ties that burned her wrists, amid the chatter of women and the rancid, milky stench of baby sweat, babies who howled in the heat of that room and who made Norma want to run as fast as she could from that place, break the binds around her wrists and escape by any means possible from that hospital, from her own throbbing body, from that mass of swollen and enflamed flesh, the bloody, shamed and soiled flesh that bound her to the damned bed. She wanted to hold her breasts to relieve the stabbing pains shooting through them; she wanted to push the sweaty strands of hair from her face, to scratch the maddening itch she felt across her stomach, to yank out the plastic tube stuck in the hole in her forearm; she wanted to pull and pull at those bindings until they broke, escape from that place where everyone stared at her with pure hatred, where everyone seemed to know what she'd done, to wring her hands, to cut her own throat and release the elemental cry, which, just like her urine, she could hold in no longer: Mama, mamita! she keened in chorus with the newborns. Mamita, I want to come home, forgive me for all that I've done to you.

Mamaaaaaaa, the man was screaming, forgive me, mama, forgive me, mamita, and he yowled like the dogs that drag themselves, run-over but still breathing, to the roadside: Mamaaaaaaa, Mamiiitaaaaaa. And Brando, huddled in his corner, in the gap between the wall and the cell toilet, the one space he'd been able to claim for himself after Rigorito's men threw him in there, thought, and not without a certain glee, that maybe it was Luismi screaming, Luismi howling somewhere in the building in the grips of all-consuming agony, Luismi bawling to the point of retching as they beat a confession out of him with wooden boards. The money, they wanted to know where the money was, what they'd done with the money, where they'd hidden it, and that was the only thing that interested the filthy pig Rigorito and the cocksucking police when they beat the shit out of Brando until he was spitting blood, and then tossed him into that cesspit that reeked of piss and shit and the acrid sweat that seeped from the skin of those miserable drunks hunched, like him, against the walls, snoring or snickering under their breath, or smoking and throwing rapacious glances his way. He'd already had to defend himself from three men who jumped him the second he set foot on that side of the barred wall; three young guys who knocked him around and told him to take off his trainers – or what, you wanna play the punk with me, faggotkiller? said their ringleader, the one who shouted loudest, the one whose hands trembled as he stroked Brando's face, a dark-skinned guy, practically all skin and bones, with a beard and one missing tooth, dressed in a shirt that was more like a tattered rag, who spoke in a booming voice that seemed to come from nowhere: Cocksucker, give me your fucking shoes or I'll fuck your ass so hard you won't know what day it is, and Brando, who could barely sit upright after the beating the police had just given him, had no choice but to remove his Adidas and hand them over to that bearded reprobate, who put them on in a flash and then did a kind of victory dance complete with indiscriminate kicks in the guts of the drunks groaning in their sleep on the cell floor. That sniveller from before, the run-over dog, hadn't stopped yelping for a second. His howls rebounded off the cell walls and were drowned out entirely whenever Brando's cellmates barked back: Shut your fucking mouth, you mangy bitch! Shut it, you butchering fuck! This junkie kills his own mother, smashes her head in on some crackhead fucking rampage then says the devil did it! I mean, Jesus fucking Christ! Someone needs to knock the shit out of you, you little bitch. Brando had curled up in a piss-ridden corner of the cell with his arms crossed over his stomach and his back pressed as close to the wall as humanly possible: hunched in the one position that stopped his swollen insides from spilling out of the almost certainly haemorrhaging cavity of his abdomen. Even with his eyes closed he could sense the ringleader loitering, he could smell the almighty stench coming off that lunatic's skin. Faggotkiller, the guy said to Brando. Look, faggotkiller, look... but Brando just covered his ears with his hands and shook his head. He'd already given up his only valuable item. What more did the guy want? His shit-smeared pants? His blood-and-piss-splattered shorts? He'd already paid for his right to be here with his trainers, hadn't he earned a minute's peace to lick his wounds? The sniveller was still yapping somewhere down the other end of the wing, probably from the tiny cell the pigs affectionately called 'the cubbyhole': It

wasn't me, mama, it wasn't me, he was screaming; it was
the devil, mama, it was the shadow that came in through
the window, the devil's shadow, mama, I was sleeping,
and the prisoners who weren't fucked or beaten to a pulp
responded with whistles, jibes and obscenities. He was
turning them on, see, and some of Brando's cellmates
went as far as to ask the guard if he wouldn't mind lending him to them for a while, so they could rough him up
a bit, ass-fuck him even, really give him something to
squeal about, you sick fuck, that's some fucking son who
wastes his own mother, how have these pigs still not
sweated you down, you son of a motherfucking bitch?
Where was Rigorito? Where were his thugs? Where
was the bucket full of piss to take this asshole for a dip?
Where were the cables and the battery to brown that
sniveller's balls? Rigorito had disappeared with his
henchmen in tow in the sole police car in Villa; he'd left
for the Witch's house the moment they'd finished knocking a confession out of Brando in that little room at the
back of the station. Where was the money? Rigorito had
spat at him, talk or I'll drown you like the rat you are;
talk or I'll cut off your dick and shove it up your ass, you
little shitdick, you faggot fuck, going on and on for
Brando to tell him where the money was, when the boy
had already sworn blind that he hadn't found a thing inside the house, that there was no hidden treasure, it was
all a load of shit, pure rumour, and he'd even wept in
front of those sons of bitches on remembering the anger
and disappointment he'd felt when they hadn't found
anything during the raid, nothing but a grubby two-
hundred-peso note on the kitchen table and a handful
of coins dotted about the living room floor; no treasure,
no chests brimming with gold, nothing but rubbish,
mouldy tat gone rotten in the humidity and piles of

paper and rags and useless knickknacks and gecko turds and starving cockroaches, because even the speakers and the music equipment from the faggot's parties had been destroyed, smashed to pieces and left scattered all across the floor, as if in one of her hissy fits the faggot had taken it upon herself to take the mixing decks and drag them upstairs for the sole purpose of throwing them over the banister and smashing them on the floor. There was nothing there, he told the police, zip, zilch, but by the time they'd stopped thrashing him on the small of his back with a wooden plank – so heavy Rigorito and his henchmen were forced to take turns using it – by the time they'd shown him the cables and the battery they intended to electrify him with, by the time they'd pulled down his piss-soaked shorts and tied his hands to a pipe hanging from the ceiling, Brando was left with no choice but to tell them about the upstairs room: the door in the Witch's house that was always locked, which none of them could open that afternoon, despite all their efforts to knock it down or prise it open. Brando was also forced to confess, when Rigorito placed the bare wires against his balls, that he'd returned to the house later that same night, after the murder, after they'd thrown the body into the irrigation canal, but without Luismi or Munra now, to ransack the place one more time, because how could there really be nothing in there, for fuck's sake? He confessed how, having searched the whole downstairs, he went back up to the bedroom and tried, again, to open the door to the sealed room, even taking a machete to it, because he was convinced there had to be something in there, something of value; if not, why would anyone go to such lengths to keep the room off limits, to prevent anyone from going upstairs? And only once he'd confessed all this, once he'd cried in anger and humiliation and from the pain all over his tender bruised body, only then were those sick pigs satisfied, and they dragged him out of that back room, threw him into the cell, piled into the sole police car and took off, straight to the Witch's house of course, to look for that fucking money, to shoot down the door if necessary, even though Brando had a hunch that Rigorito wouldn't find anything in there, and that when they realized it had all been for nothing they'd drive back to the station to take their revenge on Brando, lop off his dick and ears and leave him to bleed to death in that cell that was really a standing coffin: the notorious 'cubbyhole', maybe even in the cheery company of that crackhead who lost his shit and killed his own mother. Because the truth was Rigorito didn't give a fuck about the Witch's murder. The only thing that fucker wanted to know was where the gold was. What gold? Brando shouted, and smack, a blow to the pit of his stomach; tell me where you hid it, and ba-bam, another to the small of his back, all before he'd even had the chance to reply that he didn't know, as if the fucker could read his mind. And I can keep this up all night, faggotkiller, I do this shit in my sleep, so sing: where's the money? Where did you hide it? Brando could feel his crushed insides and the lacerated skin on his ass from all the thrashings; that's right, those bastards knew the score well enough not to hit him in the face, so the reporters could come and take his photo the next day without everyone going around saying they'd beaten Brando's confession out of him. His mother would know everything soon enough, when his face was plastered all over the tabloids, although more likely some neighbour had already gone over to tell her about how they'd seen the police beat her boy into their car, right there in front of Don Roque's shop. Faggotkiller,

159

that stinking cunt Rigorito kept calling him, the fucking
drama queen; it was only one fag they'd stabbed, it wasn't
like that was what Brando did for a hobby, and besides,
the Witch deserved it: for being a dirty fag, for being a
cunt and a bully. No one was going to miss that cocksucking witch, Brando didn't even regret what had
happened. Why should he? First, he didn't even plunge
the knife in, he just knocked her around a bit, softened
her up, right? When they first got into the house, and
then later, in the back of Munra's van. But Luismi was
the one who killed her; it was all Luismi's fault; he was
the one who stabbed her in the throat, he told Rigorito.
Brando only grabbed the knife by the handle at the end
and threw it in the canal. But Rigorito didn't want to
know about any of that, he was only interested in the
money, the motherfucking money, and nothing Brando
said could convince him that there was no money, never
had been, it was all a big con, and if he regretted anything it was not having had the balls to kill the lot of
them: that prick Luismi, and, while he was at it, the hobbling loudmouth cunt Munra, and then get the hell out
of that stinking, fag-infested town. They should round
them all up and burn the fuckers, he told the police,
burn every last one of those poofters in town, and Jesus,
the blood! Plus by now even his pummelled bladder had
failed him; so like that, covered in piss, barely able to
walk and with a metallic taste in his mouth, he was
thrown into the cell for those other grimy motherfuckers to mug him: his brand new trainers, for fuck's sake,
not fakes, the real deal – they'd cost him the best part of
the two grand he'd nicked off Luismi, the famous two
thousand pesos that the Witch had given Luismi to go to
La Zanja and score some coke, and that dumb fuck was
so up to his nuts on pills that he didn't even notice when

160

Brando swiped it from his pocket on the way, and the Witch lost her shit the next day when Luismi showed up without the coke or the money, because she thought Luismi was taking her for a ride, like he always did, and she threw him out and told him never to come back in one of those nancy-boy meltdowns the Witch was prone to having; a pathetic scene that ended with that cock-sucker kicking and screaming on the floor while the stupid prick Luismi shrieked at her that he was no fucking thief, that he hadn't stolen anything, that someone must have lifted it off him, or maybe it had fallen out of his pocket on the way because he'd been baked out of his brain, and the pair of them were so caught up in their soap opera shit that neither of them suspected Brando; Brando, who, the following week, once Carnival was over, went to the Almacenes Principado in Villa and bought himself his red and white Adidas trainers: they looked the nuts on him, and to everyone who asked whose cock he'd sucked to buy them he replied that his old man had got them for him, even though it'd been years since that asshole had paid them a visit, and he and his mother had to practically beg for the pitiful monthly allowance they barely scraped by on. He hadn't needed to explain to his mum where the trainers had come from; she was so thick she didn't even notice that Brando never wore the crappy shoes she picked up for him at the market, last year's style and cheap as shit; shoes that got holes and scuff marks after two days, pauper shoes she bought from the same shops where she picked up the tat she decorated the house with: little plastic angels, posters of the Last Supper, ceramic shepherds and cuddly toys that she propped up on the settee in the living room, to the point where you couldn't even sit there because there was no way of parking your ass on the fucking seat with all those dusty pieces of shit in your way, which is why, whenever his mum wasn't around, on the afternoons she spent at church praying the rosary with the rest of the pious old crows in town, Brando would take one of those cuddly toys, gut it and burn it with petrol in the backyard, always imagining they were flesh and blood animals, real rabbits and bear cubs and doe-eyed kittens, squealing in agony as their coats burned to cinders. It fucked him off that his mum was so dumb, so gullible; it was her fault they ate beans every day because she donated a great fat chunk of the money Brando's dad sent – which wasn't much to start with – to the seminary. And it really fucked him off that his mum spent all day, every day at church sucking up to that bitch Father Casto, whose sole purpose in life seemed to be giving Brando shit whenever he came over to the house for a meal: why didn't he attend mass, why didn't he come to confession, why did he mix with such bad company? Why wouldn't Brando to take off those clothes covered in satanic symbols, devils and skulls and profanities against Our Lord? Why didn't he bin his music, which only led him into temptation, into evil, straight into the clutches of damnation and madness? Wasn't he ashamed of tormenting his poor mother like that? On Fridays, instead of meeting up with those no-good loafers and getting drunk in the park, why didn't he go to the mass that Father Casto dedicated to all the wicked folk in town, to all those who, having chosen witchcraft over God, had succumbed to darkness, to dark forces, to the legions of daemons and ghosts that roamed the Earth; malign spirits that swarmed around looking for people to let them in: with impious thoughts, with the black magic rituals and superstitious beliefs which, to the town's shame, abounded in that place, all because of the African roots of those who lived there, the idolatrous customs of the Indians; and because of all the poverty, destitution and ignorance. Brando was no stranger to those masses: his mother used to take him when he was younger, convinced that her son was possessed. That service was unbearably long and boring as hell because Father Casto would drone the whole thing in Latin and Brando never knew what the hell he was saying, although at the end things would get vaguely interesting because there were always a few sitting up on the first pews who'd start squirming and rolling their eyes back when Father Casto flicked them with Holy Water or placed his hand on them. And there was also a tribe of crazy women who'd faint, and others who'd start speaking in tongues, their cries filled with the Holy Spirit. Brando wasn't even twelve back then and he didn't understand why his mum took him to those masses, why she was convinced he was possessed by the devil when he'd never felt any urge to shout out during mass or writhe around like a fumigated centipede like those dumb old bitches, but she told Brando that for a while he'd been talking and crying in his sleep, getting out of bed to shuffle around the house like a sleepwalker, talking to invisible presences and sometimes even laughing. If he wasn't possessed by the devil, then why had he become so disobedient, so evasive? Why did he never look her in the eyes when she told him to take his hands out of his pockets, to stop touching himself in places he shouldn't, to come out of the bathroom and stop getting up to whatever filth he was surely getting up to in there? Wasn't he embarrassed that God could see him sinning? Because God sees everything, Brando, especially the things you don't want Him to see, the things you do behind that bathroom door with your mother's glossy magazines open on the floor, the things you learned all by yourself, on sleepless nights, things you couldn't blame on the guys in the park, even if they did spend all day every day baiting you with their: So, kid, how many times have you beat one off today? You've got hair growing out of your palm, you sicko, look. Guys, did you see? The prick actually looked at his hand! Thought you didn't toss yourself off, eh? Isn't that what you said? Still, I bet you still can't get that stubby little prick up, right? And Brando, blushing, surrounded by guys smoking and drinking, some of them twice his age, shot back: Oh it goes hard alright, just ask your mum, and those fuckers would piss themselves laughing and Brando felt proud to be admitted into that circle that would congregate around the remotest bench in the park, even if those assholes spent half the time laughing at him, at his gayboy name, at his undoubtedly micro-scopic penis and, above all, about the fact that Brando, all twelve years of him, had never squirted his load in-side anyone. Dude, you're a loser! Dude, at your age I was fucking my teachers, straight up. You're full of shit, Willy, Gatarrata shouted. Are you fucking kidding me, dickhead? Don't you remember the day Borrega gave our sixth-grade teacher yohimbe, and the bitch lost her shit and started having some crazy-ass fit on the ground? She had a great fucking pair on her, man, but that day no one got to see them, let alone fuck her because she never came back. The one we did fuck in sixth grade, now that I recall, was Nelson, Mutante said. Shiiit, Nelson! Where do you reckon that poof is now? Well they say he landed up in Matacocuite and opened a beauty salon, they call him Evelyn Krystal now, he's not Nelson anymore. What a little prick-teaser! You remember the ass on him? And the way he'd strut past us acting like he didn't know we were watching him? He was pretty young when we popped his cherry, but we were sick of looking at that ass, imagining what we'd do to it, and one day we took him up near the railway tracks and between us we gave him the grinding of his life, you remember, man? The little poof was crying tears of joy, he didn't know what do to with all that cock! Serious you've never dipped it in anyone, Brando? Come on! Not even a hooker? Seriously? Not even a pig, or a lamb? Those cunts were on their knees laughing and Brando just snorted and chewed his nails, because it was true that at twelve, thirteen, fourteen years of age he still hadn't fucked a girl, he just wanked in the bathroom with his mum's glossy magazines open on the floor in front of him; magazines that later he'd have to bin because they'd ended up crusted in spunk, the semen that would finally spurt out of him, just like those punks in the park warned him, even though that crap about how the more he wanked the bigger his cock would grow turned out to be bullshit, and the truth was that Brando did worry about the size of his cock, or rather the girth; he thought his dick was probably too thin, too dark, almost purple at the base, and, well, it was also true that it did seem a bit small, especially when compared to the monster dicks on those guys in the pornos he started buying off Willy, once he'd grown tired of the bikini-clad sluts in his mum's magazines. Willy's place was tucked away at the back of a run-down apartment block next to the Villa market public toilets; it was a bodega where he stored all the pirate movies he sold on his stalls, although his real business was selling porn and pre-rolled joints, which he kept in one of those breakfast cereal tubs. Willy had laughed his head off the first time Brando showed up to buy porn off him. You'll end up with hairy hands, man, he'd say; that's why you're covered in spots, that's why you're such a lanky fuck, because you spend all day beating off, and Brando would reply: And what's it to you? And he'd swallow all his rage and all Willy's mocking, waiting to be given access to the back room to choose his movies, where he'd let himself be guided by the photos on the sleeves, blurry copies on glossy paper, before taking a couple of tokes on Willy's joint, sprinting home and watching the videos on the VHS player in the living room, getting his kicks while his mum was at mass or praying the rosary, either way she'd be out of the house for several hours, which meant that he could sit there tossing off in front of the screen, watching and rewatching his favourite scenes: the one where a colossal black dude fucked a stacked blonde over a car bonnet; the one where two slags fucked each other, ass to ass, with a giant dildo; or the clip in the same movie when a little Chinese girl tied to a bed sobbed and her eyes sort of rolled back like those possessed loons from Father Casto's masses, while two guys fucked her at once. Scenes that quickly bored him, scenes he soon grew tired of, until one day, by pure chance, either because of Willy's mistake or the people who made the bootleg copies in the capital, he witnessed the scene that would change everything, the video that would mark a turning point in his sexual life, in the world of his fantasies: the clip that appeared sandwiched between scenes from two different movies which showed a skinny little girl with short hair and a boyish face, completely naked, with faint freckles dotted across her shoulders and tiny, pointy breasts. And with her appeared an enormous black dog, a Great Dane cross wearing socks on his front paws; a slavering brute that chased the girl incessantly around the room, backing her up against the furniture

166

to burrow his black muzzle between her legs and using his pink tongue to lick the equally pink cunt of that beaming girl who was giggling like an idiot and pretending to tell off the dog in a language Brando didn't understand. The clip ended two minutes later when the girl pretended to stumble backwards onto an armchair and the dog jumped on top of her and pinned down her shoulders with those ridiculous yellow sock-clad paws, and the girl leaned in towards the animal's erect dick and, just as she opened her cherry lips to wrap them around the tip of that dog's member, the scene cut suddenly with a second of blue screen and was followed by a clip of a guy getting his cock practically sucked clean off by some run-of-the-mill fake-titted blonde. Brando let out a moan of frustration and dashed to fast-forward the video to see if the girl with the dog came back, but it was no use: he had to make do with those two minutes, playing them on loop for hours when all he really wanted to see was how the dog fucked the little bitch; how, having sucked its cock, that bitch got on her knees and let the dog hump her mercilessly until it had pumped her rosy red cunt full of sticky cream, warm dog cum running down the girl's pale thighs as she moaned and squirmed to free herself from that foul beast; an imaginary scene, which Brando would try and fail to wipe from his mind over the following months, even when he found himself in places and situations where it was truly inconvenient to get a raging hard-on: at school, for instance, all it took was for one of the girls in class to bend down to pick up a pencil from the floor for Brando to imagine himself as that enormous black dog jumping his classmate and ripping her pants off with his teeth to pin her to the ground and fuck the absolute brains out of her with his cruel and inhuman black cock. Sometimes he'd wake up in the

167

middle of the night and try to masturbate to dampen the memory of the video, but since the mental images never stopped, and since, at that time of night, with his mother sleeping in the next room with her door open, it was impossible to play the video in the living room, Brando would slip out into the back yard, climb up onto the flat roof and then back down onto the road using the iron bars on the neighbour's windows as a ladder, and he'd wander the deserted streets looking for signs – muffled barks, muted yelps – that would lead him to wherever that primitive, cyclical ritual was taking place: down the alley behind Don Roque's shop or among the flowerbeds in the park in front of the church, or at the back of the empty lots that ran right to the outskirts of town; places where the slippery shadows of stray dogs congregated to fornicate in hallowed silence, with their tongues dangling and their sexes swollen and their bared fangs commanding respect for the hierarchy dictated by the panting desire of the bitch. How did she ever choose? To Brando they were all equally beautiful: free and beautiful and sure of themselves in a way that he wasn't, nor would he ever be. Brando would watch from a safe distance to avoid scaring or provoking them, and with a little help from his right hand he would participate in the orgy from afar, spilling every last drop of the fiery poison that ran through his veins before returning home and slipping back into bed, lulled by the numb languor of that divine emptiness, the calm that washed over him whenever he was able to finally purge himself of the venom filling his balls. Maybe that was the proof, the irrefutable proof that he really did have the devil inside him, even though he never found any of the marks that, according to Father Casto, appear on the face of all possessed people; at night, in the dark, he would look hard in the mirror, standing at the sink and staring at his reflection without finding the slightest satanic trace or demonic presence, just his faded, chubby-cheeked face with the same scowl as ever, the banal image of mediocrity. He would have liked to find some malign glint in his eyes, a burning glow behind his pupils or the trace of a horn on his brow; fuck, anything was better than that stupid-ass face of his, the face of a pipsqueak who was growing ever more pinched and weedy, in part as a result of his increasingly frequent nocturnal outings, and in part because of the vast quantities of marijuana that he began to smoke more or less around that time, no longer just on Saturdays at Willy's, but in his own house, before touching himself, and also with the park rats: with Willy, Gatarrata, Mutante, Luismi and the other guys, the guys he spent his evenings with after school, drinking aguardiente and smoking weed, occasionally sniffing glue, or cocaine when they could, when they had the money and Munra agreed to give them a lift to the Pablo brothers over in the La Zanja, just outside Matacocuite, where they'd buy cheap coke cut with way too much other shit, which Brando chose to smoke in the tip of a joint or cigarette rather than strip his nostrils raw by snorting it. Brando fucking buzzed off the burnt plastic smell of the sweet smoke that filled his lungs and pleasantly numbed his senses, but he'd worked out now that whenever he was up to his tits on coke he couldn't come, not even watching his favourite clip. He could spend hours beating himself off while picturing some imaginary chase between the dog and the girl, the beautiful girl with the freckles and a boyish face and a rosy cunt that didn't look like any cunt he'd ever seen in real life, any of the cunts that, at his fifteen, sixteen years of age, he'd managed to penetrate, albeit without coming.

Because of the drugs, of course, the coke, above all the coke, which sent his mind and body to sleep, and because of those dickheads who laughed at him behind his back; but above all because of that motherfucking bitch, the one he'd barely poked his cock into because the fucking thing wouldn't go hard, how fucking embarrassing, but it hadn't been his fault: it was the coke and the booze and the lack of sleep, the first time he'd pulled an all-nighter with the gang, the first time Brando had ignored his mother's orders and Father Casto's stern warnings about Villa's pagan, debauched Carnival, a rampant coven masquerading as one great fiesta, encouraging the young people in town to fornicate and succumb to vice. Brando was sick of being cooped up with his mother, overhearing the parade music pumping in the distance, all that fun, all those people getting to spend the night drinking and dancing in the streets, the deafening snap of firecrackers, the crash of bottles smashed in late-night brawls, the baying of lost drunks, which stopped only when they paused to vomit, and the catchy tunes of the fairground rides set up each year next to the church: mechanical, metal monsters that Brando only ever got to see once they were already dismantled on the ground, their lightbulbs and neon strips grey in the cold light of day, the morning of Ash Wednesday, when his mother would force him to walk her to mass along the streets still littered with rubbish, beer cans, empty aguardiente bottles, and entire families of ragged hicks snoring in the park flowerbeds and on the confetti-strewn pavements, and Brando always asked himself how all the excitement that rippled through town in the run-up to Carnival – all that tinsel, all those fireworks – could end up in that apocalyptic shit-heap of cavemen passed out in pools of vomit. Until

170

the year Brando turned sixteen and decided go to Carnival, ignoring his mother's sobbing and bitter slurs, calling him a wicked good-for-nothing and threatening to tell his father, an idea so farcical that Brando couldn't contain his laughter, because it had been years since his dad had counted as any kind of authority figure in that house, years since the guy had even bothered to call, let alone show his face in town; Brando laughed, too, because it seemed his mother was the only person in the whole of Villagarbosa who didn't know that his father had another house, over in Palogacho, a whole other family with another woman and young kids, and that he only carried on sending money out of pity, so they wouldn't starve to death, while that dumb mother of his spent her life in church burying her head in the sand, thinking that all that praying and pleading would make things go back to how they were before, by divine intervention; that Brando would go back to being the meek, silent, almost autistic kid he'd once been, the submissive little prick who held on to her arm in the street like some kind of baby husband, while the park crew laughed and jeered from afar: Brandi-boo, does mummy still wipe your botty? Does she still give you your bath and dust you with talc and tug on your little willy to give you sweet dreams? When are you gonna stop being such a weasel fag, Brando? Aren't you embarrassed you're still spanking the monkey? Aren't you embarrassed you haven't banged a single bitch? Here's your chance, kid, those assholes said; fuck her, fuck her right now, before she wakes up, the night he went out to his first parade, his first Carnival; or rather, the morning after his first Carnival, because Brando had never stayed out till dawn with his friends, that was the first time he'd pulled an all-nighter with them, roving the streets in town,

unrecognizable in the cacophony – music of all kinds –
that blasted from the speakers on the floats. Brando ran
his drunk and dilated eyes over the bare skin of the parade show girls, over the anonymous faces in the crowds
gathered on the pavements, the scary masks worn by
children who appeared out of nowhere to throw eggs
stuffed with flour and confetti at the heads of distracted
adults. The smoky February air smelled of beer foam, of
liquid fat from the taco stands, of delicious fried food, of
joints and rubbish, of the piss and faeces slopped all over
the pavements and the sweat of the bodies bunched
against his own. The main square in Villa was also teem-
ing with police brought in from the capital specifically to
contain – albeit with limited success – the mob that
crowded around the queen on her throne: a young girl
wrapped in tulle and brocades like a princess from another century; a girl with a lost look in her eye and a
forced smile, who shimmied her slender limbs to the
syncopated beats blasting out from the wall of speakers
directly behind her: *A ella le gusta la gasolina*, with one
hand on her hip and the other holding on to her crown,
dale más gasolina, and that vacant, almost petrified gaze,
cómo le encanta la gasolina, frightened by the obscenities
that the drunks at her feet were shouting at her with
something more akin to hunger than lust, *dale más gasolina*, primed to devour their queen, to sink their teeth into
her smooth, lean flesh, if only the police allowed them
within her reach. And Brando had never laughed so
much in his life, to the point of hysterical tears, to the
point of having to hold on to the walls and his friends to
stop himself from falling over, his face flushed from the
weed and the beer and his stomach aching from laughing so hard at the spectacle of those out-and-out queens,
the vast legion of fairies and trannies who'd come from

172

every corner of the republic to let it all hang out at the famous Villagarbosa Carnival, to fag about freely on the streets in town, dressed up in skin-tight ballerina leotards, or as fairies with butterfly wings, as sexy nurses from the Red Cross, as cheerleaders and hulking gymnasts, as limp-wristed policemen and potbellied Cat Women in stilettos; queeny queens dressed as brides chasing the boys down alleys; clownish queens with gargantuan tits and asses running around trying to kiss the rancheros on the lips; powdered, Geisha queens with extra-terrestrial antennae and caveman clubs; monkey queens; Scottish queens; queens dressed like macho men, who looked like any other normal guy until they raised their sunglasses to reveal their plucked eyebrows, their rainbow glittery eyelashes, their lecherous gazes; queens who paid you in beer to dance with them; queens who fought over you with their bare hands, tearing off each other's wigs and tiaras and rolling around on the ground shrieking, shedding sequins and blood, all to the delight of the onlooking mob. And what with that demented riot going on around him, Brando lost track of time, and before he knew it the sun was up, it had been for a while, and his friends were banging on about scoring some coke to keep the party going, saying Munra would drive them to La Zanja to get the blow, and before he knew it, Brando was already in Munra's van watching the old cripple swerve and veer his way up the highway towards Matacocuite, and really it was all the fault of the weed and booze and commotion, because Brando didn't even know at what point the girl in the green dress had joined them, at what point she'd got in the van with the gang. No one knew her or her name, but she didn't seem to care; she was hammered and pretty out of it, and by the looks of things horny as fuck because she was lurching all over the place with her arms out trying to grope his friends' cocks. Willy was the one who took it upon himself to start stripping her: he pulled her tits out of her dress and started tugging on her nipples as if trying to get milk from them or something, but the girl was loving it and she began moaning and asking them to fuck her, all of them, right there in the back seat of the van, and that's precisely what those pricks did: they fucked her one by one, first that lowlife Willy, and then Mutante and Gatarrata and Borrega and Canito, all of them except Munra, who was driving and saw the whole thing in his rearview mirror, sulking because they were going to get jizz all over his seats, those nasty sons of bitches; all of them except Luismi, too, who was pilled-up to his eyeballs, passed out with his head squashed against the front passenger seat window, and all while Brando looked on with a mixture of fascination and horror. The smell of that bitch's grey, hairy pussy made his stomach turn. Was that how women's pussies smelled? Was that how the soft cunt of the girl in the dog video smelled? Fuck! He decided to look out the window instead, to look up at the pale blue sky above the cane fields, but soon enough his friends started calling him: Brandi, oh, Brandi, you're up, Brandi; put it in, kid, hurry up and give it to her, Willy was shouting, before she wakes up, because the dumb slut had fainted or suffered some kind of cock overdose, or who knows what the fuck was up with her but they were all laughing and jeering: put it in, Brando, you dickhead, hurry up and give it to her, and so Brando, grudgingly but unable to decline, climbed onto the back seat and slid his dick from his pants but without taking them down, because there was no fucking way he was going to leave his ass exposed to that bunch of fucking degenerates, and he knelt

174

down between the upstretched legs of the woman and he prayed, with every last ounce of the faith he no longer had, that his dick would get hard, even the tiniest bit, hard enough to at least be able to pretend he was fucking her, so he wouldn't lose face in front of his friends, and he was almost getting there, with his eyes closed and his mind on his girl, on his dog, tugging away surreptitiously with his right hand as he managed to slip the tip of his dick into that gummy hole, when suddenly he felt a warm squirt against his stomach. He looked down and saw a dark patch appear on the fly of his trousers and the hem of his T-shirt, and with a cry of disgust he fell back against the side door, and for a second everyone was stunned and completely silent, and then they burst into wild fits of hooting laughter as they pointed at Brando's crotch and the stream of piss still coming from the filthy slut. She pissed on him! those cunts shouted. She pissed on him while he was fucking her! The bitch, the fucking skank! Nobody stopped Brando when he launched at the woman and punched her hard in the face, they were all too busy laughing. And so it was really a stroke of luck that, just then, Munra stopped the van, a hundred and fifty feet from the Pablo brothers' patch and started bellyaching about the stench of piss, telling them to leave the woman on the side of the road, because otherwise Brando would have gone on hitting her, he would have knocked her into next Tuesday, knocked all her teeth out, maybe even killed her, for having got her rank fucking piss all over his dick and clothes, but above all for having made a prick out of him in front of the gang, in front of those pain-in-the-ass bums who for years after the event would still wet themselves laughing at Brando, and Brando just sucked it up because he knew they'd only bust his balls harder if he let on that it got to him, and maybe it was for that reason – to distract them, to wipe the incident from everyone's minds, although it was also because after so many years of wanking he'd grown tired of his own hands – that Brando got himself a lover, Leticia, big-assed black Leticia, at least ten years his senior, who flirted with him whenever they bumped into each other at Don Roque's shop. Leticia was married to an oilman who drove to and from Palogacho on a daily basis, which meant she was left alone all day, lonely and bored shitless, or that's what she told everyone who'd listen when she went to buy cigarettes. Brando never spoke to her in the shop, he ignored the looks she threw his way, usually because he was too busy trying to destroy some squirt from the neighbourhood on the arcade games that Don Roque had out on the pavement. He never spoke to Leticia but he did look brazenly and openly at her ass, and she knew as much because she'd wiggle it whenever she walked by, an ass that seemed to have been put on the earth to be spanked, bitten, punished. One day she winked and made signs at him in front of all the pricks in the park and Brando had no choice but to follow her home. You jammy fuck, they said when he came back to tell them all how the slag had opened her front door, invited him in and straightaway, without a word, hitched up her skirt from behind to show him she wasn't wearing any knickers. He'd fucked her right there, he told them, first standing in the hallway, and then against the armchair in her living room, and then later again with her peering out the window upstairs, spying between the curtains just in case her husband chose that day to come home early. The stupid cow refused to do it in the bed where she slept with her old man. She also refused to suck Brando off – she said she didn't like it, that the smell of semen made her feel sick. The smell of your cunt makes me feel sick, the boy thought, but he never said anything. He got enormous pleasure from grinding down into that negro, always either standing from behind or doggy style against an armchair in the living room. Between moans she'd beg him to pull her hair, to grab her ass, to splay her cheeks wider apart so that he could drive down deeper; to stick his cock in her ass and give it to her hard. The only problem was Brando couldn't come. But he didn't tell his friends that, obviously. Leticia herself hadn't even noticed, or maybe the slut didn't care: she was just happy for Brando to go and screw her and make her come. She said he was the best lover she'd ever had, the most generous, the one who lasted the longest – she came hundreds of times while Brando pounded away inside her, growing ever more tired, sweaty, and bored. The pleasure he felt as he entered her gradually turned to repugnance as Leticia's stench grew stronger with every orgasm, getting up Brando's nose and making him heave. It made no difference that he closed his eyes and thought about the dog-girl, about her little girl cunt – that soft, inoffensive cunt that surely smelled of raspberry honey: the pungent reality of Leticia's pussy and her rotten fish stench always made him go soft after a while, and he'd have to pretend he'd come. After that he'd pull out of her as quick as a flash and lock himself in the bathroom where he'd take off the slimy but empty rubber and flush it down the toilet before washing his hands, cock, balls, and every inch of skin that had made contact with Leticia's cunt, and even then there were times when he'd get home and have to take several more showers because it seemed to him that the smell had followed him. But he didn't tell the boys from the park any of that. To the boys in the park he spelled out every last detail of that brown ass slapping against his stomach while he banged her from behind. And he'd often recount scenes that never happened, like the way Leticia supposedly sucked his cock, or how she begged him to come on her face and tits, scenes he got from the porn movies he watched. Nor did he tell them that he regularly felt like ditching Leticia and never going back to her place or fucking her again, but the truth was that he needed her; he needed the reality of her shuddering ass, of her affected moans and her tight but infected cunt; he needed those things for material for stories, to keep entertaining his friends with his smut so they'd finally stop giving him shit over the skanky slut who'd pissed on him. Because they never let it rest – those fuckers who fucked anything that moved and who even fumbled with the queens for money to get booze and drugs, but sometimes just for shits and giggles, for the sheer pleasure of fucking the fags who came to Villa in droves for the Carnival festivities. Something that Brando found monstrous and denigrating at first, but that he soon got used to once he was caught up in the irrefutable logic of the gang's arguments: Man, don't tell me you've never been sucked off by a fag, Willy would say, his jaw stiff from coke. You don't know what you're missing, man, Borrega chimed in, they give you the head of your life and then pay you for the pleasure and buy you as many drinks as you like after. You just close your eyes, Mutante said, think of any old bitch and enjoy the ride. You've seriously never fucked a poof? they'd ask smirking. A sweet, tight little poof who even purrs like a kitty when he kneels down to suck your balls? Those pricks always found a way to turn the joke back on Brando. Even when he tried to take the piss out of them or tell them what a bunch of fags they were for putting their rent-boy asses about, his friends always

178

ended up making him feel like a poor inexperienced prick. And worse, a prick who'd had his dick pissed on by some nasty fucking whore! Fuck's sake! But it wasn't all rosy with those faggots, and Brando knew as much. Most of the punks Willy and the others screwed around with – even fucking Luismi, who'd have thought it! – were a bunch of paunchy old mincers who came along to the cantinas in Villa from Thursday to Saturday looking for fresh meat and fresh cock. Freaky, crazy fucking queens, like the Witch, fuck me, the tranny from La Matosa who spent her life holed up in that creepy house in the middle of the sugar cane fields and who made Brando's hair stand on end with some fucked-up shit that had nothing to do with all the fumbling, but with something he'd heard as a kid, when he'd play out on the street and his mother would go on and on at him to get indoors, but he never would, so then his mother would tell him that if he didn't go inside that minute the witch would come and take him away. And one day, by pure chance – Christ, what a fucking coincidence! – who should be walking down the street but the queer who'd show up in Villa every now and then, dressed all in black and with her face covered by a veil: the freak they called the Witch. And that day his mother pointed at her and said to Brando: See? Here comes the Witch to get you, and Brando looked up and found himself standing right before that grotesque spectre, and quick as a flash he darted into the house and under his bed, and it was a long time before he dared play on the street again, so all-consuming was his fear of the Witch; a fear that, over time, he pushed to the back of his mind, but which would resurface every time he had to go along with his friends to party at that piece-of-shit faggot's house. Because it was all on the Witch: the beers, the alcohol, and sometimes even the drugs, anything to get the gang to hang out at her place, which she seldom left. A huge fucking mansion built in the middle of La Matosa's cane fields, just behind the Mill complex; a house so ugly and so disgusting that Brando thought it looked like the giant shell of a poorly buried tortoise; a dismal, grey house that you entered through a little door leading to a filthy kitchen, before heading down a hallway to a huge living room full of junk and bags of rubbish, and a staircase up to the first floor where no one ever went because the fag lost her shit if she saw you going up, and just beneath the stairs there was a kind of basement where the Witch held her notorious parties; a room with armchairs and speakers and even disco lights like the ones the *sonideros* had at the raves in Matacocuite. Crazy-ass shit, because once she'd let you in and brought you down to that dungeon the poof would disappear and then come back without her veil and dressed up in shiny colourful wigs and all sorts of costumes, and then, when they were all well and truly fucked, when they were drunk as skunks and high as kites on the weed that the Witch grew in her garden and those mushrooms that flourished under cow pats in the rainy season and that the freak collected and preserved in syrup to get her visitors off their tits, properly spaced out and tripping all kinds of shit, their eyes like Japanese anime characters and their mouths agape because of all the things they were hallucinating – like that the walls were coming in, that their faces were suddenly covered in tattoos, that the Witch had grown horns and wings and that her skin had turned red and her eyes yellow – then the music would start blaring from the speakers and the faggot would get up on that makeshift stage at the back of the room, surrounded by disco mirrors, and she'd start to sing or rather warble with her shit

voice, which never hit the high notes of those songs
Brando knew only too well, because they were the same
songs his mother listened to as she did the housework,
from the local cheesy radio station, sad songs that said
things like: *y la verdad es que estoy loca ya por ti, que tengo
miedo de perderte alguna vez*; or: *seré tu amante o lo que tenga
que ser, seré lo que me pidas tú*; or: *detrás de mi ventana, se me
va la vida, contigo pero sola*, and, microphone in hand, the
Witch would hold out her arms and stare into the distance with a lost look in her eyes, as if the bitch was on an
actual stage, in some stadium, surrounded by fans, and
she'd smile and sometimes it looked like she was crying
and Brando couldn't understand why his friends – and
the other random men who went there of their own free
will, local farmers, most of them, although also the odd
washed-up mincer from Christ knows where – would all
stand there watching her, mesmerized, or maybe just in
shock, but no one dared boo or heckle the faggot or tell
her to shut her fucking trap because her singing was
shit; and the truth is Brando never liked going to that
dump of a house, because when he was on coke and all
revved up the last thing he wanted to do was shut himself inside that sunless carapace to listen to the same shit
fucking music his mother listened to, and he'd get para-
noid as anything and start thinking everyone in there
was conspiring to get him wasted and take advantage of
him, rape him the moment he closed his eyes or nodded
off, as had happened to plenty of those losers after taking the pills the Witch handed out like sweeties, which
turned them all as dumb as fuck, a bunch of brain-dead
cunts who'd just giggle and giggle with their eyes barely
open. One night the Witch had hassled Brando for so
long that he'd had to pretend to take one, or rather he'd
put the pill in his mouth but spat it straight out and left it

on the edge of his chair, and there he sat watching while
everyone else dissolved in their seats and fell to the floor,
so high they couldn't even applaud the mad old freak,
who, for her part, was jiggling about on the stage under
the disco lights like a horrible, giant wind-up doll, a
nightmarish mannequin come to life. But the real fucking news came afterward, when that poofter grew tired
of crooning her cheesy songs, and who should go up on
stage but fucking Luismi, and without anyone saying a
word, without anyone making him do it, as if the prick
had been waiting all night for the chance to take the mic
and start singing, his eyes barely open and his voice
gravelly from all the aguardiente and cigarettes, but
even so, despite all that, fucking hell, fucking Luismi,
who the fuck would have thought the guy could sing like
that? How could that skinny rat-faced runt, up to his tits
on pills, have a voice so beautiful, so intense, so amaz-
ingly pure but at the same time manly? Until that
moment Brando hadn't had a clue that Luismi's nickname came from the fact that his voice sounded like the
singer Luis Manuel – he'd assumed it was ironic, because with his curly, sun-scorched hair, his crooked
teeth and scrawny body, Luismi couldn't have looked
less like the famous heartthrob. *No sé tú*, the kid sang,
pero yo no dejo de pensar, with that crystalline voice, *ni un
minuto me logro despojar*, quivering like a guitar string, *de
tus besos, tus abrazos, de lo bien que la pasamos la otra vez*, and
Brando felt himself choke with emotion, felt his skin
prickle with goosebumps, and for a moment, with an almost cramp-like sensation in his gut, he wondered if
maybe he hadn't spat out the whole pill, if it was all just a
hallucination, a strange nightmare, a bad trip brought
on by bombing too much cheap aguardiente, by smoking too much weed and spending too long cooped up in

182

that horrible house with that crazy terrifying bitch. He never told anyone how much Luismi's voice had moved him, and he would have rather died than admit that the real reason he kept going to the Witch's parties was to hear Luismi sing. Because the truth was that even after years of hanging out there, the hair on the back of Brando's neck still stood up whenever he had to talk to that freak: so hideous and so weird, with that creepy, rigid way she had of moving her gangly limbs, like a wind-up toy that just had life breathed into it; if he'd had his way, Brando would never have so much as spoken to her; he only went to that house because the others went, although it's true: on one occasion he let the Witch suck him off on one of the armchairs in the basement, and while Luismi was singing, to shut the bitch up, because if he hadn't let her, that diva would have thrown him out of the party and Brando didn't fancy walking back to Villa through the cane fields alone in the middle of the night, so when the time came, *no sé tú*, he'd pulled out his dick, *pero yo quisiera repetir*, and let the fag blow him, *el cansancio que me hiciste sentir*, and he closed his eyes and listened to Luismi's song, *con la noche que me diste*, but he never touched the Witch, *y el momento que con besos construiste*, and he did as Borrega and Mutante always told him, he just closed his eyes and thought of something else while that tongue wrapped itself around his cock, and he never, ever let that fag touch his face or kiss him; because it was one thing for the homos to take a shine to you, to buy you the odd drink, the odd beer, or even for you to fuck them, either in the ass or the mouth, just for a while, but it was another thing entirely to be a filthy fucking animal like Luismi when he and the Witch smothered each other in kisses, their hands all over each other. It was hard to pinpoint exactly why it repulsed

Brando so much to watch them; not even that rank shit-show, the literal shit-show of Mutante fucking the old freak, was as nauseating. Maybe because, deep down, the very idea of kissing a fairy was repugnant to him, a sordid attack on his manhood, and how did Luismi have the nerve to kiss the Witch in front of everyone, when Brando had always considered him to be straight as an arrow, a man's man, alright; someone who, despite only being a year or two older than Brando, already did whatever the fuck he liked and didn't answer to anyone, especially not a hysterical, sanctimonious mother who cried every day and beat her breast whenever he came home drunk. Luismi took whatever he wanted, did whatever he pleased, and no one gave him shit because some bitch had peed on his dick on a night out. Nobody fucked with Luismi, and that made Brando jealous as hell, although he'd worked out quickly enough, back when he began going to the highway cantinas with his friends – all of them on the hunt for queens and fairy boys – that Luismi had a shadow who followed him everywhere: his cousin Lagarta, a skeletal runt with a massive hooter who'd regularly storm into the bars, slap Luismi in the face in front of everyone and pull him out of there by his mangy hair. Nobody knew what that crazy bitch's problem was or why she seemed to hate Luismi so much, and he'd just laugh a sad laugh whenever the gang gave him shit about his cousin, but he never said anything. Word had it that Lagarta spied on him because she was out to catch him with his fags; she was obsessed with the idea of making the kid's grandma disinherit him. But while Luismi might have looked like a stupid prick, he wasn't one, because he always managed to give his crazy-ass cousin the slip before he went off to fumble with his butt boys; she never did catch him, or not until the night she showed up at the Witch's house, the night Brando, by pure coincidence, had gone out to smoke a banano in the backyard beneath the bushy tamarind tree that grew near the kitchen door. He'd gone outside because the vibes in the basement had got a bit too intense for his nerves and there came a point when he could no longer stand the Witch crooning into her mic, or the whining synths in those shit pop songs, or the glare of the disco lights, and he went out to the yard to be alone for a moment and to smoke his banano in peace and just gaze into the night with his dilated pupils, with no one for company but the buzzing insects and the whistling wind that swept across the plain, the stubborn bastard of a wind that tried to snatch the burning tip of his banano where the coke mixed with the weed in the rolling paper, smoke which gave him the most deliciously mellow high. Maybe it was the blow that sharpened his vision, or maybe his eyes had just adjusted to the dark, but a second after flicking the still smouldering stub into the whirring depths of the reed beds, Brando spotted a figure approaching him from the dirt track, a stick-thin shadow moving silently, stooped along the sandy path; and, squinting his eyes, Brando immediately recognized who it was: Luismi's cousin, the one they called Lagarta. She hadn't spotted him yet, maybe because he was hidden by the branches of the tamarind, or maybe because the light hanging above the door dazzled her just as it dazzled the giant woodboring beetles that flew in crazed circles around the bulb, but Brando, in an impulsive, cruel urge, held back from speaking to the woman until she was very close, and just as she was about to put her hand on the gate to open it, he called out, in his deepest, most sinister voice: And where are you going? And the stupid bitch squawked like a wounded bird and looked so shaken that Brando split his sides laughing. She must've been shitting her pants. With a look of pure terror, she didn't take her eyes off the tamarind tree until Brando emerged from behind its branches and the light from the bulb illuminated his sneering face. Only then did Lagarta seem to recognize him, although they'd never been introduced. What were you thinking, you idiot? she croaked, her voice stifled from fright and rage. You nearly gave me a heart attack, you little shit, and Brando couldn't help but laugh again. The woman ignored him and pulled on the kitchen gate, and Brando had to step in to stop her. And where are you going? he asked again. She shrugged his hand off her shoulder and bared her teeth: What the fuck's it to you, pipsqueak? And Brando, without losing his cool, with a kind of cold fury, merely smiled at her stiffly and raised his open palms in the air: Alright, you're right, who am I anyway? he said. You go on in, but don't come running back to me screaming. She snarled at him and went into the house, but before disappearing off into the shadows of that kitchen, she turned back just to say: You're the devil, asshole. Brando chose not to follow her; he stood there by the doorway clutching the bars with both hands because he felt dizzy all of a sudden and his heart was pounding in his chest: because of the banano, right? Or maybe because he was dying to watch the scene that was about to kick off inside, when Luismi's cousin came across the basement and saw what was going on down there and launched herself at her cousin, shouting and punching him, like whenever she caught him in the cantinas. But that night Brando waited in vain, because the only sound coming from inside was the Witch's warbling: *tu amante o lo que tenga que ser, seré*, while outside, in the yard, the night grew ever darker, *lo que me pidas tú*, and the rustle of the leaves and bushes, trembling under the stubborn southern breeze, *reina, esclava o mujer*, barely muffled the toads' and cicadas' serenade to the moon, *pero déjame volver, volver contigo...* And just when he'd almost stopped expecting it to, the gate crashed open and the figure of Lagarta emerged from the murk of the kitchen, and she shoved him aside and ran up to the dirt track, not screaming like he'd warned her she would be, but running like a bat out of hell as if the devil himself were coming for her. The music hadn't stopped for a second, so Brando decided to go in and see what had happened, but before reaching the hall he bumped into Luismi, shirtless and with his jaw hanging open in fright. No fucking way, was the first thing he said. I think I just saw my cousin; and Brando, placing a hand on Luismi's right shoulder, tried to calm him down: No chance, man, chill out, I've been here the whole time and I didn't see shit. And Luismi, still confused: But I saw her right there, I saw her face poking round the door. And Brando, still smiling: Dude, you're off your head, you just imagined it; I was outside, I'm telling you, I didn't see anyone. And Luismi: But, but... And then he fell quiet, lost for words, his nerves shot, and that night he didn't want to get up on stage to sing; instead he sat drinking and drinking until he passed out, and Brando had to wait several days before he found out that Luismi had moved out of his grandma's place and gone to live with his mum, who he'd never got on with at all, and that's why it looked instead like he'd shacked up with the Witch, because he spent all day in her house, whenever he wasn't in the cantinas or down by the Villa railroad tracks behind the abandoned warehouse, although this last detail was pure rumour, truth be told; a pretty heavy rumour at that, because it was one thing to knob some queer for a wrap of coke when you were strapped for cash, but hanging out behind the abandoned warehouse, where at all hours of the day you could see men butt-fucking in the bushes, fucking and blowing each other for the sheer pleasure of it, that was something else, and frankly disgusting because everyone knew that nobody charged down by the tracks, and the truth is that Brando felt a wave of morbid curiosity to go one day and follow Luismi to see if it was true that he went to the tracks to fuck, for free, the squaddies who travelled down from the Matacocuite barracks, or to be gangbanged by them like a bitch on heat, but he restrained himself because he was horrified by the thought that if he went hanging around those parts he might get mistaken for a fag, so he just left it to his imagination. And sometimes, when the queens would take Brando to the urinals in El Metedero to pay to suck his dick, he'd close his eyes and imagine that the tongue sliding up and down and around his penis was Luismi's and his cock would grow as hard as a rod, and in turn the poof would let out breathy sighs and suck even more vigorously, and Brando would come thinking about Luismi's eyes, about the shameless look that spread across his face whenever he saw his engineer, that balding pot-bellied queen who worked for the Oil Company and who every Friday, after work, would show up at El Metedero to have a whisky with Luismi, and it was really fucking weird watching them drinking in complete silence, like those couples who've been together for years or old friends who don't feel the need to talk, the engineer the absolute picture of a gentleman with his immaculate long-sleeved shirt and gold bracelet on his hairy wrist and the latest model phone hooked onto his waistband, and that prick Luismi gazing at him like some infatuated teenage girl, his hair all ruffled and

188

his feet filthy from walking around in flip-flops, and then something would catch your eye and when you'd turn to look back at them they wouldn't be there and you'd just know they'd gone off in the engineer's pickup to fuck on some empty lot or in the Motel Paradiso further up the highway. Only once had Brando actually caught them kissing, in a corner of the yard outside El Metedero, making out in the dark like secret lovers, their lips glued together and their eyes closed and the engineer's hands greedily feeling up Luismi's scrawny little ass, like you might clutch the fleshy rump of a woman you're still horny as hell for. Fuck me! the gang cried in unison when Brando ran back into the club to tell them what he'd just seen: Luismi's the engineer's twink! Luismi, a dirty fucking queer, who'd have thought it! Fuck me! Let's see who can bang him first, Borrega said, laughing, and they all clinked bottles and started to speculate over who'd screw Luismi first, over how tight or loose his ass was, and whether he gave good head, and in silence Brando gave himself permission to imagine what it might be like, until he felt his chest flood with anxiety, and since the fags weren't biting that night, he had to leave, under no illusion of finding Luismi and the old queen still fumbling outside, and he tugged himself off with his gob-smeared hand, letting out guilt-ridden groans as he pictured what it would be like to screw Lusimi from behind while at the same time tossing him off slowly so he could come together with Brando, come on all fours like the dog he was, like the scrawny, mangy bitch he was, a horny bitch who wagged his tail each time the engineer showed up, his pansy of an engineer; because even the Witch had realized that Luismi was crazy about that old queen, he never shut up about him or how cool he was or the job that supposedly

189

he was going to get him at the Oil Company – head in the clouds shit because Luismi had barely scraped through elementary school and he wasn't fit for anything but fucking and being fucked, and no one in their right mind would give him work, not even as a streetsweeper. And who knows who went and told the Witch, but suddenly that freak turned into a real needy bitch whenever Luismi went out with the gang; crazy with jealousy, of course. And one night, a few days before Carnival, just like that she sent Luismi packing, she said he'd stolen money off her, and Luismi said he hadn't, that it wasn't true, that he'd got really fucking rat-assed and someone must have nicked it off him, or maybe he'd dropped it, he wasn't sure, and they started squabbling like a pair of bitches, in front of everyone, cussing and cursing and hurling bitter, heartfelt accusations at each other, and then, out of nowhere, the Witch punched Luismi, and Luismi launched himself at her and started throttling her, until the others came to pull them apart and the Witch was left crying on the floor, kicking and flailing her legs like some cartoon character while Luismi scrambled out of the house. Brando was hot on his heels and trailed him all the way to Sarajuana's door, where at last he caught up with Luismi and was able to calm him down, even buying a beer or two with the money he'd stolen from him, with the two thousand pesos the freak had given to Luismi to go and buy a couple of grams of coke for the party crew hitting up her house later, who'd need a good incentive to put up with her cheesy songs, her shit music, her pathetic, risible performance. And then, at three a.m., once Sarajuana's had emptied out and Luismi's voice had become hoarse from all his whining about the Witch and her bullshit, they left the bar and walked the half a mile or so to Luismi's house, to the hovel that chickenshit called his house, and there they collapsed together on the mattress and Luismi fell asleep while Brando, lying face up, listened to him breathing and stroked his own cock through his clothes, until that urge, the motherfucking urge to have Luismi grew so intense he had no choice but to take down his trousers, kneel by Luismi's face and stick the tip of his cock between the half-open mouth of his friend, those full lips that the faggot opened suddenly, letting Brando inside, all of him deep inside, right down to the base, and then come the second he felt Luismi's tongue slip past his frenulum, come with such intense spasms it almost hurt. That was the last thing he remembered from that night, the last thing he wanted to remember, because he must have passed out straight after he came; his mind must've gone blank after having felt the devastating force of that first orgasm in Luismi's mouth, and that's why it was such a terrible shock to wake up the following morning on that mattress with a monstrous headache and his pants around his ankles and his right hand nestled in Luismi's tangled mop of hair; Luismi, whose head was resting on Brando's shoulder. His first instinct was to move away from his friend, whose head flopped onto the mattress without him waking up. The second thing he did was pull up his trousers, move aside the wooden board that served as a door, and run out to the dirt track and up to the highway to take the first bus to Villa, praying that no one – above all Munra, that fucking bigmouth Munra – saw him leave Luismi's *casita*. And it wasn't until he'd got home and showered to wash off the rest of the semen encrusted in his pubic hair and was lying naked on his bed that he realized the tremendous mistake he'd made: that instead of having run away like a fucking coward, he should have taken advantage of Luismi's defenselessness as he slept to straddle and then choke him with his bare hands, or, better still, with his belt, anything so he wouldn't have to spend the whole of Carnival cooped up at home with his mother – to her delight – too afraid to meet up with his friends, who, having had the full debrief about what had happened with Luismi, would castrate him in front of the whole town, calling him a poof, a fag, a motherfucking fairy. He waited until after Ash Wednesday to show his face in the park, his hands buried in his pockets and his stomach churning, wearing his new Adidas trainers, only to discover, to his great relief, that nobody knew a thing, that Luismi hadn't told anyone, maybe because he'd been so fucked off his nut that night he didn't even remember what had happened between them, the things they'd done on that squalid mattress, or at least that's what Brando believed until, two weeks later, by now in early March, he bumped into Luismi's famous engineer in a recently opened club on the highway, El Caguamarama, and despite never having exchanged a single word with the guy, the engineer recognized Brando, he even knew his name, and insisted on buying them a bottle of scotch, and halfway into that bottle the old fag asked him to score some coke, and so together they got into the engineer's pickup and Brando directed him to La Zanja and was even good enough to get out himself and pick up a couple of grams off the Pablo brothers, and from there they drove to an empty lot to take it – as always, Brando smoking it on the tip of a joint – and once they'd polished off the lot that mincing fag let out a sigh and turned to Brando and asked him, with a coquettish smile, if he wouldn't mind taking down his trousers because he wanted to lick his ass, and Brando sat in silence for a moment because he thought he'd misheard; he thought the

192

engineer wanted him to pull down his trousers so he could lick his balls, and he was already taking his hands up to his belt to undo the buckle when he realized what was happening, what the engineer wanted, and with his voice muffled with rage he told him to go fuck himself, go lick your grandma's ass, Brando wasn't into that fag shit, and the engineer burst out laughing, an asthmatic wheeze, and started confusing him with riddles: Oh yeah? So how exactly do you know you don't like having your ass licked, kiddo? And Brando told him to fuck off again, this time even more angrily, but the engineer wouldn't drop it; he went on and on about how Brando should give it a try, that he'd like it, come on, don't play hard to get, as if Brando was one of those coy fucking poofters who'd whip out his ass at the slightest nudge, drop his pants and get on all fours for the engineer to lick his ass and then, almost certainly, stick it in, making full use of the fact that Brando was there for the taking. Go on, I'll make it worth your while, that tubby wrinkly fag was saying, even licking his moustached lips, and it was the sight of that pale tongue that made Brando explode: Fuck you, you dirty fucking queer, he said, before opening the passenger door and starting to get out, and the engineer just laughed and said: Don't pretend like you didn't know what you were coming for. Don't be a dick. Luismi already told me all about how crazy you get when someone runs their tongue over your precious little opening... and Brando already had one foot on the ground when he heard that, but instead of continuing to get out of the pickup, he hopped back up onto the seat, moved in closer to the engineer and nutted him in the face, crushing his glasses and his nose too, judging by the crunch that Brando felt against his hairline, and also by the squeals that started coming from that perfumed old fag, but he wasn't going to hang around to assess the damage: he jumped out of the pickup and flew across the highway and into a field and he ran and ran through the grasslands until he could feel his chest burning, and only then did he stop. He had also bled a little on his forehead, but the cut had already dried by the time he reached town, and it was so small nobody noticed, not even his mother asked him what had happened. Fucking butt-munching faggot fuck: that cunt Luismi, what a fucking grass. Why couldn't he keep a secret? Why did he have to go and tell that punk engineer? And why hadn't he, Brando, just killed Luismi that morning when he woke up beside him on the mattress? He should have killed him and run away with the stolen money, however poxy the sum. Those were the only two things he could think about lately: killing and running away; school was a fucking drag, a waste of time; he was sick of drugs and booze, didn't even get a kick out of that shit anymore; his friends were all a bunch of poor cunts and his mother was a fool who still believed her man was coming back one day, a fucking fool who pretended she didn't know that Brando's dad had another family over in Palogacho and only sent them money each month because he felt guilty for having tossed them out like rubbish bags, as if we were pieces of shit, Mum, wake the fuck up: what's the point in all that praying, what good does it do if you can't even see straight, if you can't see what everyone else does, you stupid, stupid woman! But she would just lock herself in her room and chant her litanies, almost shouting them to block out Brando's raging and bashing against her door, the kicking and thumping that he would have happily aimed at her rotten mug, to see if that way she'd get it through her thick skull, to see if she'd just die and fuck off once and for all to her motherfucking promised land and stop banging on at him with her prayers and her sermons, her moaning and snivelling, all that: Lord, what have I done to deserve this child? Where's my darling boy, my sweet, dear little Brando? How could you allow the devil to enter him, Lord? The devil doesn't exist, he'd shout back, or your shitty God, and his mother would let out an anguished wail followed by more prayers, intoned with even greater intensity, even greater devotion, to make up for her son's blasphemes, before Brando stormed off to the bathroom, where he'd stand before the mirror and stare at the reflection of his face until it looked like his black pupils, together with his equally black irises, had dilated so wide that they covered the entire surface of the mirror, a forbidding darkness cloaking everything: a darkness devoid of even the solace of the incandescent fires of hell; a desolate, dead darkness, a void from which nothing and no one could ever rescue him: not the wide-open mouths of the poofs who approached him in the clubs on the highway, not his nocturnal escapades in search of dog orgies, not even the memory of what he and Luismi had done, not even that. *No se tú, pero yo te he comenzado a extrañar*, went the song on the radio in Sarajuana's, *en mi almohada no te dejo de pensar*, but Luismi no longer sang those words, he didn't even hum along to them distractedly like he used to when one of his favourites came on, *con las gentes, mis amigos*, he didn't speak at all anymore, he was that pilled-up, *en las calles, sin testigos*, because the engineer had stopped answering his calls and never showed his face again in the highway clubs, and a rumour spread that they'd transferred the bastard to another station because of the worsening violence and corruption in the sugar cane region, and Brando didn't tell Luismi anything about what had gone on with the engineer the time the old queen proposed to lick out Brando's ass, nor did he give him shit for having blabbed about what had gone on between them, because to do so would have meant admitting that that night had really happened, and Brando wasn't prepared to do that, although in truth he wasn't prepared for the stupid fucking thing Luismi went and did after three full days crying his heart out over the engineer and getting high in club bathrooms and by the side of the highway, the night he showed up at Sarajuana's positively beaming with happiness to tell them all that... He'd got hitched! You're shitting me, fucker! Seriously? Hitched, like full-on married? Aha, the idiot said. She's called Norma and she's from Ciudad del Valle. No fucking way! The short-ass he picked up in the park the other day? A whole bunch of the boys had an eye on that little urchin when Luismi beat them to it and took her home, to La Matosa, and now she was his woman, well, his wife, and... Hear this, bumboys! Norma's expecting and Luismi's gonna be a dad, in just a few months! Fuck me! You're fucking shitting us! Well, congratulations! the gang cheered, and to celebrate the wedding they went on the most almighty bender, and Luismi was happy as a pig in shit, and all the fags in town fought over each other to blow the newly-wed, and Luismi well and truly got his mojo back, said he'd given up the pills and had a glint in his eyes for the first time in ages, and Brando seethed at the thought of what they, he and Luismi, had done together, on that never-to-be-repeated night, the memory of which tormented him so mercilessly he wanted to pull out his own brain; and he couldn't stop wondering who knew their secret, who else Luismi had told. Or maybe the engineer hadn't actually known a thing and he'd just said that shit to see it if stuck, to fuck with him...? Because no one else ever brought it up, no one wound him up about Luismi or ever dared insinuate anything, and even Luismi himself acted like normal, as if Brando had imagined everything that happened that night, as if they'd never touched each other, never kissed or fucked, and he treated him in the most normal way in the world, the same as ever: he raised his eyebrows by way of a hello when he saw Brando roll up at the park, and bumped fists with him, just as they usually did, and in the middle of their night out he offered him a few tokes on his joint out in the yard of El Metedero, tokes which Brando took without saying a word, without looking at him, and of course without touching him, as if nothing had happened, as if Brando had imagined the whole thing, although, of course, that wasn't possible: he was no fucking fag, right? To go around imagining that nasty queer shit... But then why did he have to force himself to take his eyes off Luismi when he went out drinking with the gang or whenever they went for a fumble with the local poofs? Why did he get the feeling that Luismi was waiting for the perfect moment to tell everyone what went on that night? Why was Brando becoming more and more obsessed with the idea of killing him before that could happen? All he had to do was get hold of a gun, which was easy enough, and kill him, which wasn't a problem either, and then dispose of the body, probably just dumping it in the irrigation canal; and after that he'd have to skip town, head for any place they'd never find him, especially not his cunt of a mother; he might have to kill her too before going, shoot her in her sleep maybe, something quick and discreet to send her off to her precious fucking Pearly Gates, to put her out of her goddamn misery. Because the truth was his mother served literally no purpose: she didn't work, she didn't earn shit, she spent her life either in church or glued to the TV screen watching soap operas or reading celebrity magazines; her sole contribution to the world was the carbon dioxide she exhaled with each breath. An utterly pointless life, a dead loss. He'd be doing her a favour killing her – an act of compassion. But before all that he needed cash, enough cash to reach another city and find a place to live, and to keep him fed and clothed until he could find work, make a new life for himself, a life as free as the one his father surely built for himself when the Company transferred him to Palogacho and he could at last be rid of them, of Brando's goody-goody, frigid mother and of the stupid kid himself who did nothing but blindly follow his mother's orders; the little squirt who every Sunday helped Father Casto at mass, a server boy, and who believed that tossing yourself off was a sin and that you'd go to hell if you ever tried it. Fuck that, he thought; fuck everyone in that shithole town, while he licked his numb lips because man, it felt good, the coke dusted onto the tip of his joint, what a rush as it filled his lungs, what a high when the glowing ember lit up each time, Jesus motherfucking Christ, Brando cracked his knuckles, fuck, it's good shit, sure you don't want some? he asked Luismi, who just laughed with his big wonky teeth and said nah, he'd given up, same went for the pills, from now on he was good with beer and weed. Willy was banging on about his escapades in Cancún, about what a great time he'd had when he left home at seventeen and went to work as a waiter down on the peninsula, and Brando felt like asking him how much money he'd need to start a new life there, but he was scared the others might see he was interested for real, that they might guess he was planning something. Thirty thousand should do it, he calculated, thirty grand should be

enough to get to Cancún and rent a room and start looking for a job, any job: as a waiter, a busboy, as a dishwasher
if he had to, whatever it took at first, just to find his feet,
and then he could learn a bit of English and look for
work in the hotels – where there'd be no shortage of
gringo fags looking for a poke – but never staying put in
the same place, always keeping on the move, drinking
and fucking and getting shitfaced by that turquoise, almost green sea. What do you say? he'd asked Luismi
when they went out to smoke a joint in the yard at the
back of El Metedero. Suddenly, who knows from where,
he'd had an idea for a way to get the money, the thirty
thousand pesos: off the Witch. The plan was to go to her
place and ask for a loan, or straight up lift it if we can;
you know what they say, Luismi, they say she's got gold
in there, old coins worth a fortune; they say some guy
once found a coin under the leg of a piece of furniture
the Witch had asked them to move, and when they went
to the bank to sell it they told him it was worth like five
grand, one rusty old coin! And the poof didn't even
know she had it, just lying around it was; she hadn't even
realized it had rolled under that table, because Brando
was sure that somewhere in that house there were chests
or sacks full of those coins, what else did the Witch live
off, if she didn't work, if those cunts from the Mill had
taken all her land; where did she get the money to keep
all the boys drunk and high when they went to her place
to get out of their skulls and listen to her shit songs and
sometimes screw her on those armchairs of hers; and
think about it, Luismi, even if we don't find the cash
there's plenty of valuable shit in that house: the speakers
and decks in the basement, the giant screen and the pro-
jector, all that's worth a small fortune and between us we
can easily get it into Munra's van, and Munra won't

mind driving up to the Witch's place if we offer to pay; think about it, she must have something hidden in that room upstairs, if not why would she keep it locked, why did she fly off the handle every time anyone went upstairs, every time anyone asked her what it was she kept up there? What was she hiding? Brando didn't have a clue. Would it be worth it? Brando had absolutely no idea; but what he did know was that they couldn't leave any witnesses, although he kept that part from Luismi to prevent him from getting any ideas before the time was right. Kill the freak and leave that dumb fuck Munra in it, and then he and Luismi would be out of there, although sooner or later Brando would have to take out his friend too, but only once they were long gone, far from Villa, far from everything they knew, only then would Brando make Luismi pay for the humiliation and misery he'd put him through this whole time, especially since Brando had to watch him with that street rat Luismi called his wife, a snot-faced ragdoll with native features, slim but with a real belly on her, who never opened her mouth and who blushed every time anyone spoke to her. She was so dumb she didn't even see that Luismi had been taking her for a ride; the prick had invented some shit about working as a security guard in Villa so he could carry on fooling about with the same tubby queens as always: the drivers and the mill workers and the so-called engineers who'd scraped their way through middle school and now threw their weight around acting like big shots because they wore the Company shirt and drank Buchanan's. Let's go get that money, Brando told Luismi when he bumped into him alone in the park, let's go over to the Witch's and loot the fucking place and get the hell out of here, for good, you and me, but Luismi shook his head and said he didn't want to set eyes on the

Witch, he hadn't forgiven her for not believing him about the money: fuck that fag if she thinks I'm going crawling back to her, after she called me a thief and a freeloader; and Brando kept on at him every day, every time he saw him he kept on and on at him because he had to get out of there and he knew that the only way the Witch would open the gate was if she saw Luismi with him, because everyone knew that crazy bitch was still crying a river over Luismi, always asking after him and pining over him, saying that if Luismi apologized she'd probably forgive him; and she might even lend Luismi the money without them having to kill her, but Luismi kept saying no, kept saying he didn't want to see the Witch, and besides, who could be fucked to leave La Matosa? Better to just stick around, something would come up sooner or later, there was no need to lose their cool, and anyway, Norma was pregnant and he couldn't risk anything happening to her on the journey, and Brando would nod understandingly, saying: Course, man, you're right, while inside he was thinking: You motherfucking son of a bitch. God I hate you, you cunt. I fucking hate you. And he'd promise himself he wouldn't bring it up again with Luismi, but the following day he'd see him and the words would just tumble out of his mouth: Come on, Luismi, let's just fucking do it, let's get the hell out of here, because he couldn't think about anything else; day and night he imagined how they'd kill the Witch, how they'd run off with the money, how they'd find a way to convert those gold coins without raising any eyebrows, and how, at last, they'd finish what they started that night on Luismi's bed, and how Brando would waste that fucker in his sleep. The Easter break came to an end and Brando didn't even bother going back to school; he didn't see any point in continuing his studies, and besides, he couldn't concentrate. His mother didn't dare bring it up, and, in fact, she seemed happy to have him there at home with her; she didn't even care anymore that Brando went off each night to drink till dawn, as long as he stayed in to watch the nine o'clock show with her; she didn't care what he did after that: she prayed for him, she prayed and she put everything in the hands of God, Jesus and the Virgin, and whatever would be would be, let His will be done. And Brando was getting more and more sick of her, of the nine o'clock show, of the imbecilic giggles from the characters in those comedies and the cloying advertising jingles and the high-pitched whirr of the fan revolving at full speed above their heads. He was sick of that town, sick of that cunt Leticia too and of her whingeing down the phone because Brando wouldn't fuck her. That nigger had got obsessed with the idea of having Brando's kid; she said her husband had no balls, that he couldn't give her a child no matter how much he fucked her, so she wanted Brando to come over and see her and come inside her to get her pregnant. She'd bring up the kid as if he was her husband's, she said; Brando didn't have to worry about anything other than dumping his load inside her and making her a baby, she said. Dump his load inside her, that stupid bitch! Make her a baby! She could go fuck herself: the last thing Brando needed was to leave something of his in that hellhole of a town. No, no fucking way – he wouldn't give her the pleasure, no matter how much she begged, no matter how much money she offered him. He could get the money some other way; then he'd leave for Cancún and work as a waiter and just follow the party, always on the move, so that he wouldn't get bored and so that they couldn't catch him. Come on, Luismi, for fuck's sake, he'd say, when no

one else was listening, because Brando didn't want witnesses. Let's do it this Monday, this Tuesday, next week,
Munra will take us if we pay him; we just show up and
knock on the door and you convince her to open the
door, and once we're inside we get the money, by force if
we have to, who gives a fuck, and we bust out of there, no
suitcases, nothing that'll turn heads, and we won't tell a
soul, just you and me, come on, Luismi; and he'd reply:
But we have to take Norma with us, and Brando shook
his head and thought: As if you give a shit about that
girl, you fucking homo, but he pulled himself together
and smiled and said: Yeah, of course, we can't leave
without your wife, right? And the word 'wife' tasted like
shit in his mouth. Luismi's negative attitude was really
starting to wind him up. At one point Brando even
thought that Luismi had smelled a rat and suspected his
intentions to take all the cash himself, to kill him once
they were far enough away, and for a couple of days he
was seriously contemplating the idea of leaving on his
own, with no money, until one Friday afternoon, completely out of character, Luismi showed up at Brando's
house. He looked like shit and hadn't slept for two days
because Norma – and here Brando could barely make
out what Luismi was saying he was clenching his teeth
so tightly – was seriously ill, his wife was in hospital and
it was all the Witch's fault, something the Witch had
done to the poor girl, and that's why Luismi had changed
his mind, that's why now he did want to go to her house
and go through with the plan that very day: today, now,
dickhead, strike while the iron's hot, Brando, today,
fucked out of his mind on pills and barely able to stand,
and Brando was about to send him packing, was about to
knock some sense into Luismi to try to make him see
what a load of shit he was spouting, but then he thought

that maybe this was the opportunity he'd been waiting for. What did it matter when they did it or Luismi's motives, what did he stand to lose when he might never get an opportunity like that again, so he said alright, they should go do it, but not before having a few more drinks to psych themselves up, to buck up the courage, and he went to his room and put on a black T-shirt – to conceal any blood, he thought prudently – and then on top of that he put on another, his Man U shirt, and, grabbing all the money he had and without a word to his mother, he left the house and took Luismi by the arm so he couldn't escape and he led him to Don Roque's shop, where they bought two bottles of aguardiente and mixed it with a bottle of orange drink, sweet water pumped with colourings and poison which they drank between the four of them, because Willy joined them on the way to the park and then Munra showed up in his van, and Brando didn't really believe that Luismi meant it; he had the feeling that at any moment he'd back out, or that he'd suddenly come out with the big talk in front of Munra and Willy and that the plan would go to shit, and that's why it surprised him that Luismi, as high as he was, had the good judgement to wait until Willy was well and truly out for the count on the park bench before asking Munra to do them the solid of driving them to La Matosa. Maybe he wasn't as high as Brando thought, or maybe he just really meant business. Munra, that total prick, said he'd take them wherever they wanted if they paid him, no less than a hundred to go to La Matosa, and Brando said fifty now and fifty later, once he'd done them the favour, it's all I've got, I'll give you the rest later and we'll all go out and get on it with what we make, and Munra said: You're on, and they left, and then that thing happened, that thing happened, that thing Brando did unaware of his own strength and he shouldn't have hit the freak so hard with that crutch when she turned to run out of the kitchen, and right on the top of her skull, for fuck's sake, because she went crashing to the floor, where Luismi proceeded to kick the shit out of her face, and after that she didn't say another word, not even when Brando slapped her to make her tell them where she'd hidden the money, she just moaned and drooled on the kitchen floor while blood poured out of the gash on her head, soaking her hair, and they had to search for the money fast. Who knows how long it took them to go through the house, because Munra may have said it was no longer than half an hour, but to Brando it felt like entire days had passed, their frustration growing with every room they raided upstairs; vacant, sparse rooms with four walls and just two pieces of furniture, a bed and a dresser, or a bed and a chair, or a table in the centre of an otherwise empty room; a small dark toilet like a latrine; curtains drawn across boarded-up windows, grey walls, unintelligible scrawls and the foul, unearthly smell of dead old woman. And who knew which of those rooms belonged to the Witch, thought Brando, horrified, or where the freak slept at night, because all of the rooms on that floor seemed unoccupied, desolate even, as if no one had slept on those hard beds under those dusty quilts for years. He went through all the rooms and the wardrobes full of moth-eaten clothes, bags of rubbish and rotten papers, until he reached the very end of the hallway, the gloomiest end with the only door in the house under lock and key, boarded up from the inside, it seemed, but no matter how hard Brando rammed it with his shoulder, and no matter how many times he kicked the handle, the door remained closed, which is how it was when Luismi came upstairs to help him, although the truth was that by then Luismi was as good as useless; the buzz he'd got from fucking up the Witch had come crashing down and now the fuckwit seemed totally out of it, and Brando began to sense that the whole thing had been a huge fucking mistake because there was nothing inside the house apart from a two-hundred-peso note on the kitchen table and a handful of change dotted throughout the living room, coins that Brando had to go around picking up like a fucking tramp because Luismi's hands were shaking so much: in the midst of all that craziness it was finally dawning on him just what they'd done, that the Witch was toast, on her way out, breathing by some miracle between snorts and grunts, and you could see she was suffering, from the way she moaned, and Brando told Luismi that they'd better take her somewhere else, throw her in the woods to make it harder to find her; he said that if they left her there the local women would all turn up on Friday and discover her and then come after them, and that's why they had to get the fuck out of there, right that second. So they covered the Witch as best they could in her own skirt and they wrapped her head with that revolting veil of hers to stop her brains from spilling out from the wound, and like that, between the two of them, they picked her up and threw her in the back of the van before driving off down the dirt track leading up to the Mill. But before reaching the river they took another turn onto a path that led to a bend in the irrigation canal, and there they got her out and dragged her to the water's edge, and Brando handed Luismi the knife, the knife he'd taken from the Witch's kitchen, the same one that had been lodged in an apple on that table for years, for as long as Brando could remember, on a plate of coarse salt; the knife Brando had kept clutched in his fist the whole

206

time as he directed Munra at the wheel from the back of
the van. And when it came to the crunch Luismi refused
to take the knife and Brando had to physically put it in
his hand and wrap his fingers around Luismi's fist to
make him clasp the handle. And Luismi didn't want to
look at the Witch, but Brando had to convince him that
the poor bitch was in pain, that they really should put an
end to her suffering and pop her, go on, the coup de
grace; only, since they didn't have a gun or any bullets,
they'd have to use the knife, stab that faggot who was
now trembling and moaning on the grass, her face covered in blood and the yellow shit that continued to gush
from the wound at the back of her head, stinking to high
heaven. Stab her in the throat, he told Luismi, stab her
before she bleeds to death, but instead that fucking pussy
Luismi just gave her a limp-fisted little jab in the neck,
which didn't hit any of the main veins; it just made the
Witch open her eyes really wide and bare her bloody
teeth, and Brando couldn't take any more and he knelt
down next to Luismi and once again wrapped his hands
around his fist and with the full force of his body he
thrust the knife into the Witch's throat, once, twice and
once more for luck, to be sure that this time, without a
shadow of a doubt, he'd pierced every layer of skin and
muscle, the walls of the arteries, the cartilage of her lar-
ynx and even her spine – on the third blow there was a
dull crack that made that faggot Luismi whimper like a
baby, the knife still clutched in his hand and blood everywhere, on their hands, clothes, shoes, hair, even their
lips, and Brando had to prise the knife from Luismi's
hand and throw it into the canal, even though he would
have preferred to wash it and keep it, maybe use it again,
that very night, on his mother and Luismi, because he'd
have to go back to La Matosa: he'd have to go back to the

Witch's place after the nine o'clock show, after the news and in the middle of the variety show his mother always nodded off to, when he'd take his bike and pedal against the swarming mosquitos trying to get into his gasping mouth, against the roots of the trees that grew up through the gnarled ground, against the brisk wind that ruffled his hair and swept the plump beads of sweat off his brow and onto the parched earth. He'd gone back to the Witch's house to look for the money, and once again he hadn't found shit: the living room was as bare as the shell of a dead snail, and filled with an alarming silence, filled with echoes, and it was the same story in the basement and the upstairs rooms, where he didn't find a thing, not even after moving all the furniture again and rummaging around in the rubbish and even ripping open some of the plastic bags piled up against the walls. Finally, he went back to the locked, sealed door which they hadn't been able to open that afternoon and he knelt down before it to peer through the gap between the floor and the wood, but he couldn't make out anything other than dust and darkness and that stench of death which pervaded the landing. He figured there must be a machete somewhere in that house, even a rusty one, and that if he took to the latch with it he might be able to break the lock, or at least smash in the wood around it, and he went hurtling down the stairs, but on reaching the kitchen he stopped dead before the yellow eyes of a huge black cat who was eyeballing him from the kitchen door, and Brando couldn't understand how that animal, who was brazenly watching him, had got in, when he had bolted the kitchen door himself with a bar so that no one else could enter while he ransacked the house. The fucking cat didn't move an inch when Brando raised a leg as if to kick him; it didn't even bat an eyelid, although from its closed mouth came a vicious hiss that made Brando step back and glance over at the table for another knife. And just then the lights in the kitchen and all over the house went out, and it dawned on Brando that this furious creature, this beast hissing in the darkness was the devil himself, the devil incarnate, the devil who'd been following him all those years, the devil who had finally come to carry him to hell, and he understood too that if he didn't run, if he didn't escape from the house that very instant he'd be trapped with that grim beast in the darkness forever, and he leaped towards the door, pulled aside the bar, and pushed with all his might, falling flat on his face on the hard ground in the yard with the demon still growling in his ears. He dragged himself across the dusty yard to his bicycle and disappeared into the whirring night, pedalling like mad along the tracks that cut through the cane fields, sweating from fear, from the terrible conviction that he was lost in the middle of nowhere, pedalling in circles down dirt tracks that, sooner or later, would come out onto the irrigation canal where the Witch would be waiting for him with her throat slit and her brains spilling out and her teeth swimming in blood... and he'd almost lost all hope of escaping, when at last he glimpsed the first lights in Villa, the lights from the houses close to the cemetery. He pedalled until he reached the main street, which was completely deserted, and arrived home half an hour later. He checked that his mother was asleep before creeping into the bathroom and washing his dirt-encrusted face and hands, but he almost screamed when he looked up at the steamy mirror and saw his own reflection: on his face, where his eyes should have been, were two burning rings shining out from the sweaty mercury. It took him some time to calm down, several minutes in which he stood unmoving at the sink with his eyes closed and his hairs standing on end and his hands raised to his face, as if he feared his reflection might attack him, until finally he plucked up the courage to take another look in the mirror, when he discovered that under the film of oily steam covering its surface weren't two demonic rings of light but his eyes – sunken and bloodshot, hollow and desperate, but totally normal – and he finished washing his face, chest and hands, went to his room, lay down on his bed and stared up at the ceiling for hours, unable to fall asleep. *No sé tú*, he was sure that Luismi hadn't been able to sleep that night either, *pero yo te busco en cada amanecer*, that Luismi was lying awake on his mattress waiting for him, *mis deseos no los puedo contener*, that he was waiting for Brando to come to him so they could finish what they'd started, *en las noches cuando duermo*, on that fetid mattress, *si de insomnio*, their unfinished business, *yo me enfermo*: fucking and killing each other, maybe the two things at once. He also thought about his botched efforts to get the money and his eyes welled up in humiliation. And finally he thought about leaving anyway, looking for a hideout somewhere. Maybe, if he could get hold of his father in Palogacho, just maybe he could stay there for a few days... Palogacho was quite close to Villa, but it was a first step if the police did come after him... And as he mulled it all over, imagining how it would feel to be far away from that hellhole town and from his mother, the sky began to dawn, and by the time he noticed the birds singing on the branches of the almond trees, and without having slept a wink, Brando got out of bed and went to the living room to look for his father's number in the little notebook that his mother kept by the phone, and he called him, and it rang and rang for a good while before the man himself answered with a cool, Yes? and Brando offered a timid hello – he hadn't spoken to his father for years and there was a chance the old man wouldn't recognize Brando's adult voice and that he'd hang up thinking he was one of those money scammers – and he apologized for calling so early and muttered a few polite, trite lines, which he didn't even get to finish because his father interrupted him: What do you two want from me? Tell your mother I can't send any more money, I've got bills to pay too... A baby started crying down the line. Brando said: I get that, look... And it's about time you started looking after your mother, don't you think? How old are you now, eighteen? Nineteen, Brando replied. His mother had entered the living room dressed in that threadbare nightie she refused to throw away and started flapping her hands making signs, trying to get Brando to pass her the receiver, but instead he chose to hang up without saying goodbye. His mother wanted to know what was going on and Brando told her to shut her mouth, nothing was going on, go back to bed, go back to sleep, and he returned to his room and put on the first thing he found on the floor, grabbed the two hundred pesos and loose change he'd taken from the Witch's, and without paying any attention to his mother's sobbing in the hallway, he stuffed a few more items of clothing in his rucksack and left the house, slamming the door behind him. From there he stormed down the main street towards the Villa exit, towards the petrol station, with the intention of hitching a lift from the first trucker who stopped. It was now or never because May Day would slow down the roads, there'd be fewer and fewer drivers willing to pick him up, and maybe, if he got a move on, he could get out in time, even if he did only have two hundred pesos to his name. It all depended on how generous the drivers felt and on how long he'd be able to

211

humour the fags, whether he could hack it all the way to Cancún, or to the border or wherever – what difference did it make now. But as he walked he also thought about Luismi and how desperately he wanted to see him before he left, to settle their score, and with every passing minute Brando grew angrier and angrier, and sadder and sadder, and before he'd even reached the highway he turned round and headed back in the direction of his house. It was four in the afternoon when he opened the front door. Without saying a word to his mother, who was praying on her knees before the altar set up in the living room, he went in and straight to his room, where he took off his dusty, sweaty clothes and lay down on the bed and slept for nearly twelve hours straight, no dreams, but no nightmares either, and he woke up when it was still dark, his body drenched in a cold sweat. Brando got out of bed and went to the kitchen where he drank an entire jug of boiled water and peeped inside a saucepan in the fridge without feeling the slightest interest in the beans he found there, before going back to bed and sleeping for another twelve hours straight. When he woke again he felt disoriented and his whole body was shivering under the sheets as if the room were cold. He felt like the walls of the house would fall in on him if he didn't get out of there, so he got dressed and left the house with an empty stomach and a buzzing in his ears. His body felt numb and the air he drew into his lungs had a thick, almost liquid consistency. He headed towards the end of the block, and on turning to face Don Roque's shop he came across a familiar sight: a local kid, a young boy with a pale face and very dark, straight hair was playing all alone on the arcade games on the pavement next to the boxes of vegetables Don Roque displayed in front of the shop, already half-wilted by

212

that time of the afternoon. Brando couldn't remember the boy's name, but he recognized him. For years he'd kept one eye on him around the place, especially because he seemed to look a bit like Brando as a boy, well, a whiter version, an improved version of himself, let's say – a kid whose mother let him go out and play on Don Roque's arcade games, and he was pretty damn good at it, or he certainly put in the effort, judging by the ferocious way he rammed the levers and buttons on the machine, shaking his pert little ass to the beat of the music. The boy's lips were pink, that's what stood out more than anything to Brando. He'd never come across another person with lips that colour, except for the girl in the dog video. He was sure that the boy's nipples, concealed under the fabric of his T-shirt, must be the same rosy tone, and probably tasted of strawberry; they'd probably bleed strawberry syrup instead of blood if someone dared bite them. Brando suddenly realized he was standing in the middle of the road so he walked to the other side and approached the boy. He was taking a minute just to watch him play, when the kid – he couldn't have been older than ten, Brando supposed, running his eyes over those baby-smooth cheeks – turned to Brando and challenged him to a game, an invitation Brando immediately accepted, despite not having played that particular combat game before – he'd lost interest in video games years ago. He went into the shop and bought a packet of cigarettes to get change for his two-hundred-peso note, and he then he went back out to play against the boy, tugging on the levers randomly, wildly, letting his opponent win every time and then draping himself over the boy to stealthily assess how strong he was, how hard it was going to be to restrain him once he'd lured him up to the tracks; and Brando had almost convinced

213

the kid to go with him, under the pretext of treating him to an ice cream – in fact his intentional losing streak had left him clean out of coins – when three uniformed police officers jumped him from behind, clubbed the shit out of him and threw him to the ground before handcuffing him and hauling him into the back of the patrol car. Where's the money, faggotkiller? they asked, punching him; and Brando: What money? I don't know what you're talking about; and Rigorito: Don't play dumb, faggotkiller, tell me where you hid the money or I'll burn your fucking balls off; and Brando had put up with the beating because he didn't want to tell them that he'd gone back to the Witch's house the previous night and that the only thing he'd found there was some fucking cat ghost, but eventually he started spitting up blood and they placed those cables on his balls and he had no choice but to tell them everything: about the locked door, the one room he and Luismi hadn't been able to get into, and behind that they'd almost certainly find the treasure they were looking for. And the second he told them, those pigs were out of there and Brando was thrown into the back of a cell, the cell full of straggling pissheads from the May Day parade; full of thieves like those three crazy pricks who took his trainers, and Brando barely set eyes on one of them, on the bony, bristly face of the ringleader, the one who was missing all his front teeth, before dragging himself into the one free space, next to the stinking toilet, curling up into a ball and gently holding his poor pummelled guts while the scrawny ringleader paced in circles around the cell, trampling on the drunks with his new trainers and growling like a caged beast, all worked up from that other wretch still howling like a wild dog, the matricidal junkie they'd had to bang up in 'the cubbyhole' to

214

stop the other prisoners from killing him. Shut up, motherfucker! the ringleader bellowed. Shut up, you fucking butcher! came the cries from the other cell. You killed your old girl! Burn in hell, fucker! The ringleader called out to Brando and gently kicked his pounded ribs, not to hurt him now, it seemed, but to get his attention, and under his breath he chanted: Faggotkiller, fagstabber, look, look, and Brando covered his ears and closed his eyes but that nutcase wouldn't let it drop: Look, faggotkiller, look, the enemy, do you believe in the enemy? And the smell coming off him was even worse than the stench of piss on the cell floor, but Brando made an effort to unfurl himself and look up at the man who wouldn't stop goading him, and murmur: What the fuck do you want, man? I've got nothing left to give you, and Brando looked to where the man's bony finger was pointing: to the space above his head on that wall covered in scrawls and scratches – names and nicknames and dates and hearts, cocks and pussies like mythological monsters, and all kinds of abominable scenes – and where now he could clearly make out a series of red lines forming the perfect figure of a devil. How had he not noticed it when he first entered the cell? The giant demon presiding over the jail like a king. The enemy, faggotkiller, the demented ringleader was saying. The enemy is everywhere. He'd been drawn with brick or some other red pigment and he had an enormous head with horns and a pig's snout and round, hollow eyes with shaky lines protruding from them like some perturbed child's depiction of the sun, and stubby goat legs and a pair of tits that hung all the way down to that monstrosity's waist, just above a long erect dick that was spurting what looked like dry blood, real blood, and the bearded lunatic, the cell bully, was now shouting at the top of his lungs and kicking the drunks to wake them up, to force them to witness the miracle that was about to take place. The enemy! he bellowed, the enemy calls for more servants! Scum of the earth: rise up! Get ready, bitches! And the drunks groaned and covered their heads with their arms, and some others over by the cell bars made the sign of the cross, but nobody dared take their eyes off the ringleader, off his macabre dance, off the delusional show of shadow boxing he performed in the middle of the cell before launching himself at Brando, not to hit him, but to deliver two punches to the wall above his head, right in the pit of the painted devil's gut; two blows that resounded in the sudden, almost mystical silence that fell over the prison. Two blows, two, muttered the ringleader's cronies, taken aback. Two, two, repeated the most lucid among the drunks. Two, two, the prisoners in the other cell began to shout, as if by contagion, and even the wild dog pleading for his mama's forgiveness contributed his shot voice to the collective song: Two, two, they cried. Two, two, Brando whispered, despite himself. The shouts reverberated between the prison walls, filling their ears, which is why Brando didn't hear the cell door creaking open, or the sound of footsteps heading towards them. In fact it was only when he tore his gaze from those blind suns on the devil's face that he realized there were three figures standing behind the cell bars. Move your asses, you pieces of shit, the guard shouted, brandishing his truncheon. How the fuck do you evil fuckers always know how many I'm bringing you? And with that he shoved two new prisoners inside the cell: a limping short man with a grey moustache who could barely keep himself upright, and a skinny, emaciated kid with curly hair matted with blood, his mouth bruised and bulbous and his eyes swollen shut. He

216

really had felt the full force of Rigorito's pigs, who clearly didn't give a fuck about the journalists or the photographers or human fucking rights: Lusimi, in the flesh, that cocksucking son of a bitch Luismi, right before Brando's watering eyes. His. Fuck. Finally his to squeeze in his arms.

VII

They say she never really died, because witches don't go without a fight. They say that, at the last minute, just before those kids stabbed her, she transformed into something else: a lizard or a rabbit, which scurried away and took cover in the heart of the bush. Or into the giant raptor that appeared in the sky in the days following the murder: a great beast that swept in circles above the crops and then perched on the branches of the trees to peer at the people below with its red eyes, as if wanting to open its beak and speak to them.

They say there was no shortage of people who entered that house looking for the treasure after her death. The moment they heard whose body had been found floating in the irrigation canal, they raced with shovels and picks and sledgehammers to demolish the walls and dig holes like trenches in the floor looking for hidden doors, for secret rooms. Rigorito's men were the first to show up; on the chief's orders they even broke down the door to the room at the end of the hallway, the room belonging to the Old Witch that had remained locked ever since she'd disappeared years earlier. They say that neither Rigorito nor his men could stand the spectacle awaiting them there: the black mummy of the Old Witch lying supine in the middle of the solid oak bed, the corpse that began to flake and crumble right before their eyes, ending up a heap of bone and hair. They say those spineless cowards skipped town never to return; although some people claim that's not true, that what really happened was Rigorito and his men did in fact discover the famous treasure hidden in the Old Witch's room – gold and silver coins, priceless jewels and that ring with a rock so big anyone would assume it was glass – and that they swiped the lot before taking off in Villa's sole police car. They say that, at some point after driving through Matacocuite, greed go the better of Rigorito and he decided to kill his men so he wouldn't have to share the bounty. They say he told them to hand over their guns and then shot them, one by one, in the back; they say he cut off their heads narco-style to throw the authorities off the scent and then sped off with all that money to an unknown destination. But others say that's impossible and that Rigorito's men must have killed him first, six against one; probably what happened was those policemen came face to face with the first of the Raza Nueva crew making their way down from the north, sweeping up the mess that the Grupo Sombra left behind at the oilfields, and that they were the ones who knocked off those officers and probably also the chief himself, whose body will turn up before long at the scene of some shootout, perhaps also mutilated, showing signs of torture and bearing cardboard signs with messages for Cuco Barrabás and the other members of the Grupo Sombra clan.

They say the place is hot, that it won't be long before they send in the marines to restore order in the region. They say the heat's driven the locals crazy, that it's not normal – May and not a single drop of rain – and that the hurricane season's coming hard, that it must be bad vibes, jinxes, causing all that bleakness: decapitated bodies, maimed bodies, rolled-up, bagged-up bodies dumped on the roadside or in hastily dug graves on the outskirts of town. Men killed in shootouts and car crashes and revenge killings between rival clans; rapes, suicides, 'crimes of passion', as the journalists call them.

Like that twelve-year-old kid who killed his girlfriend in a jealous rage on discovering that she was pregnant with his father's baby, down in San Pedro Potrillo. Or the farmer who shot his son when they were out hunting and told the police he'd mistaken him for a badger, even though everyone knew the father had his eyes on the son's wife, he'd even been creeping around with her behind the kid's back. Or that headcase from Palogacho, the one who said her children weren't her children, that they were vampires out to suck her blood, which is why she bashed those kiddies to death with planks of wood that she wrenched from the table, and with the wardrobe doors, and even the television set. Or that other miserable bitch who suffocated her little girl, jealous of all the attention the husband gave her, so she just took a blanket and held it over the girl's face until she stopped breathing. Or those bastards from Matadepita who raped and killed four waitresses and whom the judge let off because the witness never showed, the one who'd accused them. They say he was bumped off for being a grass, and those cunts are still out there, like nothing ever happened...

They say that's why the women are on edge, especially in La Matosa. They say that, come evening, they gather on their porches to smoke filterless cigarettes and cradle their youngest babes in their arms, blowing their peppery breath over those tender crowns to shoo away the mosquitos, basking in what little breeze reaches them from the river, when at last the town settles into silence and you can just about make out the music coming from the highway brothels in the distance, the rumble of the trucks as they make their way to the oilfields, the baying of dogs calling each other like wolves from one side of the plain to the other; the time of evening when the women sit around telling stories with one eye on the sky, looking out for that strange white bird that perches on the tallest trees and watches them with a look that seems to want to tell them something. That they mustn't go inside the Witch's house, probably; that they mustn't walk past or peek through the yawning holes that now mark its walls. A look warning them not to let their children go looking for that treasure, not to dream of going down there with their friends to rummage through those tumble-down rooms, or to see who's got the balls to enter the room upstairs at the back and touch the stain left by the Witch's corpse on the filthy mattress. To tell their children how others have run screaming from that place, faint from the stench that lingers inside, terror-stricken by the vision of a shadow that peels itself off the walls and chases you out of there. To respect the dead silence of that house, the pain of the miserable souls who once lived there. That's what the women in town say: there is no treasure in there, no gold or silver or diamonds or anything more than a searing pain that refuses to go away.

VIII.

The Grandfather sat puffing away on a tree stump while
the boys from the morgue finished unloading the ambulance. One by one he counted them all, even those that
weren't in one piece, the faceless, sexless remnants of
people: the calloused foot of some peasant who'd probably tried to clear the hillside brush while drunk; fingers
and lumps of liver and strips of skin, post-op scraps
from the oil company clinic. The first intact corpse they
brought out was clearly a tramp: his skin was sallow and
shrivelled like someone who'd spent half his life on a
driftless rant under the harsh sun. Next, the young lady
who'd been chopped to pieces. At least she wasn't naked,
poor thing, but wrapped in sky blue cellophane; presum-
ably, the old man thought, to prevent her severed limbs
from sloshing out all over the ambulance floor. Then
came the newborn, the little creature with a tiny head
like a custard apple, almost certainly abandoned by its
parents in some clinic before the little lamb had even finished dying. And finally the heaviest and most unwieldy
of the lot, the one the workers had to wrap up in sheets
because the skin kept coming away in flaps whenever
they tried to tie its hands and legs; the one that was going to be more of a headache for the Grandfather than
the rest of them put together, even more than the dis-
membered girl, because not only had the bastard been
violently slashed to death but he was still whole, rotten but whole, and those were always the hardest work:
as if they refused to accept their fate, as if the darkness
of the tomb terrified them. But those two cretins from
the morgue weren't interested in any of that. They only
wanted to sponge smokes off the Grandfather and talk
shit, see what they could get him to say. Plenty of work

on the way, the lanky one said. They just found the missing pigs from Villa: well and truly ripped to shreds, heads and all. The Grandfather continued taking long, measured drags from his cigarette, his eyes fixed on the bodies that the boys had flung into the hole, calculating how much sand and lime he'd have to throw over them. You may as well start digging the next hole, the other one said, the *güero* who hardly ever spoke, the one who would just stand there staring at the Grandfather with a gormless smile on his face. Still room for a good twenty in this one, replied the old man. The lanky one laughed: That's what they said in Villa, Gramps, and what do you know? We've had to bring the bodies all the way here – no room at the inn. The graves down at the cemetery look like pitcher's mounds. The Grandfather merely stared at him through squinting eyes. Why not bury them upright? the *güero* proposed, flicking his butt into the bottom of the grave. The stupid boy was joking, but the Grandfather knew that would never work. They put up a real fight if they weren't laid down flat, nice and snug one on top of the other: they couldn't get comfy and they'd toss and turn and no one would be able to forget them and they'd end up trapped in this world, causing mischief, wandering around among the tombs, terrifying people. The Grandfather lit another cigarette and simply shook his head gently from side to side while the boys from the morgue in Villa watched him expectantly. No doubt they were waiting for him to tell one of his stories, but the old man wasn't going to give them the pleasure. What for? So they could go around telling everyone that the Grandfather had finally lost it? To hell with that! The lanky one especially, the one who first spread the rumour that the Grandfather spoke to the dead, and all for something the old man had told him in confidence, thinking the little dipshit would get it, but no: he'd left the cemetery and told anyone who'd listen that the Grandfather was hearing voices and had lost his marbles, for fuck's sake, when he'd only wanted to explain to the kid that you had to talk to the bodies as you buried them; because in his experience things worked out better that way; because that way the dead person felt that a voice was guiding them, telling them how things worked, and this seemed to console them a little, to stop them going off and hassling the living. That's why he waited till those two kids drove off in the now empty ambulance before daring to say a word to the new arrivals. You had to reassure them first, make them see there was no reason to be afraid, that life's suffering was over now and the darkness would soon fade. The wind was lashing across the plain, stirring the leaves on the almond trees and whipping up little dust devils that swirled between the graves in the distance. Rain's coming, the Grandfather told those dead men and women while he watched, with relief, as fat clouds drew a dim veil across the sky. Glory be, the rain's coming, he repeated, but don't you worry. A solitary plump raindrop landed on the hand gripping his shovel. The Grandfather drew it to his lips to lick the sweetness of the first rain of the season. He'd better get a move on if he was going to cover the bodies before the heavens opened: first with a layer of lime, then a second of sand, and then laying chicken wire over the entire pit and placing rocks on top of that so the stray dogs didn't come digging up the bodies in the middle of the night. Don't you worry, don't fret, you just lie there, that's it. The sky flashed with lightning and a muffled boom shook the earth. The rain can't hurt you now, and the darkness doesn't last forever. See there? See that light shining in the distance? The little light that looks like a star? That's where you're headed, he told them, that's the way out of this hole.

Acknowledgements

To Fernanda Álvarez, Eduardo Flores, Michael Gaeb, Miguel Ángel Hernández Acosta, Oscar Hernández Beltrán, Yuri Herrera, Pablo Martínez Lozada, Jaime Mesa, Emiliano Monge, Axel Muñoz, Andrés Ramírez and Gabriela Solís, for the generosity with which they read and commented on the different versions of this novel. To Martín Solares for the same reason, and for having recommended *The Autumn of the Patriarch* at precisely the right time. To Josefina Estrada, for the leads she gave me without meaning to in her remarkable crónicas, *Señas particulares*. To the memory of the Costa Rican writer and activist Carmen Lyra, author of many short stories, including 'Salir con domingo siete', a very moving version of the popular folk tale of unknown origin which I took inspiration from to rewrite another version of the same story in these pages.

To the journalists Yolanda Cruz and Gabriel Huge, murdered in Veracruz under the government of the vile Javier Duarte de Ochoa, whose crime stories and photographs inspired some of the stories in *Hurricane Season*.

To Lourdes Hoyo, for all of her affection. To Uriel García Varela, for the little light that shines in the distance like a star.

To Eric, Hanna and Gris Manjarrez, for being the best family in the world, and allowing me to be part of it.

Fitzcarraldo Editions
8-12 Creekside
London, SE8 3DX
United Kingdom

ISBN 978-1-913097-09-7

Design by Ray O'Meara
Typeset in Fitzcarraldo
Printed and bound by TJ International

fitzcarraldoeditions.com

Fitzcarraldo Editions

This book has been selected to receive financial assistance from English PEN's 'PEN Translates' programme, supported by Arts Council England. English PEN exists to promote literature and our understanding of it, to uphold writers' freedoms around the world, to campaign against the persecution and imprisonment of writers for stating their views, and to promote the friendly co-operation of writers and the free exchange of ideas.

www.englishpen.org